COMING CLEAN

"You tremble," he observed, his tone husky.

In truth, she did, and from the center of her soul to the outermost parts of her, but she would not admit the cause to be his touch.

"I am chilled. The water has long since lost its heat."

He would not allow such deception from her.

"But you have not." And with his hand he lifted her chin so that she could not escape the penetration of his smoky eyes. "You are as warm to my touch as sun-baked steel."

With no words of warning or intent, William lifted her from the bath and stood her upon the rough floor, the water sheeting off her to soak the boards. Briskly, he rubbed her dry, the linen sheet quickly becoming wet through.

Dizzy from the heat of the water, the proximity to the fire, the length of her time spent soaking . . . or was it the heat of his hands, her proximity to him, the length of him almost rubbing against her upthrust nipples? She could not say, but she could not find the strength to stand.

He caught her against him and then set her back upon her own feet, holding her by the waist and looking deeply into her dark eyes.

"Are you clean, lady?" he asked, his own eyes dark.

Other *Leisure* books by Claudia Dain:
TELL ME LIES

THE HOLDING

CLAUDIA DAIN

LEISURE BOOKS   NEW YORK CITY

A LEISURE BOOK®

March 2001

Published by

Dorchester Publishing Co., Inc.
276 Fifth Avenue
New York, NY 10001

ISBN 0-8439-4858-2

The name "Leisure Books" and the stylized "L" with design are trademarks of Dorchester Publishing Co., Inc.

Printed in the United States of America.

Visit us on the web at www.dorchesterpub.com.

THE HOLDING

To Patience, who cried over it;
To Natasha, who believed in it;
To Alicia, who printed it.
To each of you, my heartfelt thanks.

THE HOLDING

Chapter One

England, Winter 1155

William le Brouillard, Greneforde's new lord, would not be pleased with his prize. That was Kendall's first thought upon beholding his overlord's lands. Kendall reined in and cast his eyes around him, letting his breath out slowly. Nineteen years of war had taken its toll on William's hard-won holding.

Fields that should have been cleared and turned were broken wastelands of scorched earth dotted with struggling seedlings of oak and hemlock. The forest was encroaching steadily on the cleared land; forest that had once been beaten back to the fringes and held there diligently by sweat-soaked effort was relentlessly advancing on what should have been Greneforde's prime food source. There would be no corn this winter. A wet gust of wind blew against his face, and his stomach rumbled in protest at the assault; it would be a hungry season.

Leading his squire on, Kendall was struck by the absence of huts. Where were the villeins? Was that why the land lay fallow? Was there no one left to work the land? His stomach rumbled again, this time in trepidation. He did not want to be the messenger who brought William the news that his holding was a name on the Domesday Book and nothing more.

As if to mock him, Greneforde appeared suddenly out of the gray gloom looking reassuringly solid. The battlements were sound and the roof intact; there was even rising smoke from within the enclosure. The curtain wall, although of wood, looked sturdy, and one tower had been constructed of stone. Kendall's stomach ceased its complaining: Greneforde Tower was sound, but what was a sound great tower with no food to sustain the inhabitants?

Just then a woman appeared on the battlements, a woman where there should have been only battle-ready men. Silently they studied each other. At this distance, he could not make out her features, and there was something in her manner that warned against riding any closer to the curtain. He could see that her hair was fair and that she held herself erect; her mantle went beyond ordinary to be indescribably plain. They watched each other as warily as prospective opponents, and he found himself unnerved by her silent regard. It was almost ghostly the way the tower had appeared out of the fog and she with it. His squire mumbled uncomfortably behind him, stirring him to action.

"I am from King Henry II of England, overlord of Aquitaine, Normandy, Maine, Anjou, Touraine, Poitou, Guienne, and Gascony." Hearing no response, Kendall continued: "In light of Cathryn of Greneforde's orphaned state, the king has pledged her in marriage to William le Brouillard, who even now approaches to fulfill the king's command."

After a pause that could be counted in heartbeats, the woman on the wall nodded sharply, making no other response to his royal proclamation.

Kendall squirmed in his saddle, adjusting his sword, liking the reassuring weight of it in this desolate place of thrashing branches against a leaden sky and a woman who stood far too silently in the face of such news.

"Do you understand?" he asked awkwardly.

Again he saw her nod.

Kendall could sense more than hear his squire backing his horse away from him, away from the woman on the wall, away from Greneforde. Being a knight of some renown, he could not allow himself the same indulgence, else his renown would be for his cowardice rather than his skill at arms.

The clouds that had covered the sun in a thick mat thinned suddenly, and multiple shafts of warm light pierced the air around the tower. Kendall caught his breath. What the gloom had hidden, the light revealed. The soil beneath him, broken though it was, was rich earth, earth that would welcome any seed. The great tower was constructed of yellow sandstone with arched wind holes and buttresses at the angles. And the woman . . . Her hair was of palest gold, warm and rich, hanging to a length beyond his view.

On impulse, Kendall asked, "Are you Lady Cathryn of Greneforde?"

As he was coming to expect, she did not speak, answering with a brusque nod, and then she did something new: she vanished. It seemed an odd reaction to news of her marriage.

Turning his mount, disgusted to see that his squire was by now a mere dot in the distance, Kendall reflected wryly, "At least William is not to be cursed with a shrewish wife."

The river Brent was swollen with rain, but William and his men eventually found shallows by which to cross. They were upriver from Greneforde in his estimation, and so eager was he for his first look that he did not wait for those who followed, but charged up the opposing bank and turned westward, praying that the light rain would not obscure his first glimpse of Henry's gift.

William snorted under his breath. Gift it hardly was after the years he had spent in proving his worth to the future monarch of Britain. Many had flocked to Henry's banner when it was decided and agreed upon by Stephen that Matilda's son would assume the crown at his death. Maud and Stephen had wrestled through their prime years for the right to rule England—battled with the tide turning first in favor of the one and then the other until they were both too old to fight, with the land and people of England the hardest hit in their struggle for power. There would be peace now, God willing, with Henry II on the throne—years of peace and time for England to heal. William prayed that Henry's rule would be long and prosperous—long and prosperous for them both.

Many had gathered themselves around Henry when he was named successor, hoping to advance their own plans, but Henry of Anjou was no fool, and of the many who had pursued him for their own selfish reasons, few remained. William had followed Henry across the miles and fought under his banner willingly, for he had seen a man who, although no warrior, was an able administrator. And in the course of time, he had attracted Henry's attention and eventually his confidence, and, as was the way of things, he was rewarded for his loyalty and his ability.

Greneforde was his reward.

Greneforde, hidden somewhere ahead in the mist, washed with rain. Greneforde, which had survived the civil anarchy of Stephen's reign as king, but in what state? William shook off his gloom, blaming the murky weather for his sudden malaise, and patted the large bag of seed he had carried with him. During the years he had roamed the continent, he had been quietly preparing for this day, the day when he would have land of his own. Everywhere he had gone, from the hot sands of Damascus to the mountains of Bavaria, he had searched for the best seed, the best cloth, the best spice for his future home. And now his home had a name: Greneforde.

"A beauty, according to gossip at court."

William turned to look at Father Godfrey, the

priest who had been with him for a handful of years and who would perform his marriage ceremony. He wore a cotte of black wool that shed the light rain and had hiked it up to his knees to sit his mule. An unusual priest, one who had studied with Abelard, he believed that the average man could only benefit from knowing the Holy Scriptures, and to that end had spent many a dull evening coaxing William and his retinue to memorize God's sacred word.

"I thought men of God did not notice the beauty or lack of it in a maid once they wore the cloth," William commented dryly.

Godfrey smiled slowly as he gazed down at his coarse woolen habit. "We notice, but perhaps we do not give it the importance a knight-in-arms would."

Ulrich, William's squire, moaned dramatically. "We have been roaming the land for so many years in the company of men that my own grandmother would look fair."

William grinned. Ulrich, all of ten and seven years and with the gangly look of a half-weaned pup, imagined himself quite irresistible to women. In fact, when he had fulfilled the promise of his wide shoulders, he would most likely not need to imagine. He was a fine-looking lad with his smiling eyes and rich brown hair.

Godfrey, swaying upon his mule, said, "Then you see a woman with gentle eyes, which is as you should."

Ulrich only rolled his gray-blue eyes up and sighed.

William smiled, amused by Ulrich, as he often was. His training of the youth was thorough but not harsh; his own term as squire had been under a stern and humorless man, and he could not see that he had benefited from it. The physical demands of knighthood were heavy enough without crushing the spirit under an additional and unnecessary weight. But his thoughts were not long on Ulrich. Again he searched the shifting mist, eager for sight of Greneforde.

Godfrey rode quietly and watched William. His thoughts were of Greneforde, that was plain, but there was more to Greneforde than the great tower and the land, and if William did not remember that, he did.

"She has been an orphan for many years," Godfrey remarked.

William jerked slightly in surprise and said absently, " 'Tis so."

"These have not been easy years for England," Godfrey pointed out.

"Also true, but whatever is amiss will be made aright with my coming," William answered confidently.

Rowland, William's comrade in arms, joined them, nudging Ulrich to the back. His dark eyes looked first at William's back, and then his gaze skipped to Father Godfrey. The priest returned his look briefly, but long enough to see that they were of a similar mind.

"Lady Cathryn will no doubt be cheered to know it," Rowland said quietly.

William's only response was to grunt. He gave the distinct impression that he had forgotten her entirely. It was more than an impression; it was closer to fact. Cathryn was a small spur on the body of his thoughts, and he would have been the gladder for her plucking. A wife had not been his intent, for what room was there in his thoughts for a wife when hunger for land had taken the whole? Still, he was of an age to marry and Greneforde could not be taken without her. So he would have her. But his thoughts were of Greneforde.

"War is hard on the land; you have seen enough of warfare to know that, William le Brouillard," Godfrey pointed out casually. "And you have also seen how effectively a sword can send a man to stand before his God. How think you an orphaned maid has survived a score of years of civil war?"

He had not considered it, at least not overmuch, and he was not thankful that Father Godfrey had pointed it out to him. What mattered the maid? It was Greneforde, the land that came with her, that consumed him. It was Greneforde that he had striven for and Greneforde he had won. Yet Lady Cathryn awaited him as well as Greneforde. It seemed that she could not be forgotten, though he had tried.

Kendall, riding out from the center of the mist, happily distracted him.

"You found Greneforde?" William asked when Kendall was within shouting range.

"Yea, William, I found your holding."

"And how did you find her, this land that is mine?" he pressed, instantly uneasy with the brevity of Kendall's response.

Kendall looked down as he removed the mufflers from his hands. "The land is rich, the great tower is well constructed and sound, and the Lady Cathryn is preparing for your imminent arrival."

Reminded of her again, William felt obliged to ask, "And how did you find the Lady of Greneforde?"

"When I related that the king had pledged her in marriage, she received the news with calm acceptance," Kendall carefully recited. He had been rehearsing his exact wording for over an hour and was pleased with the blurry truth of it.

"Did I not tell you that she would respond so?" William smiled at Rowland.

Rowland only smiled and nodded his dark head in acquiescence.

"The lady will be ready when I arrive?" William asked specifically, anxious to be past this possible point of conflict.

"When I told her that she was to be wed to William le Brouillard by order of Henry the Second, she said not a word against the match and disappeared straightaway to begin preparations," Kendall replied, telling the technical truth.

"She sounds a woman of remarkable self-possession," Godfrey said softly.

"Yea," William agreed, "a valuable trait in a wife. As you have pointed out," he continued, directing his conversation to Godfrey, "there have been many years of war, and she is clearly gladdened to know that she will soon have a husband who can defend the land and give her children. 'Tis what all women want," he finished authoritatively.

In response, Kendall fussed with the placement of his mufflers, which seemed to be giving him unaccountable trouble. Father Godfrey fingered the rosary beads hanging from his belt, his expression deeply contemplative. It was all the response William was going to get. Their manner puzzled him. Why such buried discomfort over Kendall's news of her readiness to receive him?

"Come, Rowland," William demanded, "you have been a husband. Do not all women yearn for safety as men yearn for conflict?"

"That has been true of the women I have known," Rowland answered simply.

Thus ended the discussion of Cathryn. William was about to question Kendall more thoroughly about Greneforde when Kendall volunteered, "We enter Greneforde land, William; in fact, you were on your own land when I reached you. The great tower is but a moment's worth of hard riding due west."

There was no time for Kendall to say more. William had urged his mount into a run and was riding hard, due west. Rowland followed apace, for even with Henry on the throne, the land was rife with men who ignored the law.

It took considerably more than a moment to see the solid outline of Greneforde's tower materializing through the uneven rain, but William hardly noticed. The tower, licensed and built during the reign of Henry I and therefore not destined to be demolished with the myriad castles that had been built during the years of anarchy, had originally been of motte and bailey design. The great tower stood on a raised mound that dropped off sharply to the river. The curtain wall was of wood, but well constructed, and a tower had been added to the southeast corner, overlooking the river. The curtain would need to be rebuilt of stone, but it was not in derelict condition and would withstand attack during the rebuilding process. William was busily calculating the cost in time and money of construction and concluded that it might be accomplished in a year if he could find an able engineer. With William approaching from the west as he was, the tower on the wall looked impressive; the walls were crenelated, as was the great tower, which rose to an impressive height of four floors.

So involved was William with his first sight of Greneforde that he did not immediately note that the land lay untended, that the forest was encroaching on cleared land, that there was no village. So pleased was he with his holding that when he did take note of the air of neglect that Greneforde exuded, he could not let it concern him overmuch. Greneforde had a lord again and he would see to all her needs and happily.

William was home.

Chapter Two

Marie did not take the news of her mistress's imminent marriage calmly; in fact, she was horrified.

"What will you do, lady?" she said shakily.

Cathryn looked up from separating the flowers from the leaves of the yarrow she had just gathered. "Marry," she answered succinctly.

Marie knotted her hands together in the folds of her gown and choked out, "But, Lady Cathryn—"

"Marie," Cathryn interrupted, carefully brushing off the flower heads that she was preparing to dry, "Greneforde needs a lord." Looking into Marie's lovely blue eyes, she said calmly, "My duty is to see to the safety of Greneforde; I have known this since bread first replaced the taste of my mother's milk." When Marie only stared with frightened eyes, Cathryn smiled softly and asked, "Have you not seen what my orphaned state has brought to

Greneforde? Surely you have been as hungry as I? Will we not all benefit from a knight's strong arm raised in our defense?" Gathering Marie's chill hands in hers, Cathryn said, " 'Tis past time for me to marry, and the king is within his rights in selecting a mate for me."

"But the man he has chosen will be one of *his* men," Marie protested.

"Can King Henry be worse for England than King Stephen has been?" Cathryn countered. "Can this man, this William le Brouillard, be worse for Greneforde than no husband has been?"

Marie had no answer for her mistress, at least none that she dared voice. It was true. Times had not been good, but it was not Greneforde that she thought of; it was Cathryn herself.

"And when you are this knight's wife and he is lord of Greneforde, what then, Lady Cathryn?" Marie whispered, her heart in her eyes.

Cathryn turned again to the yarrow plants, the flowers still amazingly white and delicate, though soon to turn brown, the leaves lacy and green, long and slender. Alive and taking nourishment from the soil in one moment, and the next plucked to serve the needs of those who inhabited Greneforde, for yarrow served those who bled and those who could not draw air into their lungs, even those who shivered with fever. But yarrow had first to die to heal the people of Greneforde. And Cathryn, pushing all memories to the bottom of her thoughts, lived to serve Greneforde. Running her hands over the leaves, letting them slide through her loosely closed hand, Cathryn answered her young servant without raising her dark eyes.

"Then Greneforde will be safe, Marie, for as long as he can lift a sword and mount a warhorse."

Yea, Greneforde would be safe, Marie thought as she watched her mistress leave the herbs and proceed to the kitchen, but what of Cathryn?

What could be done to dignify the castle in its present state was being done. None wanted it said that Greneforde did not greet its new lord with head held high. John the Steward was supervising the preparation of six hens, two ducks, and half a pig; the herbs used in cooking were becoming scarce, but there was still enough parsley and primrose to be respectable, and when Lady Cathryn arrived with a small bag of cloves she had hidden away, there were smiles all around.

The bustle of activity, from the beating of the tapestries to the replacing of the rushes, from the sharpening of the plows to the mucking out of the stables, all infused Cathryn with a ripple of energy. Greneforde was coming alive again, coming alive in anticipation of a new master, and the sight gladdened her.

Finding that John had the meal well in hand, she rushed across the yard and up the stairs to her chamber. Cathryn walked quickly and quietly across the room to the massive polished chest that contained her worldly possessions and carefully opened it. The small knife that had always rested on the top, the knife that her father had given her as a parting gift, had been absent for three months, and she surprised herself by thoughtlessly reaching for it. Pushing aside the memory, she worked through the trunk, considering first one bliaut and then another. The absurdity of her behavior suddenly struck her, and she rocked back on her heels in silent laughter; to choose the worn cendre which made her look as appealing as a cold hearth or the faded castor gray? How did it happen that all her clothing was of a grayish cast? Shaking her head ruefully, her plaited hair brushing the floor with the movement, Cathryn decided that the least odious was the undyed wool. Shaking it out, she checked it for damage. Happily, it was in good repair and did not look too plebeian; the black cord edging gave the soft white of the wool a crisp look. It did not add much to her appearance, the lack of strong color seeming to draw the warmth from her complexion, but it was clean and did not look to be the sort of thing a servant would wear. It was the best she could do. She did want to look pleasing to the man who even now approached to marry her, though she could not think why. They would marry no matter how he found her, pleasing or no; it was the king's command. It was how Greneforde looked to him that mattered, after all.

Arranging her clothing with nimble fingers that shook almost imperceptibly, Cathryn stood for a moment fingering the heavy fabric. Below, she could make out the sound of footsteps on the stair. Someone, she could not distinguish who, was calling to Albert as he manned the tower gate, and Albert called back in the negative. William le Brouillard had not yet arrived. But he soon would. Gradually, almost cautiously, she moved to the wind hole and looked out at the courtyard stretching away to the curtain. Alys was stretching to reach an apple high on a tree in the orchard, the basket at her feet only half-full. Tybon was whisking a comb through the long coat of the only remaining inhabitant of the stable, fussing over her as if he were a powerful warhorse and not a tired mare. From the corner of her eye she watched Marie slide along the shadow of the kitchen, her eyes downcast and her shoulders bunched up to her ears, looking for her, Cathryn was certain. She smiled, touched more deeply than she should be that someone cared so tenderly for her. Yet for Marie's peace of mind, for all the people of Greneforde, she dared not admit that the coming of le Brouillard frightened her.

He would arrive at any moment; it was unlikely that his messenger would have preceded him by more than half a day. By nightfall she would be wed, and on the heels of that . . . She could follow that line of thought no further. He could be any manner of man, one who took without giving, one who would strip Greneforde of its struggling life and leave for richer holdings. She did not know, could not know until she had looked into his eyes and taken his measure, and the not knowing consumed her. One thing she knew: she would protect Greneforde in any way she could until she discovered the caliber of the man King Henry had contracted for her.

She did not think of protecting herself.

Breathing deeply and straightening her shoulders, she walked down one flight of steps to the lord's chamber. It would be the chamber of her new husband. The bed was dressed with the best Greneforde had to offer. A fire had been laid. The washstand was ready with fresh water. Not looking at the bed again, Cathryn nodded curtly in approval and left the room. It was past time to check the progress of the meal.

Alys carried the apple basket into the kitchen and plopped it on the dirt floor.

"The trees are truly naked now," she announced.

John looked at her over his shoulder and remarked softly, "They have given up their bounty for the best of causes."

"I would not have her disgraced in any way that we can prevent," Eldon declared, speaking for them all. "The new lord and his men will eat and eat well, even if we do not eat at all."

"We will eat," Lan offered as he cut into the pork, "but it could well be stew."

Alys wiped her hands on her apron before she began preparing the fruit for baking.

"A hot meal is always welcome," she remarked in her straightforward way.

"Will a new lord be as welcome?" Lan asked.

"With a new lord comes the means of procuring more meat," John responded. "He shall improve our lot, for which we shall be grateful."

"Perhaps," Lan persisted, his knife hacking into the flesh of the pig, "but perhaps not."

"Nay," John interjected, kindly but firmly, "there will be no questioning, no speculation, no doubting as to that. A new lord comes and he will be welcome. Think on our lady: an orphan at the dawning, betrothed at the first meal, and a wife before close of day. Nay," he repeated more forcefully, "not a whisper will pass your lips of 'perhaps not' for the sake of Lady Cathryn, if no other purpose will serve."

Lan said no more after that, stricken that his careless tongue could have caused Lady Cathryn to bear a heavier burden than the one she already bore. John's words had been well spoken and well received by all who toiled in the kitchen preparing a feast from next to nothing to celebrate the coming of King Henry's man. John's warning had been well timed, for Cathryn entered the kitchen just moments later.

Watching her as she checked the progress of the oatmeal pudding bubbling in the cauldron or debated with John the precise amount of precious clove needed to spice the pork, they drew comfort from her composure. She was the keel to their boat, keeping them from floundering in panic and fear. But until today, their boat had been rudderless. William le Brouillard would change all that. Watching her, Alys could scarce believe that in hours she would be wed, so calm was she. Watching her, Eldon knew with growing confidence that the Lord of Greneforde would protect the land and the people from attack. The image began to solidify for each of them that having a lord again would mean hunters to provide meat and men to scan the horizon from the curtain walk; their world, upended for so many years, would be set right again. Cathryn's visit had achieved its purpose.

And then, from the walk, Albert's cry bounded off the walls to echo through the courtyard, an echo that seemed to reverberate in Cathryn's very soul.

"He comes!"

All eyes turned to her, all preparations halted; the sweat running down the column of Christine's neck, the blood dripping from Lan's knife, the rolling boil of the cauldron, the rapid blinking of Eldon's light blue eyes were all magnified and crystallized for her in that moment. It was an eternal moment, a moment when time ceased. It was the moment between freedom and bondage, maidenhood and marriage. Nay, she inwardly scolded, it was the moment between vulnerability in a hostile world and safety, hunger and a full belly. That was what she must remember, what she must believe. With her next words, eternity ended.

"He comes," Cathryn repeated and then she smiled softly, "and I shall go to meet him."

With measured tread, she turned and left the kitchen, standing for just a moment on the threshold. The sounds of frantic activity resumed with the force of unexpected thunder and she smiled. Taking a deep breath, she stepped into the gray wind that swirled within the enclosure, enjoying the cool wetness of the air in her nostrils. Truly, she was enjoying every moment as if it were her last. Today she would marry. Her bridegroom even now approached, and she would wed by order of the king. The thought careened in her head like a stone in a barrel until she nodded firmly, setting her scattered thoughts to rest. With strictly enforced peace holding her terror captive, Cathryn marched across the courtyard.

Out of the corner of her eye, she saw Marie, huddled against the stone of the great tower, her eyes unseeing circles of summer sky in an ashen face. Stepping into her line of vision, Cathryn made a quick motion with her hand and Marie was gone, gone to hide in the shadowed corners of the great tower. For a moment, a small moment, Cathryn wished for someone to give her permission to hide away from the coming encounter, and then that rebellious wish was cast down with a firm nod.

"Open the gate," she called calmly to Albert. "The lord of Greneforde is come."

Cathryn stifled the overwhelming sense of vulnerability that assailed her upon seeing that open gap in the wall. She could hear a horse approaching. Squaring her shoulders, she waited, alone in the wide courtyard of Greneforde, for William le Brouillard.

Chapter Three

The gate in the tower that rose in solid splendor over the river Brent opened as William approached. It strengthened his impression that he was home. In the future, he would have a solemn talk with the keeper of the gate, for it was foolhardy in the extreme to open Greneforde wide to an unidentified knight and his retinue, though his men were far behind him. Even Rowland, who rode with him, had been left behind as he had urged his horse to greater and greater speed the closer he drew to Greneforde.

Riding into the courtyard, William drew up suddenly, and for the first time in many days, Greneforde Castle left his thoughts entirely. Mayhap it was not such a hardship to marry.

She stood alone, the wind pressing against the soft white of her bliaut and causing her rich brown cloak to flutter out behind her. She was as golden and slender as a single flame. Hair of light gold hung in ribboned plaits to fall to her knees. She had delicate features, her nose delightfully small, her lips gently full, all covered in skin the color of palest honey. Amidst the delicate golden glow of her, dark brown eyes stood out, looking almost black in the paleness of her skin. It was then that he noticed the scar that marked her, skimming the fringe of one dark brow. It was recently earned, if he could trust the pink that colored its center. She had the coltish look of a woman not yet matured to the role, and yet he had been told she was full-grown; the heavy white wool of her gown fell without any familiar break or bulge of obvious womanhood.

She was Cathryn of Greneforde.

In that moment of discovery, he wanted her just as fervently as he wanted Greneforde. He had not wanted a wife, but he wanted her. Soon he would have her. The king had offered her to him and he had agreed; the king had commanded her to marry and she was Henry's to command. Aye, she would be his. There was no turning away from this alliance, this bonding; by day's end, he would have her.

She stood alone and suddenly he grew suspicious. He had ridden in alone, without his men, and he could see none of the men of Greneforde. It would be a perfect trap, did she choose to spring it, though she would be a fool to stand against the king. Henry was not Stephen, a king to turn away when those he ruled rebelled against his will. Mayhap she did not know the fiber of the man who now ruled England.

"I am William le Brouillard," he declared without

raising his helm, "sent by Henry the Second to secure Greneforde and marry the Lady Cathryn."

His stony monotone was hardly encouraging, but Cathryn smiled slightly and replied, "Welcome, William le Brouillard, Lord of Greneforde."

Rowland charged into the courtyard, his horse blowing clouds of pearl into the air and his hand going immediately to the blade at his side. Quietly he spoke.

"I see no men-at-arms, William."

William clasped the hilt of his own blade, gripping the handle with mailed fists. Not one link of mail would he remove until he was certain no treachery was afoot. With his helm in place, his eyes scanned the curtain walk and the portals of the outbuildings. "Where are your knights, your squires, lady?"

Though she could not see the scowl that framed his eyes, she could hear the harsh edge to his voice.

"Dead, my lord," she answered quickly. "All dead."

William's eyes swung back to hers, and he asked her brusquely, "How long?"

"The last knight pledged to me died three months ago, my lord," Cathryn answered in a strange monotone.

Kendall, Ulrich, and the others were riding into the yard, the clink and squeak of their coming almost drowning out the softly spoken words of Lady Cathryn. Her eyes had left him as she searched the faces of the men who rode with him, eyes that seemed to seek the measure of each man they touched, and then he saw her face brighten.

Strangely he was annoyed. Following her look, he realized that she was staring at Father Godfrey with a look of keen anticipation. Did she hunger for the wedding then? If so, why not look at him thusly?

With his men about him, fully armed and ready, William relaxed his guard. Whether her men were dead or not, he and the knights who followed him would take possession of Greneforde. It was the simple truth that he had never been bested in battle.

It was also the simple truth that he wanted, suddenly and quite urgently, for Cathryn to see the man she would call husband. He wanted her attention. He wanted all of it. He wanted her eyes to be as riveted to him as his eyes were to her. Releasing his grip on his sword hilt, William lifted off his helm with one hand.

When the new lord of Greneforde removed his plain iron gray helm, Cathryn followed his movement, more pleased that he was not so prepared for battle than eager to see his face. When she did see him, he very effectively arrested her attention.

His hair was black and curled and cut short in the manner of the Norman French. Black brows, thick and sweeping, arched over abundant lashes that encircled eyes of polished gray. A straight nose, blunted at the tip, pointed to a wide mouth. The skin of his face was the color of rich cream and shaved, also in French fashion. If not for his thick neck and his obvious bulk, he would have been beautiful. As it was, he was striking.

Though he had removed the helm that had hidden his face from hers and so assumed a less aggressive posture, still his gaze as it held hers was silently challenging and unrepentantly proud. Her eyes did not waver from his; she did not blink or flush or shift her feet in the face of his challenge. And he was challenging her, though she could not fathom why. Her composure would not allow him to see her confused reaction to his beauty, which was causing her inner parts to heave and roll without mercy. He was lord here, but he would not so easily be lord over her. She was no fool to be bested by simple good looks. Greneforde he could have, as he would soon have her by all that was legal and binding, but her thoughts and her heart were her own and would remain so. Greneforde would be his; Cathryn would not, and if she was clever, he would never know that she eluded him. Male pride crashed against the strength of willful submission to roll over her as harmlessly as waves roll over sand.

And so she faced him, this man who would be lord over her by day's end.

Cathryn curtsied deeply to the waiting company.

"Greneforde welcomes you," she said clearly, though her voice never rose above normal pitch. "We will see to your comfort if you would dismount."

William, watching closely for her reaction to him and nonplussed that she seemed only momentarily disconcerted, now looked and saw that men had materialized out of the shadows. There were not many, but then, he did not know if these few represented all Greneforde had to offer. Certainly those he saw were nothing remarkable. In fact, the more closely he looked, the more he was sure that the only thing noteworthy about the men who came forward with such hesitation was that they were filthy. Clothes that looked better suited to be rags draped their spare bodies; lack of good cloth he could understand, but not the lack of washing, not with a river so close at hand.

Rowland studied William's face, his eyes shining with mirth, but when he spoke his tone was well modulated.

"How does the lord of Greneforde find his villeins?"

William grunted softly, removing the mufflers that sheathed his hands.

"I find them in need of washing," he answered in a quiet rumble.

"Will that be your first duty as lord? Preparing baths for your people?"

William shot Rowland a frigid glance, but said good-naturedly, " 'Twould not be time ill spent, not when I will be in such close proximity."

Rowland smiled and dismounted, handing his reins into the grimy hands of a hunched-over man long past his prime. He watched as the man carefully led his mount away into the stable; for all his dirt, he seemed capable.

"The Lady Cathryn is clean. You should have no reason for complaint when in close proximity to her," he said dryly.

William did not answer immediately, his gaze resting upon the woman who would soon sign the marriage contract. After her initial greeting, she had paid him scant attention; her face had been drawn to one man only, and that man was Father

Godfrey. She spoke with him now, her expression earnest though composed, leaning toward the good father almost . . . conspiratorially.

"What think you of her lack of knights, William?" Rowland continued as they walked across the courtyard.

William's eyes never stopped in their circuit of the bailey of Greneforde. The outbuildings were in good repair, though not without signs of hard use. The orchard was well tended. The yard was free of debris. The great tower, in its four-storied splendor, was magnificent. Most towers were of two floors, and some boasted three, but Greneforde, *his* tower, was a colossal four.

" 'Tis well I have knights pledged to me," he answered Rowland. "Until the curtain wall is rebuilt of stone, Greneforde is vulnerable. 'Twas my plan to engage an engineer I heard of in London; now I also wonder if laborers should not be hired from other parts than these. The men I have seen look hardly strong enough to lift and heft a river stone."

"Lack of food does not make for strength," Rowland remarked quietly.

William looked at his friend and nodded solemnly. He, too, had noted that the fields were empty, having a look of neglect that spoke of more than a season of idleness. Greneforde and its people had indeed suffered during Stephen's reign of anarchy. Money would be needed not just for the curtain wall, but for food. Still, these discoveries did not dampen his enthusiasm over Greneforde; if anything, they accentuated it. Greneforde needed a strong lord to see to her protection and survival. She had one in him.

In the course of his conversation with Rowland, William had let his eyes stray repeatedly to Cathryn, still deep in conversation with Father Godfrey. Though he could not hear what was being said, her manner spoke clearly of urgency. As before, when she had stood alone to greet his arrival, William's suspicions were fed like dry kindling to a new fire. Godfrey would perform the ceremony and officiate during the signing of the marriage contract; could it be that she sought his help in finding a means of escape from this coming marriage? She had been in sole charge of Greneforde for many years, and he knew enough of women to know that few would gladly relinquish that kind of autonomy. She, like all women of her class, had been reared and trained to manage an estate in the absence of a responsible male, just as he had been trained to fight and command. Cathryn of Greneforde was a fool if she believed she could thwart his ownership of the land; he would command her as he would command Greneforde, with the king's hearty endorsement, and by the struggling look of Greneforde, the land itself might well call out its thanks at his coming. Yes, Lady Cathryn would bear scrutiny until the marriage contracts had been signed and witnessed, at which point she would be powerless to rebel against him. William sighed restlessly as he watched her enter the great tower, her twined hair fluttering above her knees as she walked.

Ulrich had no eyes for the condition of the outbuildings or the land; he noted only one thing and lost no time in voicing his observation.

"It has been ten leagues and more since I beheld a woman under two score years," he almost whined. "When you bring in food for Greneforde, William, could you not also bring in some comely women?"

"You insult your lord, Ulrich, to say such when his bride has just been revealed to you," Rowland said with mock seriousness.

Ulrich blushed immediately to the roots of his hair and stammered angrily, "I did not mean . . . Rowland, you know . . . Lady Cathryn is most beautiful, most desirable. . . ."

When William's black eyebrow rose in inquiry and Rowland shook his head somberly, Ulrich blurted, "Not that I find Lady Cathryn beautiful . . ."

William's other eyebrow rose a notch at that awkward insult.

"Nay! 'Tis that she is to be your wife!" Ulrich nearly shouted.

At those words, William smiled slightly as he stood in the portal of the stair enclosure.

" 'Tis so," he said simply. Then, his gray eyes piercing the darkness of the stair, he added quietly, "And 'tis time to see that Lady Cathryn is likewise sure of it."

He mounted the circular stair quietly, clad in metal though he was, passing through the ground floor storeroom until he reached the hall on the first floor. He was well pleased with what he saw there. The hall filled the whole of the first floor and was well lit by wind holes. A fire roared in the mammoth hearth, emitting waves of heat that warmed the chill stone of the room. The wooden planks of the floor were well swept, the rushes woven into a neat mat and clean. Directly behind the lord's table, pristine in its white linen, a large tapestry depicting a knight in full armor beneath the shadow of Christ's Holy Cross fluttered sporadically in the breeze from the wind holes. Lining the perimeter of the room, tables and benches for soldiers and servants provided ample seating; it was the place he had always occupied before. Before today. Today and for always, the high table would be his.

Again he sought out Cathryn. She had abandoned her post by Father Godfrey and stood in yet another earnest conversation, this time with a servant—by the look of him, the castle steward. William, his own face quite earnest, moved across the room to speak with Father Godfrey. He would know what they had spoken of and he would know it now. This niggling doubt as to Cathryn's obedience to the king would be killed—and quickly.

Keeping his voice low, he bluntly demanded of the priest, "Your conversation with Lady Cathryn was long. Did she seek your counsel in avoiding this marriage?"

Father Godfrey could not keep the spark of amusement from his eyes as he faced William, nor did he try overly hard.

"Nay, William."

It was hardly a sufficient answer, to William's mind. He pressed, "Does she try to delay the signing? For there will be no delay. My mind will not rest until this matter is settled."

"Nay, William, we spoke not of the marriage," Godfrey answered with a smile.

"If she wanted to know something of the man she is pledged to, it would have been better to—"

"William, we spoke not of you," Godfrey interrupted with a wide smile.

William le Brouillard, known on three continents for his fighting ability and his beauty of from, frowned down at the priest.

"Lady Cathryn," Godfrey supplied, "is quite anxious for me to say a mass for the dead." At William's blank look, he added, "That is all that we spoke of, William."

"Then you must say one at the soonest opportunity," William answered calmly, his composure back in place.

Godfrey nodded in acquiescence, his own expression carefully bland.

William, hearing Rowland approach, turned to face him, more than glad to abandon his conversation with Father Godfrey. They scanned the hall together. It was not the hall itself that occupied his thoughts now, but the inhabitants. Servants moved briskly about the space, intent on their purpose, talking and mumbling and directing each other without pausing for breath. Rowland watched for William's reaction. Ulrich's words rang true; there was not a man or woman who was under forty years of age, and each and every one was filthy. Their clothes were encrusted and stiff with the grime of months, if not years. Streaks of dirt smeared faces, trails of meat fat ran along the sides of mouths, and fingernails were black instead of white.

The servants of Greneforde stank.

Of them all, only Lady Cathryn was clean, and in

her white gown she stood out as a beacon fire on a black night.

Rowland looked again at William. Across Syria, Armenia, Cappadocia, Phrygia; in Antioch, Edessa, and Dorylaeum; from Moldavia and Bohemia and Saxony; in the lands of Champagne, Blois, and, naturally, Normandy, William le Brouillard was well known for his fighting skill, his beauty, and . . . his cleanliness. In the arid sands of Damascus, where water was more precious than pearls and men sold their horses for a mere cupful of it, William had been clean. It was not that he had an unmasculine fear of dirt and hard labor—no one who knew him long could make that accusation. It was just that he could not abide slovenly habits in himself or in those around him. One had only to hear Ulrich complain to know the truth of that. And now William had his land and his estate and his people, and the people had passed dirty six months ago. If Rowland had been of a lighter temperament, he would have laughed.

William watched Cathryn as she spoke with the steward. She was thin, with the willowy grace of tall grass moved by the wind, but he could see now that she was a full woman. It was not the look of her, for she was as slender and shapeless as a child, but the manner she possessed. She was in full command of the hall and its people; for all the hurried activity of the folk brushing past her, each and every one looked in her direction not once, but often. Sometimes she would nod or make eye contact, sometimes she did not acknowledge them at all, but still they looked to her. William, watching her, suddenly felt distinctly unnecessary.

"The hour is past for the main meal, my lord."

Her voice was low and soft, yet carried to him clearly across the clamor of the hall.

"Yet a full table has been prepared for you and your company so that you might refresh yourselves after your journey to us."

He could see that it was so. The high table was being set with steaming trenchers, and the goblet that was positioned in the place of the lord's chair was of finely worked silver. There was nothing in her words or her manner to feed suspicion. He was hungry. His men were hungry. The food had clearly been prepared in advance of his arrival. Still, he could not ignore the alarm that jangled in the heart of his thoughts. For all of her sweet words and her open-door welcome, he did not quite trust the lady of Greneforde. Something was amiss, and if he did not know now what it was, he was certain he would know ere long. Until he did know, marriage to her was his best security against open warfare with the people of Greneforde. Armed battle was not how he wanted to begin his lordship. From such a beginning it might take years to heal.

"Lady," he began, "your hospitality is welcome as has your welcome been most hospitable, yet I would not delay the signing of the marriage contract and the nuptials that will join us as the lord and lady of Greneforde." William paused to smile. "I am Henry's man, and he has sent me here to secure the land in his name; I would be a churlish knight if I chose my own comfort over quick obedience to the king's command."

Cathryn heard his words without any wisp of expression crossing her features, but her very lack of response was response enough.

"Lady Cathryn," William continued, "you have prepared a fine banquet for your betrothed." He paused again to smile, but his eyes shone like unsheathed steel. "I would have it be our wedding feast and eat it with my wife beside me."

In those long and silent moments, Cathryn regarded William le Brouillard as she had not yet done. Courtly of speech he was, certainly, but the steel of him was a barely concealed blade that, while not aggressively seeking to hurt, also would not hesitate to do so if provoked. He seemed a strong man, one not accustomed to having his will thwarted, who would fight, even if gently, to achieve his purpose. All this she thought as she faced him and heard his prettily spoken words that all the same said that he would not eat now, that he would not eat until Greneforde was lawfully his.

This glimpse into the character of the man who would rule Greneforde did not dismay her; indeed, such traits would serve Greneforde well, if Greneforde's welfare was important to him. Of herself and how she would fare with him, she did not, would not, ponder.

"Your duty rules you, my lord, and I am ruled by it," she answered simply with a graceful nod. "Your chamber awaits you. When you have changed out of your battle gear, you will find me in the solar; if that is in accord with your desires."

He would rather have gone directly to the chapel and signed the contracts immediately, but he did not want to risk offending her by marrying in armor after she had capitulated without argument concerning the meal. Subduing his anxiety, he smiled with all of the courtly charm that he had acquired during his years of soldiering and answered, "That you seek to gratify my desires pleases me, Cathryn, and so I would please you."

For all that his imminent wife was adept at self-possession, he did not miss the slight widening of her dark eyes at his answer. She was an innocent, unused to the seductive speech used at court; it was to be expected in light of Greneforde's remote location, and he was pleased by it.

"I will dress in robes that will add honor to the ceremony that will join us. You will not have long to wait, lady."

No reply was necessary, for which she was grateful. There was a lump in the center of her chest that pushed against her lungs so that she struggled to draw breath. He was strikingly handsome, this man who would rule her; his eyes glowed and sparked like newly worked steel, and his finely words wound around her like a net. She hoped he did not know that she found his words beguiling, for it would not do for him to gain so firm a foothold and so quickly.

Turning swiftly, Cathryn led the way to the stair and on to her future husband's chamber.

It was just above the great hall below, but half its size. The room had been divided in the past to make two rooms: one, the lord's chamber, and next to it, the solar. It was an unusual arrangement. Usually the lord's bedchamber served as solar, since space inside a great tower, even a large one, was at a premium, but, even divided, the bedchamber was ample in size. A large bed dominated the room, draped in pristine white that almost touched the floor. The bed, surmounted by a canopy structure, was bare of the canopy itself, but that could be easily amended. On the far side of the bed was the hearth, with a fire crackling brightly and dispelling the damp cold that infused the stone walls. Before the fire was a padded stool and a plain bench that had been artfully carved but had seen rough handling during its lifetime. On the opposing wall, closest to the curtained entrance to the room, was a simply carved chest of royal proportions, and next to it was a washstand with a pitcher and bowl. William nodded his approval of the room; it was large, it was well-appointed, and it was clean.

Before he could speak, Cathryn stepped back into the curtained alcove that separated the door from the room; it was a very effective means of keeping down drafts that could rise with stormlike force in the narrow confines of the stair tower. A pair of men carried in a deep wooden tub and set it before the fire, nodding and touching hands to forelocks as they passed the new lord of Greneforde. On their heels came a stream of servants carrying buckets of water, unloading their heavy burden into the tub and quickly leaving the room. The servants, each and every one, had two things in common: each cast Cathryn a questioning glance before leaving and each was covered in grime. It did not pass William's notice, and while the one aroused his never-sleeping suspicions that something was afoot in Greneforde, he commented only about the latter.

"A bath before a warm fire will be most welcome, Lady Cathryn," he said. "You are most kind to think of it. It has been many days since I last washed," he added, looking pointedly at the last departing servant and the dirt tracks he left in his wake.

Cathryn only nodded, refusing to follow where his eyes led.

"During the time I traveled in the Way of the Cross I learned a great deal," he continued, moving more deeply into the room. "The Saracens, by example, taught us much in the way of warfare and architecture and, for myself, the comfort of cleanliness. I highly recommend it."

Cathryn stayed at her self-imposed post by the doorway, and though her answer was mild, he felt the deeply hidden barb within it.

"You are fortunate, my lord, to have learned so much. Not everyone has had the advantage of traveling far afield in God's work."

William, remembering with vivid clarity the dirt, the depravation, the starvation and thirst, but most of all the violent death that had been part and parcel of that traveling, wondered if she truly understood what she was saying.

"I concede that not many were able to follow the Way, and far fewer to return," he answered with equal mildness. "Therefore, my insights are all the more valuable for their rarity."

"An interesting perspective," she murmured.

"And one I devoutly hope you will come to share," he said with pleasant force, his eyes glowing like polished pewter, "as we will share all things."

Cathryn, backed into a corner both literally and figuratively, clasped her hands before her and nodded pleasantly and . . . forcefully.

"Lady"—William smiled—"it is my wish that the people of Greneforde bathe. Often."

"And so they shall," she responded calmly despite the escalated pounding of her heart. Bowing slightly, she said, "I will leave you to the care of your squire and your bath." And she disappeared as Ulrich entered in a flurry of motion.

Descending the stairs gave Cathryn time to slow the racing of her heart. Her initial estimation of William le Brouillard had been correct, and this second encounter only supported her conclusion: he would be a strong force in Greneforde. He would demand, in his honeyed fashion, that his wishes be made law. She smiled slightly to herself as she reached the bottom stair. The rain had become heavier and more chill since the arrival of le Brouillard. It struck the already muddy earth, sending up brown spikes of impact with each drop. Clutching her white gown up to her knees, she hugged the wall of the great tower and dashed to the kitchen. There were ways to deal with such a man, and the earth itself would instruct her. As the rain beat against the soil, seeking to change its very nature, so le Brouillard would beat against her. But, in the end, the rain blew away with the first steady wind and the earth was left as it had been, unmarked and unchanged by the water thrown against it. So it would be with them, and she would be the victor, though the victory would be a gentle one.

The kitchen staff would be nervous—that she knew without even thinking—so she entered with a smile, shaking the water from her hair with a laugh. It was well she did so, for they had cause to worry.

"He has ordered baths, has he not, lady?" Eldon asked. Of course they knew what had been said, at least in essence, in the lord's chamber. There were no secrets in the closely confined world of tower and wall.

"Yea, he has expressed his wish that bathing be a part of Greneforde life," she answered softly.

"What will we do, lady?" Marie whispered from a far corner of the room.

"We will bathe, Marie." Cathryn smiled. "The lord of Greneforde has spoken, and I have acceded to his wishes, as is right."

They looked at her in bafflement. It was Cathryn herself who had ordered that not one of them should bathe, no matter how dirty they became, even including the washing of their garments. It went beyond comprehension that she should have changed her position so quickly at just a word from the stranger who had entered their gate.

Walking to the hearth and casually stirring a pot of stew, Cathryn just as casually remarked, "What William le Brouillard has not said is *when* this bathing will happen."

Smiles, slow at first, lit the faces of the servants. Marie, in particular, breathed easier. Lady Cathryn would not be bested so easily; this they had known, but the fresh evidence of it was welcome.

Turning to Lan, Cathryn instructed, "There has been a delay in the timing of the meal, but I trust that you will be able to lay an impressive table."

Before he could answer, she turned to Alys. "Perhaps this delay will give you the time you need to do something remarkable with the apples, Alys."

"Aye, it will, my lady. I have it in mind even now," Alys assured her, and turned away to begin her work.

"John," Cathryn said, "I have been concerned about the eggs. They will harden at this delay. Could we not prepare them—"

"It has been seen to, Lady Cathryn," John answered calmly.

"Thank you, John," Cathryn responded, and then added in the same quiet and composed way in which she had said everything else, "for it must be a special meal, since it marks my marriage."

Marie, of them all, marveled at Cathryn's composure, and secretly, in her dark corner, she shivered in black apprehension.

Chapter Four

Rowland entered William's chamber without knocking, a habit he realized he would soon have to break. Ulrich was in the final stages of dressing William, and, as always, Ulrich was more than a little flustered.

The room had changed in one regard since William had first seen it: next to the chest that had been in the room originally, a new one had been added just to the other side of the washstand. William's chest. It was in this chest that Ulrich was buried up to his very impressive shoulders.

"You had best find it, boy," William murmured in low tones. "I had it made to wear for just such an occasion as this."

"Mayhap he left it in Burgundy when his brain was befuddled while wooing that comely redhead," Rowland offered cheerily.

Ulrich came up abruptly at that, holding the sought-after item in his fist.

"I was *not* befuddled!" he declared stoutly. He added with an engaging grin, " 'Twas she who was by the time we left. And here is the mantle you desire, Lord William."

Shaking it out, he laid it over William's shoulders. It was a magnificent garment, truly worthy of royalty. Lined in ermine, the mantle was of white samite so fine that it seemed to absorb all the light that touched it and cast it back subtly altered. William's tunic was of his favored gray, but gray shot with silver thread, and the hem of the piece was edged in a silken band of deep crimson. Rowland watched as Ulrich fastened the ruby clasp at William's right shoulder. That ruby alone was worth a tidy ransom, and as a ransom it had been paid. It was the size of a child's fist, encircled in beaten silver with gold filigree laid atop. It was an extraordinary piece of extraordinarily fine workmanship, even for the Saracen who had fashioned it.

William shrugged once and his clothing fell into perfect place. Ulrich was amazed, as always, at William's effortless elegance. It was true that William gave much thought and care to his wardrobe, but it was also true that he looked good in anything.

Rowland had ceased to be amazed long ago.

Dismissing Ulrich, William motioned for Rowland to join him by the fire. Sweeping his mantle out of the way, he sat on the padded stool, leaving the bench for his friend. Rowland did not hesitate to relate what he had learned.

"The dirt you saw, but they also cower when anyone not known to them approaches." Rowland leaned forward, resting his elbows on his knees. "They are a beaten lot, William, men and women both."

William leaned forward, his gray eyes searching the dark brown ones of his friend. "Was word spoken as to what has beaten them, Rowland? 'Tis clear the last years have been hard on Greneforde, but what could have crushed their spirits?"

"Months without food, without peace, can crush the stoutest spirit, William," Rowland answered quietly, reminding William of what they had both seen following the Way of the Cross. William needed no reminder, nor would he ever; the images of that time were burned into the core of his mind to live until he died.

"Yea, 'tis so," he quietly agreed, "but I am suspicious that more has happened here than burned cottages and bad harvests."

Rowland looked intently at William. William's instincts rarely misled him, and Rowland had learned not to question their accuracy.

"Is there more that you can say?" he questioned.

"Nay," William murmured, looking into the fire, "but I shall not be at ease until Cathryn is my wife in fact." Looking up suddenly, William pierced Rowland with the icy intensity of his eyes. "It is odd, is it not, that of all the cowering folk of Greneforde, one stands straight and tall without sign of distress?"

"Lady Cathryn is a woman of admirable self-possession," Rowland answered simply.

"She is that," William muttered, looking again

into the fire, vividly aware that he was much less pleased by that trait than he had been just hours ago. She seemed a cold woman, cold to the very heart; it was not such a desirable trait in a woman he would soon have to bed. "She is also of Greneforde and yet not, for she does not behave as Greneforde folk do."

"She is a lady," Rowland said.

"Being a lady is not always such a difference."

"It is with Lady Cathryn."

"So the evidence shows," William answered softly. "Yet . . . I am . . . unsure."

"Do you fear betrayal? The loss of Greneforde at her instigation?"

"Odd that you use the word 'betrayal.' I had not thought of it in such terms, yet the word seems to mold itself to her in my thoughts. But the loss of Greneforde Tower?" William asked, his eyes alight with cool sparks. "Nay, I do not fear the loss of Greneforde. It is mine," he said with authoritative finality.

Rowland leaned back against the worn contours of the wooden bench. "The means to set aside at least part of your uneasiness is within your grasp; the lady awaits you in the solar, as she promised. You have only to reach out your hand and take her."

"Yea, you are right," William said, standing suddenly, his mantle swirling around his calves in a rich cloud. "I have only to take Cathryn to take Greneforde; they are two sides of the same coin, are they not? Whatever pricks me will be plucked in good time."

William turned and strode to the door of his

chamber, Rowland following in his wake. The solar was but steps away and he was eager. Father Godfrey and George, the cleric William had hired in London, were waiting at a small table covered with a fine piece of red cloth. The tower was unusually quiet; the dogs had been chased out, the servants withdrawn, and even the rain had ceased its staccato beat. As he was coming to expect, Cathryn stood in earnest conversation with Godfrey. His black brows drawing low, he covered the space that separated them with long strides.

"Then you are sufficiently rested to say the mass?"

Godfrey studied Cathryn's face before he drew breath to answer her. Such intensity, such suppressed energy, in so slender a frame. He had been in Greneforde for just hours, and yet the only topic that had sprung from her lips was the funeral mass. He would have thought, as a woman soon to wed, that she would have had questions about the man she was to marry, but no word had been said of William.

Godfrey bit back a smile. He knew William well enough to know that her lack of curiosity would pinch his pride. William had enjoyed the lion's portion of female appreciation for many years and he had come to expect it as his rightful due; Cathryn of Greneforde was making a severe dent in his armor, though he doubted that she knew it. Therein lay the problem: she treated William as no more than a necessary inconvenience, to be handled and relegated to obscurity as quickly as possible. It was an odd way for a maid to behave on meeting her betrothed, but Godfrey was not a man to seek trouble. He would wait for her confidence, allowing her the freedom to choose her moment. From such benign passivity grew the deepest confessions. He would wait, but he could feel the heaviness of her soul. Godfrey said none of this, but asked Cathryn a question of his own.

"I feel quite vigorous, Lady Cathryn. The mass will be read at the soonest moment, but I am curious." He paused to study her face again, for she seemed on the point of withdrawal, then questioned conversationally, "What has happened to Greneforde's priest?"

"He accompanied my father on pilgrimage," she answered.

"But that was many years ago, was it not? Do you mean that he did not return?"

"Nay, he returned with news of my father's death, but felt the need to journey to Canterbury on a pilgrimage of his own some months ago. He has not returned."

And Godfrey could sense in her manner that she did not expect him to. The situation was most unusual; no house could function long without a priest. Cathryn's manner, always so urgent in her dealings with him before, was now abrupt and slightly evasive. It was odd indeed.

"I have yet to ask, but who shall the mass be for?" he asked, looking for more solid ground.

Looking down at her clasped hands for the space of a heartbeat, Cathryn answered softly, so softly that Godfrey could barely make out the words: "For someone held dear by me."

Godfrey might have had difficulty hearing her heartfelt words, but William heard her clearly enough. Her choice of words did not please him. She was an orphan; who could hold place in her sheltered and innocent heart? There was just one acceptable answer: no one.

Aware of his presence, Cathryn drew slightly away from Father Godfrey and faced William. Her urgency over the funeral mass would have to wait until after the ceremony and the signing of the contracts; it was for that very reason that she was eager to be finished with the formality of the marriage contract. William le Brouillard was lord of Greneforde; Henry had decreed it. He was in possession of Greneforde. That Greneforde was his was an accomplished fact. The marriage ceremony would merely be the seal on an already finished document.

She faced him with neither relief nor urgency, but with the calm control and lack of emotion that he now associated with her. Could anyone be "dear" to such a bloodless woman? She had no word for him, no sign of recognition; she only noted his presence and turned away to hasten the steward in providing wine. Her movements were supple, graceful in a way that reminded him of meadow grass, and, despite her cool demeanor, he found pleasure in watching her move. Her silk-entwined plaits swung as she moved, the pale golden strands capturing the light of candle and fire.

Godfrey had been right: she was a beauty. She was as the troubadors described beauty: slim and small and fair, and though her eyes were dark instead of the expected blue, he thought her beauty the more highly charged for it.

And she had not noticed him, not really noticed him, not as a maid watched a man she wanted. William twitched the edges of his magnificent mantle in suppressed annoyance. He could not remember the last time he had been so ignored by a woman, especially since it had never happened before. In all the years of his life, even during his gangly years of almost manhood, he had never lacked for women's sighs when he was near and groans when he left. Running his hand over his jaw, he adjusted his mantle with a brisk swipe of his hand and straightened his spine. With a curt bow, he accepted the goblet of wine that Cathryn handed him.

Rowland watched William bury his irritation and, correctly guessing the cause, smiled as he accepted a goblet from Lady Cathryn's hand. He was suddenly quite pleased that there were no wars to distract him; life at Greneforde watching these two in their silent sparring would prove entertaining enough.

"Let us begin, Father," William ordered gently, "that we the sooner conclude and feast at the table so richly prepared for us." He politely nodded to Cathryn, wondering if she would seek to delay the matter.

She did not.

"To this marriage I bring," she began softly, "Greneforde Castle, encompassing land twenty leagues north, ten leagues east and west, and bordered by the river Brent to the south; also Blythe Tower, eight leagues distant from Greneforde's western boundary." Looking first at Father Godfrey and then at William, she added without apology, "I have not been to Blythe Tower and do not know in what condition you will find it."

William nodded and said, "When I find it, I will determine its condition and do what is necessary."

"Also," she said, plowing on, "Greneforde village, as you know, is no more. It was ravaged repeatedly in recent years and vanished completely two years ago. The survivors live inside the curtain wall."

"Though there are few to feed, Greneforde's food stores are dangerously low," Rowland interjected softly.

Cathryn stood as straight and slim as a seedling before a gathering wind as she faced the men across the bloodred table that separated them. She stood alone, yet she did not falter. Her next words resonated in the space for all their brevity.

"It has been a hard year for Greneforde."

"So it has been if you have lost all of your household knights in the last months," William said.

Despite the evidence, he could not believe that Greneforde Tower had stood unmanned for so many weeks in a land overrun by wandering mercenaries who answered to no one. Especially in light of Rowland's observation; where had the food gone with so few people to consume it?

Cathryn did not voice an answer to William's observation, but stood silent and still. It was Father Godfrey who directed the conversation back to the marriage contract.

"Is there anything else included in your dower, Lady Cathryn?"

Her composure unbroken, Cathryn answered directly to William, her eyes not leaving his.

"There is no coin, no jewels, no plate. What my father did not take with him on pilgrimage, the years of war have eaten."

She brought little in the way of liquid wealth to the bond, but she brought what William desired most: a home and land. Looking at her, straight-backed and clear-eyed, he could not but feel pride at her honor and her dignity in telling them of Greneforde's poverty.

Father Godfrey looked now at William, checking first to see that George had recorded Cathryn's portion.

"And now an accounting of what William le Brouillard brings to the union."

Cathryn took a slight step forward, her eyes intent on William's. Noting her tension, William thought he had a glimpse into the workings of her mind. By law, their portions must be of equal value. If his portion did not equal hers, the marriage could be canceled. With a large measure of pride and a deep breath, he held her eyes and began.

"For my portion I claim a dinner service of hammered silver, twelve plates of gold, five hundred gold pieces, a trunk of spice, a trunk of woven cloth from the East, twelve warhorses, a small bag of gems with settings of gold and silver, and a bag of seed."

At the mention of the seed, and only of the seed, Cathryn's eyes lit with dark fire and she looked at William hungrily. So she cared little for his gold and much for his seed. They had that, at least, in common, and he remarked upon it.

"These seeds I have gathered from many lands to someday enrich my own land," he said warmly. "We share an interest in agriculture, it seems."

Cathryn tried to ignore the warmth of his tone and the way his eyes suddenly shone upon her like fine silver plate.

"You bring many fine and costly gifts to our marriage, my lord, but the prospect of food when one is hungry is most welcome." Smiling politely, she added, "I am certain that I will appreciate the golden plate when my stomach is full of roasted goose."

William had known hunger as too close a companion not to appreciate her sentiment; he had known great hunger, endless hunger, following the Way. He smiled fully in agreement.

And Cathryn forgot about the seed.

Never before had she seen such dazzling beauty in a man. His smile lit the world as the sun never had, and she wondered why the intensity of it did not blind her.

The world shrank to only him. All sound ceased. All thought fled. He was consuming her and she stood motionless, unable to breathe. A stillness unlike any she had experienced rose from within her—not a self-imposed control of emotion, but a frozen stillness that came from the center of her and cascaded out, almost freezing the very air around her.

William le Brouillard had touched the core of her; he had snared and caught the emotions she kept so protectively guarded—and he had done it with a smile.

But all that William saw was Cathryn's deathly stillness, which seemed to him to be remote serenity. Defying reason, he was disappointed with her response to him, and then chided himself for his folly. She would be Lady Snow to his Fog. They were well matched; after all, the land was his goal, and it seemed they shared a love of the land.

Flicking his cloak back and over his arm with courtly elegance, William leaned down to sign the completed contract. It was with satisfaction that he watched Cathryn do the same.

Greneforde was his.

Father Godfrey then began the ceremony that would bind them in the eyes of God.

"It only remains for me to solemnly demand from you your consent to the marriage. This is the moment for you to reflect . . . and to think of he who blessed all marriages. . . ."

Cathryn heard only snatches of the ceremony. She fought against William's touch on her soul, so casually achieved. She would never survive this marriage if he could touch and hold her with such ease. His deep voice rumbled and she heard: "Yea; I, William, take thee to wife."

Her hands clasped in front of her, the image of feminine submission, Cathryn responded softly.

"Yea; I, Cathryn, take thee for my husband."

Cathryn was his.

Father Godfrey produced a ring of gold studded with rubies and topaz that caught and held the flickering light of the candles.

"May the creator and preserver of all men, may the giver of grace and eternal life cause His blessing to descend on this ring."

William took the ring from the priest's hand and put it successively upon three fingers of Cathryn's right hand, gently pulling her clasped hands free of each other, and said each time, "In the name of the Father, of the Son, and of the Holy Ghost."

Taking her left hand solemnly in his two large, callused ones, he looked into her eyes upon saying the final words of the contract. Dark brown eyes absorbed the glitter of gray as he said, "With this ring I thee espouse." Cathryn felt her stomach lurch.

His voice husky now, he continued, "With my body I thee honor." The stillness within her shattered like icicles when they struck ground.

"With my goods I thee endow."

Unable to look away from him, she could only try to recapture the peace of rigid control.

Then, with Father Godfrey leading them and Rowland following, they crossed the solar silently and climbed the stair to the chapel one floor above. Of all the rooms in the tower, it alone had the luxury of glass. Reaching the center of the nave, Cathryn felt William's gentle tug on her hand and then they lay prostrate, the extended hands of Father Gregory held over them.

The wooden floor was cold and rough against her cheek, and she welcomed the sensation. She wanted to block it all out: the poverty of Greneforde, the hunger, the fact that her home had been given to a stranger and that stranger was now her husband. But she couldn't. Emotions long suppressed rolled through her prostrate form until she thought she would be sick. This man would rule her; her life lay in his hands by the authority of both God and king. If she displeased him, he could beat her, imprison her, starve her. And she would displease him, of that there was no doubt at all. The priest's next words caught her off guard.

"May God bless you, and Himself teach you to worship one another in your bodies and in your souls."

Had God blessed her with William le Brouillard as husband? She had said as much to Marie and John and all the rest, but in her heart of hearts, did she believe it? Would God, indeed, instruct her in worshiping her husband—for he was husband now—with her body? How could her body, the house of her pain, be used in worship? It could not be, yet the priest had said so. The tremors that had begun with William's words rocked against her lungs and all her inward parts. Standing with William's aid, she clasped her hands tightly and stilled the tides that pounded against her. She was Cathryn of Greneforde and she would not falter.

Standing on William's right, close enough to his hand that she could almost detect the blood flowing through his veins, she heard the mass for the first time as a married woman.

And then it was finished, or she thought it was. William advanced to the altar, his black hair coldly shining in the faint light admitted through the glass above them. He was very tall. Why had she not noticed that before? He was beautifully clothed, his cloak falling smoothly from wide shoulders. She fingered the coarse texture of her wool bliaut; it was hardly fine enough for a wedding, yet it was the best she had.

William leaned down and received the kiss of peace from Father Godfrey, who was no small man himself. Tall and broad he was, yet not a bullish figure, but wide at the shoulder and narrow at the hip with thick arms and long legs. . . . Why had she not seen the full measure of this man before? Because his cold gray eyes had captured her, she answered herself; his cold eyes and his winning smile and his black hair and . . . She was doing it again and she must not. Not now. Not when he was walking toward her, his eyes both solemn and joyous. And then she remembered. He would transmit the kiss of peace to her!

William towered over her in no way menacingly, for he was there to give the kiss of peace, after all; yet the shadow of the cross fell between and over them and she shivered. Smiling encouragingly, as though to soothe a frightened hound, William placed his hands on her shoulders. His movements were slow and deliberate and suffused with gentleness, and in spite of that, she jumped at first contact. He must think her doltish, she scolded herself silently. Breathing in slowly, she raised her face to accept his kiss.

It was a chaste kiss and meant to be nothing more.

It was a chaste kiss, truly, yet too long and too warm and too . . . close. His breath was pleasantly warm and sweet, his lips firm and soft, his chin rough against hers. She did not like to be touched. She did not like the way she felt physically surrounded by him. She did not like his breath mixing with hers. She did not want to feel his body press against hers so that she could smell the essence of him. She did not want him to touch her. Breaking away, she ended it.

And now, surely, the ceremony was complete.

Father Godfrey smiled warmly at her. William's comrade, Rowland, clapped her husband on the back once and smiled with quiet humor. She watched them congratulate William, feeling for just a moment like an outsider at her own wedding, and then all three turned to her, expectantly.

Nodding firmly, she said, "The meal awaits," and without waiting for them, hurried to the stairs.

Rowland looked askance at William as he watched his new wife rush from the room.

" 'Tis an efficient wife you have, William, and one who does not let emotion rule the day."

Pulling his eyes away from the spot where he had last seen Cathryn, William spared Rowland a glance.

"Yea, and what man would not wish for such a wife?" he asked, his voice unnaturally even.

"None in this room, surely," Rowland agreed pleasantly.

Nodding in unintentional mimicry of his wife, William marched to the stair and quietly descended with Rowland and Godfrey just a few steps behind. The meal was, in fact, waiting for them. Ulrich had produced the gold plate, at William's direction, and it added a richness to the meal that the food alone could not provide. The hall seemed to shine with the gleam of metal; the table glinted with silver, pewter, and gold, and the knights who were sworn to William cast their own dull sparkle with sleeves of mail and burnished swords.

If Cathryn was startled to find armed men at her wedding feast, she gave no outward indication of it, and that only tilted the scales of suspicion against her. If she was innocent of treachery, she would be insulted. If she was guilty, she would be dismayed and try to hide it.

Fie on wives, he growled silently; who could read the heart of a woman? Cathryn was a master of contained emotion, or perhaps possessor of none. No, he was being harsh in his judgment. She was anxious and eager for the meal to come off as planned; that much was obvious, and was so typically womanish. She stood off to one side, head-to-head with the steward, pointing and directing the stream of servants as they entered with their hot burden of food. And suddenly she was directing him.

"Sit, my lord. You have had a long journey in wet weather; sit and eat."

It was a kind offer, yet an offer he could not take. Cathryn was lady as he was lord. He would not sit at table without her. And, as eager as he was to sit at the lord's place in Greneforde Tower, he would not take that place; she would have to lead him to it and give it to him of her own will. He not only wanted her people to see her relinquish Greneforde in this public way; he wanted her to personally hand him Greneforde.

But she had already turned away, fully expecting

him to do as she had bidden. Truly, the lady had been too long without a lord.

How many minutes had passed before she looked and saw that neither he, nor Rowland, nor Godfrey had moved a step deeper into the hall was uncertain, but the look of surprise on her face was one he would not forget. It was the first glimpse of any emotion that he had seen her display in all the hours he had known her.

"Is there aught amiss, my lord?" she asked quickly, her anxiety clear.

"Yea," he answered softly, "we wait on thee, lady."

"There is no need," she assured him. "I am but seeing to—"

"Lady," he cut her off, his voice deep as it rumbled past his throat. "I wait on thee."

For Cathryn, the only gleam, the only glitter in the capacious hall originated in William's silver eyes. The air was charged between them. She could feel the force of his will upon her, even in the crowded room that had of a sudden grown very quiet. And she knew that she would do as he asked. No, he did not ask. He willed. But he was her husband and her lord and she would submit with good grace. In this.

And with graceful movements she drew near to him, her steps suddenly loud in the quiet hall. John came to her rescue when he called for the salt. The noise level escalated to its previous and normal level as the servants again jostled each other moving to and fro from the hall, down the stairs, to the kitchen and back again.

The Holding

He held his hand out to her and with hardly a shiver she placed her hand in his. His was warm and dry while hers felt cool and damp, but no matter, the table was before them and he did not hesitate to lead her to it. Such a fuss over her accompanying him to the high table; she had scarcely thought a fighting knight would trouble himself over so small a detail, but he was also unlike any knight she had ever known. He followed the code of etiquette and chivalry to the letter. He was an oddity in her experience, which was admittedly limited.

William was pleased—no, more than pleased that Cathryn had not balked in seating him at the high table in the lord's chair. What pleased him just as much, though he hardly spared a thought for it, was that she had rushed to his side at his request and was now seated placidly to his left. To his mind, they presented a united front to the people of Greneforde, both hers and his, and solidarity was his goal in image as well as fact. The contracts had been signed, the marriage vows spoken and witnessed, and Greneforde secured. Only one thing remained: consummation.

His loins burned at the word.

He had not expected that, but Cathryn had been a surprise. She was warm beauty and chill manner, delicate of bone and firm of will; he was drawn to her even as he felt her withdrawal. He wanted her and did not want to, sensing that she did not want him.

It was an entirely new experience for him.

He turned to look at her finely drawn profile, the

burning in his loins clearly revealed in the gray
sparks of his eyes. And Cathryn, feeling his gaze,
turned and was impaled on the cold heat of those
silver eyes. It was a look she recognized all too well.
Without any marked effort, Cathryn retreated even
more deeply into calm composure; the outer layers
of her thoughts and wit folded inward as a turtle
into its shell.

Married less than an hour and knowing her for
less than a day, William still had no difficulty in
seeing that she had withdrawn from him more
fully, yet he could not reason why. She was safely
married, her holding secure now that it was in his
grip, and he was not unpleasant to look upon . . .
Why should she not be gladdened by what this day
had brought to Greneforde?

Lifting the goblet, he carefully raised it not to his
own lips, but to hers. It would have been expected
of him if she were a woman unknown to him; that
she was his wife—and his wife of just minutes—
made his act of chivalry imperative. Also, he would
win a smile from her. His vanity demanded it. It
was enough to sour the meal to have her behave so
churlishly at the celebration of their joining. Cathryn reacted as if dazed. The look in her brown eyes
labeled him either a lunatic or an imbecile. He was
neither; at least he had not been before meeting her.

Smiling, his manner cajoling, he murmured for
her ears alone, "I would serve you, Cathryn. 'Tis the
French way, if not the English."

When she only stared into his eyes like a bayed
deer, he added, "I would honor you, lady."

To his relief, she allowed him to give her a drink

from the cup they would share for the feast. He did her honor, yet her manner did not warm to him. Taking back the goblet from her lips, he held her eyes with his while he drank from the portion of the cup that she had heated with her lips. She paled and stared at the hands she held so rigidly in her lap, the jeweled ring he had given her twinkling joyously against the white of her gown. It was the only thing about her that did shine with goodwill. Truthfully, she perplexed him.

"By law she is no more a maid," Rowland said softly into William's ear. "She now must wait until day's end for the fact of that to take place."

Of course. He was an imbecile not to think that she would be uneasy about the bridal bed. He suddenly almost felt pity for her. The day had a different look when seen from a maid's sheltered eyes. She was wed to a stranger, though that was not so unusual, yet hers had not been handpicked by a loving parent. Her betrothed had been decided by an unfamiliar sovereign with martial haste. It would be enough to cast any young girl's emotions adrift.

"Come, Cathryn," he said gently, his sympathy aroused now to mingle with his desire. "I have cut the finest portion for you." And he held it in his hand before her mouth. Her mouth remained firmly closed as the clear, red juice of the meat ran down the side of his hand. " 'Tis a fine bridal feast, lady; I would have you taste of it."

Hesitantly, reluctantly, she opened her mouth to him, and as the meat grazed her lips, her tongue flicked out to meet it, and William knew that he had never fed a lady with such sensuous overtones. Yet such had not been his intention. Until now.

"Yea, Cathryn," he whispered encouragingly, " 'twas moist and tender, was it not? The juice ran freely and fulfilled a hunger that grows keener with being fed, did it not? Do you desire more?"

"Nay," she answered abruptly when she had swallowed, almost choking.

"Nay?" He smiled slowly. "You eat sparingly, lady. I would have a wife with healthy appetite and feed her hunger till we are both satisfied."

Cathryn was breathing rapidly through her mouth. She was certain that if he did not stop staring at her with those eyes, those piercing steel eyes, that she was going to vomit all over the fine linen of the table. All his talk of meat and juice and hunger . . . It had her stomach in a coil. It would be his just due if she did spill her stomach in his lap. A fine bridal feast this would be then.

John saved her in the only way he could: he provided a much-needed distraction. Coming in close to William, he poured more wine, lifting his arm to just above William's face. The look of repugnance that swiftly crossed her husband's features restored her composure entirely; actually, it was an effort not to laugh. John took his time with the wine, moving his arms and clothing around much more than necessary for that simple act. Cathryn was ready for William's remark the moment John left the vicinity of the table.

"There is," he began, looking almost accusingly at her, "an odor of the unwashed mingling with that of the meal. Do you agree?"

What a fine knight she was married to, to find

such distaste in a little healthy sweat. But she did not say so; nor did she reveal the direction of her thoughts in the expression on her face. Looking blandly at her husband, she answered, "The preparation of the bridal feast has quite consumed what time they had. Particularly with the delay," she added pointedly.

William did not pursue it. Instead he studied her face. It was a beautiful face, certainly, but without any warmth or sparkle in the eyes. Well, that would change, and right quickly. Cathryn was terrified of the bedding to come; once that was behind her, she would bloom like any other woman. Fear ruled her; he was sure of it.

Unfortunately, he was quite right.

Chapter Five

Cathryn stepped out of the small room that jutted off the chapel, smoothing invisible wrinkles out of the heavy wool she wore. It had been too long since she had spoken with a priest of God, and she felt better for it. At least for the moment.

Looking up at the simple cross, she remembered Father Godfrey's words. She and le Brouillard were one in God's sight; it was not such an unpalatable thought. Truly, she was bone weary of carrying the weight of all Greneforde on her shoulders. It would be good to share the burden and the decision making. And William could travel the distance to Blythe Tower as she could not; who would attack a knight of such strength? Blythe Tower could be just a mass of rubble after so many— She pulled her scattering thoughts back. It did her no good to think of Blythe Tower, yet it was time to know just what remained and what could be salvaged. Having William le Brouillard as husband would be good for Greneforde.

Cathryn suddenly had a vision of his face as he had looked down upon her from the back of his warhorse; a shiver trailed down her spine that she struggled to control. He was a man of high pride; there was no disputing that. The priest had not even pretended to. Father Godfrey had also said that William was a godly knight with a keen devotion to God's inspired word and manifest will. There was comfort in those words, for was God not known for His forgiveness and mercy?

And His righteous anger?

She could not allow her thoughts to travel there. Truly, she had never had such trouble controlling her thoughts until the arrival of William le Brouillard. What was it about him that weakened her willpower? Whatever it was, it was most annoying. She did not think it unlikely that he did so on purpose; he was French and they were an obdurate race.

Father Godfrey had been kind and comforting. He knew her husband well and had not lost faith in him even after hearing her confession, although his own composure had slipped for just a moment. Shock had been in his eyes, swiftly drowned by compassion. He was a kind man. Surely, if her husband had been in the company of such a priest, having been instructed in spiritual matters by him for many years, surely some of that kindness had taken root in him? It was a logical, if unconvincing, argument, but it was useless to ponder it. All would be well because all must be well. The words comforted her, for she lived in a world not of *should* but of *must*.

Godfrey left the tiny room with slow steps that stopped completely upon seeing Lady Cathryn standing alone in the chapel. Dressed as she was in white, with hands clasped before herself in meek supplication, she looked the penitent pilgrim. He thought it a particularly apt comparison.

William, seeking her, appeared in the portal as silently as ever. Odd that it was William and not Father Godfrey that she was instantly aware of. His dark hair curled abundantly on his head; would it be soft or springy? Would it be as blue-black in the summer sun as it was in the winter fog? Catching her thoughts before they flew away with her, she laughed inwardly; it would be wiser to ask if his jaw would be as resolute and his eyes as penetrating six months hence. She did not know what she hoped for in answer to her unspoken question.

As he was coming to expect when he came upon her unexpectedly, he had eyes for none save her. He did not see the penitent pilgrim that Father Godfrey saw; he saw a strong woman, a woman in full command of herself and everyone else. But as cold as she seemed, she drew him in. It was folly—he knew it was—but she drew him to her as the earth draws the lightning bolt.

And then another thought struck him hard: she seemed ever to stand alone.

Godfrey broke the moment of intense contemplation between them. With a gesture, he welcomed William into the chapel, his expression unaccountably serious. Again, rising like the tides, the knowledge that something was amiss in Greneforde swept over him. The sensation never left him completely, but was only enhanced or subdued. The sensation was strong now.

"I am glad that you are both here, for there is something I would like before this day of your joining is out," Godfrey said.

Taking Cathryn's hand in his own, Godfrey held it tenderly, both hands surrounding hers as in a paternal caress; then he placed her hand in William's. Her husband's hand, far surpassing the priest's in both size and strength, engulfed hers so that all that was left visible was her protruding wrist.

Cathryn was not comforted.

But Godfrey spared her not a glance. His gaze—and it was a fixed gaze of serious intent—was reserved wholly for William.

"Remember you the scripture regarding how a husband should love his wife, William?"

William had not been expecting that, and it was a moment before he answered.

"Yea, Father, if you refer to Saint Paul's letter to the church at Ephesus, but now is not the time for one of your tests of my concentration and memory."

" 'Tis more than that, William. I would hear you speak the words of our Lord concerning a husband's duty to his wife. I would wish for Lady Cathryn to hear them in your voice."

William searched Father Godfrey's face for an indication of where he was going with this odd request. He saw nothing there save earnestness. Cathryn was looking curiously at the priest, so she did not appear to have any clearer notion as to the cause. Normally William would have cheerfully and politely refused Godfrey's request, putting him off for another time, but today he had obtained a great prize after years of labor. He submitted to the priest with a smile. The sense of unease that he had had when first entering the chapel was waning and he was glad of it; he had Greneforde and he had Cathryn. What could be amiss?

"Yea, Father, I remember it, and if you seek proof I will gladly supply it."

William began, " 'Husbands, love your wives, just as Christ loved the church and gave himself up for her to make her holy, cleansing her by the washing with water through the word, and to present her to himself as a radiant church, without stain or wrinkle or any other blemish, but holy and blameless.' "

William stopped for breath and noticed that Cathryn had her hands clasped tightly in front of her gown and that she was staring wide-eyed and mute at Father Godfrey. Of course, that irritated him. What was wrong with the woman that she always looked to the priest and never to the husband God and king had given her? Eager to finish, William continued at a faster pace.

" 'In this same way, husbands ought to love their wives as their own bodies. He who loves his wife loves himself. After all, no one ever hated his own body, but he feeds and cares for it, just as Christ does the church—for we are members of his body. For this reason a man will leave his father and mother and be united to his wife, and the two will become one flesh.' "

"Thank you, William," Father Godfrey interrupted as William stopped again for breath.

Cathryn's cheeks were flushed with color, and, though she had not looked at him since he began his recitation, William was enchanted by the sight of her. Perhaps Godfrey's request of a recitation of Holy Writ had not been ill founded; saying the familiar words had put him in mind of the pleasures of the marriage bed. Come morning, he was certain that he would make his wife's cheeks flush with becoming regularity. The longer he watched her, with her breath coming in near gasps, the more certain he was that Cathryn's blood would be warmed in bed.

"That is Holy Scripture?" she said softly, her eyes locked with Father Godfrey's.

"Yea, Cathryn," he answered seriously.

"How comes he to know it?"

More insulted at being so ignored than he cared to examine, William answered for himself with as much chivalry as he could summon.

"Nay, do not ask, Lady Cathryn, for this shepherd of God drives his lambs with a will. You would faint away if I related the hours he spent in drilling me and my comrades on the particulars of God's word, as I near fainted with weariness when he poured the words through me."

" 'Twas not words, but the spirit of God that poured through you, William," Father Godfrey corrected pleasantly.

Cathryn had hardly looked at William as he spoke, which did nothing to sweeten his mood.

"You speak the word of God at . . . open fires?" she asked incredulously. God's ways were inscrutable to all save the clergy, God's anointed, fit for the people only in the solemnity of the mass . . . or so she had been taught.

Again William answered for Father Godfrey.

"Father Godfrey, in his youth," he said with a smile, "spent considerable time with Abelard."

At this piece of illuminating news, Cathryn could only stare blankly.

"You have not heard of Abelard?" Godfrey asked in surprise.

"Nay, I have not."

"Perhaps of his Heloise?"

"William! She was not 'his' Heloise, but the prioress of Argenteuil and highly respected. . . ."

"Yea, Father"—William smiled cheerfully—"yet the tale of their love has already passed beyond the border of France. . . ."

"And now into the heart of England," Godfrey finished.

William bowed deeply and murmured, "Your pardon, Father." The effect was completely ruined by his beaming smile.

Too much information coming at her too quickly; that was what was wrong with her. Abelard and Heloise, who was or was not "his." All that about being blameless and clean, washed and spotless—that was what had her pulse shooting through her body like a falling star. Who would have thought that a well-seasoned warrior would spout Holy Scripture like a bubbling fount? There was too much to absorb; that was why she could not seem to breathe. It was the power and surprise of those words from God in heaven to man below, for she had never imagined that the king of heaven would instruct that a husband love his wife's body as his own. That was it, for how could William love her body and cherish her and even become "one flesh"? It was impossible. Impossible for her, and so impossible for him. She had to clear her mind of those words and the love and security they seemed to promise, for that promise was not for her. If she could bury those words deeply enough they would not entangle her and steal her resolve, her will, her control.

If William would not smile again, she just might survive.

Of her inner turmoil, the men saw just a rippling on the surface of the waters, which was quickly calmed to a glassy stillness. William did not let it discourage him; he had seen the fire in her cheeks. Her body coursed with blood, just as the rest of God's creations, and he was confident that he could make it rise again, with sweeter results.

"Supper will be called, my lord," Cathryn said meekly, then proceeded them out of the chapel and down the stairs, obviously fully expecting them to follow. They did. But William did not do so without a scowl. His wife was ever quick with her declarations and even quicker to expect his obedience; it was what happened when a woman was not wed at a younger age. But she was not too old to learn; nor was he too old to teach her.

Supper had been laid: wine, plover, bread, and cheese—light, but pleasant. What was less pleasant was the atmosphere.

With the waning of the day, the servants had become more anxious than they had been upon his arrival. It was a curious response. Why the tension now? Now, after he had been welcomed by the lady and was now her husband, after the bridal banquet, meager as it was, had been eaten, and the mass read? Yet he could feel their tension, their . . . fear, it almost was, and he could feel their eyes upon him as he supped. Looking up, he caught John the Steward staring at him. The servant glanced quickly away, but the sense of being watched would not leave him.

William trusted his senses.

Did they worry that he would rage over the lack of dishes at his table? He did not hold them accountable. The poverty and struggle of Greneforde was obvious, though he did not want them to know that it was so easy to read. All men had pride. It was most likely that they feared he would slash their pride over the care they had given to his new home. Any words he offered on the matter would only defeat his purpose. He could only wait until they knew him better; then they would know his mind and be at ease.

Now, Cathryn . . . she showed as much anxiety as a cloudless day. Would that she had a little more of their emotion and they had less. He watched her as she ate lightly of the trencher they shared. For a woman who chimed the dinner hour as she did, she ate remarkably little. A small bite of cheese washed down with a great gulp of wine. A mouthful of bread and a healthy sip of wine. The longer he watched, the more he concluded that what she ate served only to bob around like gulls on the great ocean of wine she had swallowed. But she was a beauty. She also appeared to hold her wine well, sluggish wine that it was, and so full of grit that he used his teeth to strain away the worst of it.

When Cathryn had drunk her fourth cup, William could no longer ignore the uneasy atmosphere in the hall. Knowing that he would get no satisfaction from his wife, he turned to the man whose company she sought above all others, the man whose loyalty to him was beyond question: Father Godfrey.

"I ask you plainly," he began softly, "and I will have a plain answer: what has Cathryn said to you?"

Godfrey, in earnest prayer since Cathryn's third cup of wine, turned stricken eyes to William. This was not a conversation he wanted to have; in fact, he had been praying that his effort in the chapel had bridged the gap between them. That William sensed the tension surrounding them did not surprise him; William was too astute a warrior to miss it. That Cathryn was losing herself in wine surprised him, for she had so far displayed courageous self-control; yet, knowing now the whole tale, he should rather be surprised at her calmness. These circular thoughts rolled like troubled snakes in his mind so that he could only stare at William in something like shock.

"Does she plan how to worm her way out of the marriage before it is consummated?" William asked under his breath, his eyes lit with suppressed fire.

Relieved that he could answer truthfully, Godfrey answered, "Nay, William. She is not planning anything to endanger the marriage. Lady Cathryn is well set to obey the king's command. I put the three questions to her and she answered well; she is old enough to marry at ten and eight years, she has no parent or relative to hinder her union with you. . . ."

"And the third requisite? Does she give her free consent to this marriage?"

Godfrey nodded readily, hoping to cool William's anxiety. "Yea, she has spoken her consent freely. The marriage is valid."

That, at least, set William's mind at rest, if only for the moment. The Church stipulated that unless a woman on the brink of marriage answered all three questions with the right answers, the marriage would not occur. It was a worthy attempt at preventing a young maid from being forced into a marriage not of her liking. But still, Father Godfrey was radiating waves of tension.

"Yet something regarding her troubles you, Father." Striking with blind accuracy, William asked, "Is it the girl's bedding?"

Father Godfrey jumped as if struck and looked at William with wide eyes.

William only laughed lightly and patted his old friend on the arm.

"Worry not, Father. I shall be gentle with her. Lady Cathryn shall not receive rough handling from me."

Godfrey pounced on those words as a hunting hound on a hare.

"Woman is the weaker vessel, William; I am heartened that you remember it."

William turned upon hearing those words to find that Cathryn had risen and was making her way to the stair. The time for retiring had come. Her servants—nay, his now—made way for her, their eyes never leaving her. With measured step and head held high, she left the hall, her bliaut a heavy white wake rippling behind her. William had no desire to argue with Father Godfrey, but he thought his wife as weak as iron.

Cathryn brushed aside the drape concealing the door and entered the lord's chamber. The bed had been hung in cadis edged with silk banding of scarlet, amaranth, and aureate since she had last seen it. It was a bed that spoke eloquently of housing a wealthy lord. It was a bed to keep the warmth of fire and body. It was finer now than when her mother and father had lain in it. Marie, who had been waiting nervously for her since the beginning of the last meal of the day, hurried over and began to help her disrobe. There was enough daylight left that no candles were yet needed, but just barely. The sun sent its rays upward to slice through the bare treetops across the river, creating a pattern on the rough ceiling of the room. Dusk was approaching and subduing the harsh contours of the sleeping land and bleeding all color until every tree and bush and hillock was masked in murky gray. With full dark would come the bridal bedding.

"He has dressed the bed," Cathryn said.

"Aye, his squire was sent to see to it," Marie remarked. "What color is that called, that one that is more blooded than violet?"

"It is called amaranth," Cathryn answered.

"Lord William has noble tastes."

"Lord William has rich tastes," Cathryn corrected.

"Did he send you up?" Marie whispered sympathetically.

"Nay, he did not," Cathryn answered bluntly, then added wryly, "but I could read him easily enough."

"Ah, lady," Marie said with poorly sheathed pity, "it is this moment that I have feared since we first heard of this arranged marriage. Your bravery has left me breathless and terrified, for though the day brought the marriage, the night brings the marriage bed."

It may have been the large quantity of wine she had drunk with her scanty meal, or it may have been the tattered fingers of sunlight retreating across the room, but Cathryn could not listen to any more of Marie's well-meaning murmurs of sympathy. Her nerves were strung as tight as lute strings; now she needed the strength of calm reserve more than ever on this long day. It would not do. She must get Marie to speak of something else but the coming bedding.

" 'Tis not bravery to obey a king, Marie, and that is all I have done. But tell me—I trust you have spent some of your time this day prowling the shadows. Do you know how William le Brouillard came by his name?"

If it had been Marie's wedding night, the last person in the world she would have wished to speak of would be her warrior husband, who might at any moment come bounding up the stairs, but she was not Lady Cathryn. If her lady wished to know more of this man she was wed to, then Marie would tell her all she knew and then keep her ear to the ground for more.

" 'Tis said that he is silent in battle, not voicing cry as other knights do to heat their blood and strike fear into the enemy. Also," she added hesitantly, not comfortable with the subject matter, "he comes to envelop and encompass his opponent as silently and completely as the fog enshrouds the land."

"So they call him 'the Fog,' " Cathryn said softly; then she added under her breath, "I had thought it might have been for the color of his eyes."

Marie offered nothing more, sensing that Cathryn was lost in thought, but what those thoughts were, she could not say. Lifting her head suddenly, Cathryn spoke again.

"But tell me more. Surely you know more than I, for none of his people would dare to speak to me of him as they would speak among themselves, and I would know all I can of him."

Marie did know more, but it was not information she thought Lady Cathryn would be cheered to know. She had not come by her knowledge of William le Brouillard in any straightforward fashion; she had heard bits and pieces as she kept to the corners, and overheard even more as his men settled themselves in Greneforde. In truth, she had been nearly caught more than once, but she had escaped detection. If being prideful was not a mortal sin, she would have been proud of her ability to hide in plain view.

"Most of the talk was of his fighting skill, my lady."

"To be expected among knights, surely," Cathryn answered.

"But I heard little of—"

"Tell me," Cathryn pressed quietly. "There is nothing that you could say that would not be of keen interest to me."

"His fighting skill was spoken of most highly," Marie began hesitantly. "He has fought in the Holy Land and in many of the lands between here and there, and was always the victor. It is for this reason that King Henry values him so highly, that and for his loyalty." Seeing that she had Cathryn's rapt attention, Marie continued with more confidence. "His family lands, in Normandy, have been lost to him through some misstep of his father's. His childhood was spent wandering, and he has been land hungry since his accolade. The king knew this; in fact, I gathered that anyone who has spent even a little time with him would know his hunger for land of his own. Greneforde was gifted to him for his service to King Henry."

Marie had said nothing that Cathryn had not known or astutely guessed; in truth, his personal history was not unlike many, yet to hear the words—to hear that Greneforde was gifted to him—struck a nerve that she could little soothe.

"So," she began with thinly concealed pain, "Greneforde was given to him, and with Greneforde comes Cathryn."

Marie realized instantly that she had blundered in her recitation, for Lady Cathryn had never before shown even a hint of the raw emotion that was seeping out of her now. To lose one's home to a stranger was bad enough; to lose oneself to the same stranger as an afterthought of little value was worse. But she said nothing; she simply retreated from the subject as if it had not been broached.

"Would you like to bathe, my lady?"

Marie could not know it, but she had given her lady the means to regain her composure with that question. Would she like to bathe? Knowing, as she did, how her new husband cherished the act of bathing? Knowing that he had commanded her that all the inhabitants of Greneforde should bathe?

With a serene smile, Cathryn answered, "Nay."

Almost as an afterthought, she added, "And avoid bathing yourself, Marie, as you continue to keep yourself hidden from sight. I would be more familiar with le Brouillard's men."

"Lady," Marie began nervously, "he is your husband and your lord. Is it seemly that you refer to him so?"

Probably it was not, but she was past caring, and Marie's high tension was causing her own nerves to stretch to the breaking point. Wanting to be alone to calm herself, she spoke the words that would give her solitude.

"Marie, you have done me good service in distracting me whilst I prepared for bed, but now you must depart, else my lord will find you on the stair."

No more needed to be said. With blue eyes as round as a startled owl's, Marie fled the room, closing the door softly behind her. The drape scarcely moved in her wake.

There was little left to be done. Moving to the padded stool, she sat before the fire and unbound her hair with rapid fingers. Picking up a comb of ivory, one of the few fine possessions left to her, she dragged it through her long hair, lifting the ends onto her lap so they would not hang on the floor. It was a job she enjoyed, usually. The act of combing her hair was soothing in its very repetition of movement, and she loved the feeling of her hair hanging free of constriction. Tonight she found no pleasure in it, rushed as she felt.

It seemed that every moment she heard heavy feet on the stair or the latch turn or the curtain move. But the moments passed and she had the room to herself. This privacy could not last long. She knew the look in le Brouillard's fog gray eyes. He would be here soon.

Putting the comb carefully on the seat of the bench, she ran to the bed and scrambled to the middle of it, sitting small and straight in the pristine white center of it.

When her feet got cold, she got under the blankets and held them securely around her hips. At first she stared at the fire. The room was in complete darkness now, save for the fire and the lit taper near the door.

He would come any moment now, this le Brouillard who was so silent when faced with an enemy. And how would he face her? If he was silent, did that mean he saw her as a foe? By his look at the table, he had reconciled himself to a wife. He wanted her, that was clear enough, but did he want her for a night's sport or as a true wife? She was not so innocent that she did not understand that a wife could be nothing more than a warm body to

90

her husband and a vessel for his heirs. She had always wanted more than that, but when she had done her wanting and her dreaming, she had not been the wife of le Brouillard. Did she yearn for a fuller union with him?

The silence of her soul was the only answer she could lay hand to.

How long she watched the fire and thought of him, she was not certain, but certain she was that the fire had burned down. It was full dark. She turned her head to watch the doorway, almost expecting to see him there, but he was not there. Was he such a man to dawdle on his way to the bridal bed? Strange men they bred in France, and not at all as the troubadors sang of them.

Fie on the man! She could not—would not—sit and wait like a dumb animal for the ax that would cleave its skull. Scrambling out of the big bed, she hurried to the warmth of the fire, but could not stand still to enjoy its heat. Pacing, measured, graceful, unhurried, but pacing nonetheless, she expended some of her excess energy. The cold numbness of her feet forced her back to the relative warmth of the bed, and she climbed in, with less care to the smoothness of the coverlet than she had at first shown.

How much time had passed? Surely all must be abed by now. No sounds of laughter or the scraping of a bench reached her ears, yet it had been a quiet wedding feast. One might even say somber. No matter. The meal had been well prepared and artfully presented, even if the quantity was not abundant. Her people had naught to be ashamed of. And she?

She who had worn plain, uncolored wool to her wedding while her betrothed had worn clothing that would not have shamed him at royal court? No, she had worn her best; she could do no better than that. And now the bedding. She had forced the thought from her mind since first receiving message of her marriage from the curtain walk, and now it was upon her. She could not but think of it now.

He was a large man and well muscled, this stranger who now laid claim to both Greneforde and her. Greneforde he had wanted. But Cathryn? Even after Marie's words, she did not need to ask. His look of desire was clear. And after the bedding?

Cold or not, Cathryn bolted out of bed. She did not seek the fire, for she could not force herself to stay near it. Like a caged animal, she prowled the confines of her chamber, her stride long and swift, her hair flying out behind her like a golden banner of war.

No, he did not wish for a wife, though the gift of a woman he would not turn aside after a cold day in the saddle. Greneforde had been his goal and Greneforde was his prize—a gift for faithful service. What matter that she was part and parcel of that prize? What matter? Of no matter at all! It was absurd even to contemplate. She and Greneforde were one. It had been told to her many times and she believed it; how could she not when to have Greneforde meant to have Cathryn? And le Brouillard had breached the outer defenses of Greneforde as he would soon be charging up the stairs to breach the final barrier: the one between her legs. Oh, yes,

she and Greneforde were one—both voiceless
prizes to be handed to the strongest warrior. Why,
it put her in mind of a tray of succulent meat being
passed at table, offered to anyone with a hand to
grab.

And without her quite realizing that it had happened, Cathryn's control, the control that ruled as
well as protected her, broke. As ice cracked and
melted beneath the heat of the sun, her composure
ran down and away and she was powerless to call
it back.

It was then that the curtain parted and William
le Brouillard entered.

The sudden flaring of the fire was her only clue
that something had changed within the room.
Whirling, her hair swirling around her in a golden
nimbus, she faced him. Cathryn had as little control
of her emotions as a cornered animal, and all of her
helpless fury and frustrated despair was reflected in
the dark brown depths of her eyes.

Of all the possible reactions William had anticipated from his bride, this was not one of them, and,
for a moment, he did not recognize what he was
witnessing. She was Cathryn of Greneforde, as
emotionless as the earth waiting for the plow. He
knew that about her. Yet here she was, fists
clenched and blowing hard through her mouth, her
eyes alight with a strange, licking fire.

With slow steps, he entered almost cautiously
and, in truth, he did not wish to alarm her. She was
a bride of but hours and faced with the prospect of
a bedding. It was maidenly nerves that had her

strung so tightly and he would deal gently with her, as he had assured Father Godfrey.

Her eyes never left him. She watched him as warily as any opponent he had faced on the field of battle. The comparison did not sit well with him. She was his wife. He did not want to begin this marriage, this bonding, as adversaries. Moving toward the fire and toward her, he watched as she watched him. Watched as she backed up at his approach. Watched the unfamiliar glitter that shone from her dark eyes.

With a smooth motion, he removed the ruby brooch that held his mantle and swept it from his shoulders. His eyes never left hers, as hers did not leave him. She backed up a small step and then lifted her chin. It appeared that she had determined not to give ground to him again.

Ah, but she was a beauty, and this new side to her, a side he had little anticipated, only whetted his appetite for her to a sharper edge. Her eyes glowed from within. Her hair fell to her knees and covered her slight form like a priceless golden cloak. The thin linen shift she wore hid nothing of her form, particularly since the orange light of the fire was at her back. Her breasts were heaving as if she had run a great distance, and they pressed against the light fabric. The dark outline of her nipples was plainly visible. The desire he had felt for her during the meal was magnified a hundredfold.

She read his desire as clearly as if he had spoken of it.

"The conqueror comes to claim his final victory,"

she said, her tension and bitterness unmistakable. "The easiest one yet."

William stopped for a moment at her words, then threw his mantle over the chest with intentional carelessness.

"The conqueror called William has already made his mark on this isle," he answered softly. "I am the William known as the Fog, and I am here as a husband newly made." He took a step closer. "I do not come to conquer."

"But to claim," she finished for him, not moving from her place by the hearth.

William continued to stare into her face, trying to read the torture he heard in her words but seeing only dark eyes and the faint trace of a scar. With careful movements, he unbuckled his belt and laid it on the foot of the bed. His words were as slow and careful as his motion.

" 'Tis the way of things for a husband to claim his wife, especially on the day they have been wed."

He removed his tunic and placed it atop his belt, revealing wide shoulders and narrow hips and the space between the two covered with black and curling hair. Her breath had been coming in deep gulps before; it now came in erratic gasps. He was ringed with muscle, from shoulders to arms to chest to belly. To name such a man "the Fog" was ridiculous in the extreme; everything about him was as solid as stone. And his beauty, for beautiful he truly was, escalated her fear to new heights.

"And if I reject this 'claiming'?" she spit out. "For to me it seems more of a final conquest, and you have had your share of victories this day."

He had promised to be gentle with her. It was a promise made with the best intentions and for a noble purpose: to soothe a frightened maiden about to lose her maidenhead. But the woman who faced him now, speaking in riddles of conquest and victory and claiming, was pushing him beyond reason.

He thought of Margret in that instant, the memory of her delicate beauty tempering his impatience; William took a breath to steady his raging emotions. He was determined to show his bride nothing but chivalric gentleness. He would treat Cathryn with the tenderness a new bride deserved.

She was a new bride, but was he not a new husband? Was he not to look forward to his lawful rights with the woman he had pledged his life to? She knew what was to come, knew what was wanting to make this marriage complete. And with the thought came fresh suspicion.

He had not been completely at ease regarding her and her calm acceptance of him as lord of Greneforde, not since she had stood in solitary welcome in the yard. If he understood her, she did not intend to consummate the marriage, whereupon it would be invalidated. It was a devious and bloodless way to have his claim on Greneforde annulled, as she would have the marriage annulled. He would lose Greneforde—and her—in one stroke. But it would not be.

And with that thought, he found himself quite certain that Father Godfrey had not told him all he knew in regard to Cathryn.

"Nay, Cathryn," he said with quiet force, the way clear in his own mind. "There is one victory left to me this day, if that is what you choose to call it, and it will not be denied me."

As he spoke, he removed what little remained of his bridal finery. He stood now before her at the hearth, as naked as the day his mother first beheld him—with one difference. His shaft, engorged and full, pumped rhythmically in her direction as a sword sought to find the weakness in an opponent.

Staring first at his throbbing sword and then into his steely eyes, Cathryn began to laugh the hysterical laughter of the deranged.

"I doubted it not." She laughed, the sound crashing against the ceiling. "Nay, I but hoped; but you have battled and won against greater odds than I could offer you." Flinging her arms wide, she stepped back. "Have you not won Greneforde? And since Greneforde is already won, then so am I, but this last victory will not taste sweet to you. Perhaps because I am not as sweet a prize as Greneforde!"

He reached for her and grabbed her arms, pinning them to her sides and holding her still. With gentle force, he pulled her up against him so that his pulsing member was embraced by her curves.

"Not taste sweet?" he said harshly. "Nay, Cathryn, this will taste the sweetest yet."

This time it was no kiss of peace he offered her, but a kiss of war—a war he would win; neither of them had any doubt of that. But it was a war against her resistance that caught her unprepared, for he did not deal harshly with her, no matter that he had been sorely prodded. Nay, he did not move directly against her mouth—did he fear she would bite?— but instead set his mouth against the tender spot near her ear. His hands moved from her arms to capture her breasts in a gentle and beguiling embrace, and as his thumbs teased her nipples to reluctant life, his mouth, warmer now than before, traced a path along the line of her chin. She stirred against him, against the onslaught of touch and emotion, pressing her locked arms against the width of his chest and pushing hard. He did not move. She had not really thought that he would, but it was all that was left to her. And she kept her eyes wide open. He would not win her. She would not lose herself in the sensations he was striving to tap. She was Cathryn of Greneforde and she would not melt for him.

His mouth, moving constantly, reached hers, and now he did take that strategic point. His effort was valiant in its persuasion and perseverance, but she kept her lips closed against his, no matter what wiles of tongue and breath he used. There would be no sweet taste there for him to savor, just the bitter gall that filled her own mouth.

At last he understood that there would be no winning her, that she would not yield to his touch and grow soft and warm for him. He had the small satisfaction of knowing that this, at least, was the Cathryn he recognized. There would be no parley, no compromise; she would be breached tonight. She would be wife in full measure, no matter her distaste for the act, for he would be lord of Greneforde. Besides, with practice, she might grow to like it.

He pressed his hips fully against hers and rubbed against her. She arched her back so violently away from him that he wondered if she would do herself an injury before submitting quietly to his touch. But she was quiet, as was he. Their battle, for it was nothing else, was waged in silence. Desperate silence.

He could do naught else. The time for him to penetrate her had come. It would be best to get it over with as quickly as he could; pleasure would come with subsequent beddings.

Pushing her onto the bed, he fell atop her, keeping the bulk of his weight off of her with his raised arms. Trying once again to coax pleasure from her, he kissed her, feeling gently with his fingertip for the small slit that would receive him. She was as dry as bone and as stiff. And still she watched him with eyes wide and panic-filled. In truth, he found he had the compassion to pity her.

With his pity, and those eyes staring in such horror at him, he felt himself grow soft.

Muttering a curse, he yanked up her shift, tearing it in the process, and stared at the delicate beauty of her golden nakedness, carefully keeping his eyes from hers lest she unman him again.

She was a beauty of fine proportion and fashionably slim—too slim, in fact. More food and less wine would serve her better. But her breasts were perfectly round mounds surmounted by dusky pink peaks of generous size. Her nipples were large and greatly extended, despite her apparent lack of response; perhaps she was not as unmoved as he had feared. Feasting his eyes upon her, he felt his manhood grow until it pressed against the soft skin of her inner thigh. It was time.

"The first time there is fear and pain," he said softly, his voice low and gentle. "Let us get the first time behind us, Cat."

And she went wild beneath him, clawing and twisting so that he knew she meant to draw his blood before he drew hers. So great was the strength of her panic, she almost succeeded in tossing him from the bed. The rest of her shift was ripped away as she battled him. But he had had enough. The marriage would be consummated. Greneforde would be his without any doubt—and so would Cathryn.

"This marriage will be consummated!" William thundered, positioning himself between her legs, pressing his weight against her so that she could not shift position. When one of her fists rocked against his face, he held her hands above her head in one gigantic fist, while with the other he spread wide one leg. She was helpless.

With one thrust he breached her and he roared out, his voice rebounding off the walls of the room. But his cry was not in ecstasy or in victory.

Cathryn of Greneforde was no virgin.

She lay still beneath him, as unmoving now as she had been volatile before. Eyes wide, she looked straight up with an unseeing, unblinking stare. Her legs were splayed out across the disheveled bed. Her hands clenched even as they were held in William's fist. She felt nothing, except that perhaps this was what it was to be dead.

William felt much, much more. His manhood was again gone, and this time he did not care; the marriage had been consummated, if just. He slid out of her and escaped the bed, hastily arranging his clothing. He did not look at her. He thought that if he did, he just might kill her.

She had known a man before him.

A tidal thrust of betrayal and fury rose to choke him. He had been on the mark when he suspected her of betrayal. His instincts were never wrong, but how he wished—and not for the first time—that they could be more specific.

She had lain with a man. At least one man. If she had soiled herself with one, she could have been with many, for how was a man to know when once the wall had been breached how many poured through the gap?

William walked to the fire, just a flicker of embers now, and stared, his body as cold as his heart. What manner of woman was he shackled to for the remainder of his days? But he need not be. He could have the marriage annulled if he chose. His wife had been unclean upon the marriage bed. The pope himself would endorse his claim.

And he would lose his claim on Greneforde. Henry had made it clear that Cathryn and Greneforde were one. Relinquishing Cathryn would equal relinquishing Greneforde. Was she worth losing all he had struggled for?

He turned to look at her. She had not moved. She lay spread wide on the bed, shamelessly. Her eyes were as calm and as dry as any harbor whore's, and as cold.

No, she was not worth it. Greneforde was his and would remain his.

William walked past the bed to the curtained doorway. Not once did he glance at her. It was just as well; the icy metal of his eyes would have pierced her through.

At the curtain he stopped and, staring into the darkened portal, informed her coldly, "I had no wish for a wife. Greneforde was the prize. Since you cannot be separated, I will keep you because I desire your hall, your people, and your land."

A rustle of the curtain and he was gone.

When he had been gone for a long time—how long she did not know—Cathryn slowly curled into a small, tight ball in the middle of the bed. The room was cold and dark, the only light coming now from the taper near the doorway.

She turned her back to the light.

Wrapping her arms around herself, she began to shake, the tremors rising from the black pit in the center of her soul to rattle her teeth.

Recalling William's bitterly spoken words, she whispered into the darkness, "Verily, 'tis true, and truly I know it."

Tears ran silently in a steady and never-ending stream down her face until they were soundlessly absorbed into her tangled hair.

Chapter Six

Hearing William's roar, his hands clasped fervently to his chest, Father Godfrey hastily resumed his prayers.

John, having loitered in the hall long past the final meal of the day, heard the lord of Greneforde's cry. With solemn eyes, he quietly left the hall for the kitchen.

Rowland stopped in the act of polishing his sword before the great fire in the hall. As William's roar faded away, he smiled and resumed his methodical polishing.

The door to the chapel opened with unearthly quiet. It was only when the candles before the altar flickered that Godfrey looked up from his prayers. Only one man could move about so quietly, and he always did so when his warrior instincts were running high. Father Godfrey looked up to find William's hard face before him; the look in his cold gray eyes set Godfrey's hands to trembling.

"You knew." William barely spoke, his words making a small cloud of fog in the cold air.

Godfrey could not find breath to answer. He hid his shaking hands beneath his robes and prayed for God's deliverance.

"And I had a right to know," William said with just slightly more force.

Swallowing heavily, Father Godfrey answered, "I had no right to tell you."

"She told you in confession."

Godfrey could neither confirm nor deny that statement; to do so would be a violation of his vows.

"Confession is between a soul and God," he tried, "and I am but—"

"I need to know!" William cut him off, his eyes blazing points of cold light. "Was it one? Ten? Every man within the curtain wall?" His left hand clasped the sword hilt with whitened knuckles, and it was then that Godfrey saw that the lord of Greneforde was armed. "Was it love or only an unruly woman with no man or priest to control her?"

Godfrey saw the pain etched on William's face. To know only part of the truth was eating away at him like a worm.

"I cannot say," he choked out. "You must find your own way in this. Think on what she has said, on what I have said," he tried.

William did think on it. Truly, there had to be a way for him to decipher this mess that lay before him, if only he could shunt the pain of her betrayal to one side and concentrate on all that he had seen and heard since riding through Greneforde's gate. But it was harder than any battle he had faced. She, with the fine-boned face of a saint, had lain with another. She, with a heart as cold as winter turf, had warmed another man's bed. No, she was not cold. She was cold only to him.

"Think, William!" Godfrey charged.

William tightened his grip upon his sword and trained his thoughts to pursue the path he directed. Snippets of information flew up from his mind like birds flying wild from a pack of dogs. The serfs were beaten, Rowland had said. The land was barren and war-torn. There were no knights, no squires. And Cathryn had a stone for a heart.

"She said," he forced himself to repeat, "that it had been a hard year for Greneforde."

Godfrey clutched those words desperately. "Verily," he said with force, "she said the truth of it." And he willed William to continue.

"And you said," William repeated with suppressed anger, "that I should treat her as part of my own body."

Godfrey, to his credit, did not back away from that indictment. " 'Tis the Lord's word on marriage. . . ."

"Ah, the Lord's word," William repeated bitterly. "Did you not teach me, 'If thine eye offend thee, pluck it out'?"

"Nay, William!" Godfrey admonished, his eyes wide in horror, unsure just how far William intended to follow that analogy. "She is the weaker vessel and has been . . ."

"Filled with another man's seed before mine!" William all but shouted.

". . . sorely used," Godfrey said over him.

"And not I?" William choked out, his eyes almost glazed with pain. "I have been gifted an empty donjon near ruin and a wife ruined complete." With a hard and mocking laugh he added, "Verily, service to one's sovereign yields bitter fruit of late."

Godfrey reached out his hand and laid it atop the hand that clenched the sword hilt.

"William," he beseeched, "love her. You have become one flesh in the eyes of God."

The pain in William's eyes died as quickly as a fire on winter ice. With cold calculation, he responded, "Nay. I will love Greneforde and give my body's strength to its flourishment." His eyes as cold and lifeless as hammered steel, he added, "To Greneforde only."

Turning swiftly, he departed as silently as he had come.

John opened the door that entered on the kitchen. The fire had been banked for the night, and the capacious room was as tidy as Lady Cathryn liked it to be. John sighed wearily. It had been a long and busy day. First the messenger from King Henry and then the arrival of the man who would take charge of both Greneforde and Lady Cathryn. The wedding feast had been prepared in the midst of frantic cleaning, and then good time spent in surreptiously studying the men in William's service while delaying the presentation of the meal. It had been a full day. Yet not one eye was closed at this late hour,

and surely they all knew that dawn came early
enough.

John was not surprised that they were not abed,
despite the lateness of the hour. In truth, he would
have been more than a little disappointed if even
one snore had greeted his arrival. And now that he
had left the great hall, they turned questioning eyes
to his, knowing why he had come.

"He knows," was all he said.

Silence greeted that pronouncement, for there
was no surprise in it. Indeed, they had been waiting
for this moment since William le Brouillard had
first crossed into Greneforde's enclosure.

"And now?" Eldon asked for them all.

"And now we see of what mettle Lord William is
truly fashioned," John responded quietly.

"What of Lady Cathryn?" Alys asked.

"He has not harmed her," John assured them all.

"Yet," Lan added tersely.

"I do not think it in him to hurt her," John mused
aloud.

"Nor do I," Alys added.

"Then he is a rare man," Lan said.

John's head jerked up at that, and he studied Lan
before answering, "Aye. It is in my mind that William le Brouillard is a rare man."

"And if he is not?" Lan pressed.

"We shall be here and will stand for her as we are
able."

The assembly nodded in agreement. They stood
with Lady Cathryn, as they always had and always
would, but Greneforde needed a strong lord to
guide and protect her. God willing, le Brouillard

was that man, but they would stand between Cathryn and her lord if need be, God willing or no. They would allow no harm to befall her, for they had learned the price of passivity, and the price was too dear.

Across the enclosure, Rowland sat in silence as he polished his weapon. It was a time of contentment for him. William had his land and his wife, and he was happy for him. After so many years of fighting and searching, he deserved this moment of complete victory. Tomorrow would bring fresh trouble in the way of food shortages and rebuilding the village; tonight he could enjoy without shadow.

After that, Rowland's thoughts drifted and he drifted with them, uncaring where they brought him. It was of little matter. His thoughts always brought him to the same place eventually, and he had ceased to fight against them long ago.

William emerged slowly from the far shadows of the hall and crossed the wide floor until he stood just paces from his friend. He had strong need of a friend this night.

Rowland did not look up, did not hesitate in his polishing, but it was with a trace of amusement that he remarked, "Strange for a man to leave his bedchamber on his wedding night."

William gazed into the fire, unwilling to look away from the mesmerizing play of multihued flame.

"What had to be done, is done," he said with brusque simplicity.

Still not looking up from his task, Rowland said,

"And with that chore behind you, you find yourself in search of a new one. My shield would welcome the feel of your hand wielding the polishing cloth."

Rowland's words passed over him without penetrating. The fire licked and swirled within and around the logs, playing with the wood even as it consumed it. Such was life, playing with a man's dreams until it handed him ashes, though he had not thought so even an hour ago. He had hoped for much, planned for much, after the wreckage of his childhood. Through all the years of toil and striving and blood, he had fed the dream of again having his own land, his own bulwark against whatever man could throw against him. He had striven to prove his worth to an overlord who could reward him with land, since Henry of Anjou had land aplenty. He had fought and fought and fought again, both the Saracen and the Christian, and now he had to fight anew—against his own wife.

The need to be with Rowland, to hear his friend's even voice and to speak his own thoughts, lay heavily upon him, but he would not speak of Cathryn and what had been revealed on their wedding bed. She had betrayed him, but he would not betray her. They were bound in the sight of God, and he would honor his vow—not to her, but to God. What passed between them was private and would remain so.

Rowland continued with his task, careful not to look into his friend's eyes, careful to give him the time and the privacy he needed to speak his thoughts. His sword had ceased needing care long ago, but he did not halt in his precise handling. He waited for William. He would wait all night and rub his sword down to a dagger if need be.

"The sum of my plans lie there," William said softly, pointing to the ash that ringed the glowing yellow fire.

Rowland chose his words carefully, remembering a night when he had first learned how fragile were a man's plans when brushed by the mighty hand of God. Indeed, it was not so far off in his thoughts even now.

"A man's plans often lie charred and crumbling in this life, yet God will have His way," he said quietly.

"I vow this is not God's way!" William argued, his voice urgent in its intensity. "And if it be His, then it surely is not mine!"

Rowland smiled sadly and looked up from his sword. " 'Tis rare the two are one."

William looked deeply into Rowland's eyes and found himself smiling reluctantly. "That is truly so and truly said." When he turned back to the fire, his smile collapsed. "Yet 'tis mortal hard to release the dream."

"Even if all you release is a fistful of ash?"

William looked again into Rowland's dark eyes, and now he did not smile. "Even so. Yea," he answered with wistful intensity.

Rowland answered him with equal intensity: "Then construct a new dream, William, and brush the ash off your warrior's hand. If God wills, you will succeed."

William sat on the bench opposite Rowland, trying to heed the wisdom of Rowland's words—words he knew Rowland had lived himself.

"And if God wills not?" he finally responded.

Rowland smiled gently. " 'Tis said there are dreams aplenty."

But what men said and what they believed often had little in common, and so it was true of Rowland's counsel. The two sat in companionable, if solemn, silence, alone in the vast darkness of the hall, each lost in the mystery and beauty of the flames. But William could find no new dream among the ashes at his feet.

Chapter Seven

Cathryn awoke just minutes before the dawning, alone in the bed. The rain of yesterday had stopped, but the mist and low clouds remained to block the rising sun. Fog ruled the day.

Someone had covered her, tucking the cover around her as snugly as one would bind a child, and the fire blazed hotly in the hearth. Marie. She could not remember actually falling asleep last night, but she knew the fire had been out before William had left the room and that she had been curled on top of the coverlet. With the thought of William, an overwhelming sense of loss and lethargy pervaded her. Their marriage had begun much as she had feared; she should be thankful. She had no bruises to sport throughout the day. It could have been worse—much worse. But then, who but God knew what this day would bring? William might have decided to leave Greneforde for a richer holding. He might have decided to publicly humiliate her and was even now waiting in the hall to deride her in the presence of his men. He might have tired of sheathing his anger and would strike her when next they met. He and his men might kill them all for their duplicity and treachery. . . .

Such thoughts were not helping her malaise. She had to rise and be about her daily affairs, husband or no. Marie's quiet entrance spurred her to action.

Throwing back the cover with more energy than she felt, Cathryn rose from the bed with a smile for Marie. Truly she felt no desire to smile for herself.

"Ah, lady, you are awake," Marie said with some surprise. "I had thought you would not want to be up so early this day." The pity in her voice was unmistakable. Cathryn could not allow it, for if she did, she would hide away all day and cry herself sick.

"And why should I linger abed, Marie?" she answered with determined cheer. "The sun will not wait for me, and there is much to be done this day, as there is each day."

"Aye, lady," Marie acquiesced quietly, "yet—"

"Come," Cathryn interrupted, eager to be off this topic, "choose a gown for me, for I stand here shivering, despite the warmth of the fire you laid for me and for which I am grateful. The sun will not slow its passage and I must be about my tasks."

Marie said no more, but hurried forward with a worn bliaut of faded green for her lady to wear. The effect it made with the soft white of Cathryn's undergarments was not displeasing; if the green had only retained its original hue, the effect would have been quite fresh and gay, especially with the belt of amber that had once been worn with the garment. But that had been long ago.

Her toilette finished, Cathryn left the bedchamber without noticeable hesitation and descended the stair to the hall. She paused briefly at the curtained entrance to the great hall, the sounds of talk and soft laughter coming to her faintly from beyond the worn curtain. She could not distinguish le Brouillard's voice from among them, but that was not surprising; she hardly knew the man, husband though he was. Then she chided herself for her self-deception; she hardly knew him, but she would know his voice at a thousand paces—that was the truth of it.

She waited a moment longer, her anxiety at having to face him rising with each breath. It was absurd. He was lord here; she must face him eventually, and the sooner the better.

Pushing back the curtain, Cathryn entered the hall. A quick scan revealed that he was not present, nor was his shadow companion, Rowland. The men gathered there turned to see who was entering, and she braced herself for their scorn or derision or cruelty or whatever else a man could think to do when his lord's honor had been sullied.

These men did nothing. Some nodded in her direction, but that was the most overt act any of them committed. Cathryn let her breath out with conscious effort, hardly aware that she had been holding it. Before she could draw another, even before she could step more fully into the room, Ulrich hurried over to her, his eyes lit with eagerness and good cheer.

"Good morn to you, my lady," he began with a smile, coaxing her more deeply into the hall and leading her courteously to the table so that she could break her fast. "My lord has been up since before the dawn to inspect the fields and determine if they are ready for seed." It suddenly struck him that she might take offense, thinking her skill at managing an estate had just been questioned. "You had not yet arisen when he yearned to be off, and Lord William is ever eager to be up and away come the morn. Rowland is with him," Ulrich thought to add, in case she would worry as to her husband's safety, "and they plan to search the wood for game. Would you not like fresh game for dinner, Lady Cathryn?" he asked.

Ulrich had not been idle during his recitation of her husband's business; nay, he had seated her, cut her meat, and placed her portion in a pleasing display on her plate. He had finished by pouring her wine and now stood ready to attend her future needs at table. Perhaps William's anger of the previous night had been but momentary. Perhaps he had schooled the boy, only a year or two younger than she, to take tender care of his wife. It was a hopeful thought.

"Yea, Ulrich," she responded smiling up at him, "fresh meat would be most welcome. Think you that your master can provide it?"

"Oh, lady, 'tis as easily said as done for my lord

William," Ulrich boasted happily, his hands folding across his chest with confidence to match his words.

"So?" Cathryn prompted. It was all the prompting Ulrich needed.

"William le Brouillard is a great warrior, my lady, though it does not surprise me that you would not be aware of it, Greneforde being not on the main path, so to speak," he explained self-importantly. "Did you not know that he saved Rowland's life? And Rowland himself is a knight of no little fame."

"Nay," Cathryn answered softly, her smile gentle for the young squire who tutored under a knight he found so grand. "I did not know it."

" 'Tis a great tale, Lady Cathryn. Would you hear it?" he asked eagerly, the words clearly ready to spill forth from his lips.

"Yea, I would."

"Ah, lady, the sun was hot, as it always is in that far-off land," he began, his eyes focused on the pale shaft of light coming through the high wind hole. "The fighting had lasted many a day, but the walls of Damascus were strong, impenetrable, and high. Rowland, feared by many a Saracen for his valor and his stamina, attacked again and again, and though he could find no breach, he did not admit defeat. Nay, not even when he lay spent beneath its walls, his body wasted for lack of water. For did you not know, lady, that there is no water in the land of our Savior and that the soldiers of God found it is more precious than the most costly gem?" Ulrich did not wait for her response; indeed, none was needed. "But William did not hesitate to ride to the aid of his countryman, though they knew each other not and though the arrows of the Saracens flew about him as thick as flies on the . . . uh, as thick as snow," he rallied, remembering his audience. "William spurred his horse to greater speed and slipped in swift silence to the very base of the walls of defiant Damascus and lifted Rowland to his feet. With gentle care, he placed Rowland on his charger and then mounted behind, his back an easy target for the archers on the wall, and rode away as silently as he had come. The Saracens were amazed and swore aloud that their God and ours protected this man, this William le Brouillard."

Ulrich had recited the words with fervor in his eyes. It prompted Cathryn to ask, "Did you serve William in Damascus, Ulrich?"

Ulrich's eyes cleared and he looked in surprise at Lady Cathryn. "Nay, lady, for I was but a child at that time. 'Tis a tale well known and oft repeated by knights everywhere."

"I see," she said, wondering how much truth was in the tale.

Ulrich recognized her doubt for what it was and changed the topic to more recent feats of bravery, determined that William's wife would know the prowess of the man she had wed.

"May I tell you of another battle, one in which I played a small part?" he asked with charming eagerness.

Cathryn could not deny him his wish, he was so transparent in his desire; and she also was curious to know what she could of William le Brouillard.

Claudia Dain

"Please continue," she prompted with a smile of encouragement.

"I have been a squire to Lord William for three years now and have seen him perform wondrous feats of war." Cathryn had to smile at that odd word pairing. "On one occasion, we surprised a band of mercenary knights pillaging a poor village on the banks of the Rhine." And now Cathryn did not smile, for this tale pierced her heart and pricked her memory. Greneforde had been such a village, and because of lawless knights, was no more.

"They outnumbered us three to one," Ulrich continued, his eyes glowing with the memory, "and I was but a squire newly made, my strength not as it is now, yet William and Rowland did not pause to debate whether they should ride on or stay to fight. With my lord there is but one course, and he follows it true," he said with pride. "The disgraceful band did not run at seeing us—indeed, they may have wondered if we meant to join them—but William quickly disavowed them of that thought when he unleashed his sword and urged his charger to run upon them. Rowland was at his side, as always, when they charged into the lawless band, but lawless though they were, they were fierce warriors and did not run. Nay, they returned stroke for stroke until my lord broke away to begin his charge anew. His arm was cut, lady, at the joint where arm meets shoulder, but he did not think to draw away."

Ulrich's voice had fallen to a whisper and he seemed mesmerized by the dust motes as they swirled in the warm light that shot through the

118

wind hole. In truth, Cathryn was a little mesmerized herself at the telling of this tale.

"My lord's eyes grew black as death itself in the
whiteness of his face. He uttered no cry, no voice of
battle to chill the foe and cause his blood to falter;
nay, he was as silent as the grave, and the men he
fought began to murmur that he was no man but a
wraith sent to strike terror into their sinful hearts.
But one of them saw the blood that ran in a steady
course down his arm to pool on the ground and
shouted that he was but a man as they were and
would die that day. My lord William did not reply.
Staring at the man who had pronounced his death,
he gripped his shield with renewed strength in his
bloodied arm and, with visor up, charged the man.
There was a shout from them that all the flames of
hell were burning in my lord's eyes, that he had no
soul and had been sent from hell to seek and replace
that holy part of man that he had lost. And my lord
kept riding, his sword glinting in the weak sun, riding to hurry those knights to their appointed hour
with God."

Cathryn's eyes were riveted on Ulrich, her breath
held, waiting for him to finish this tale of bravery.
In time, he did, his voice so low and soft that she
strained to hear him.

"They clashed hard, for those men were fighting
not only for their lives but for their eternal souls.
Never have I seen such battle," he said softly in remembered awe. "Rowland was ever at my lord's
side, his sword as swiftly flying as the falcon, seeking blood and finding it. And when they could not
best William, they cut his horse from beneath him,

hoping to render him helpless." Ulrich smiled. " 'Twas folly, for no such simple strategy as that would best my lord. He never lost his footing, not even for a moment, and fought them standing on his feet, the blood a red and ever-growing pool around the spot he would die to hold."

Ulrich was so silent for so long that, if Cathryn had not seen William for herself and been wedded to him just yesterday, she would have sworn that he went down that day.

"Yea," she prompted, "and?"

Ulrich cast his eyes upon her briefly and smiled in apology.

"And it was not long before his shield was struck from his arm, the straps torn from their mounting with the force of that blow. Yet did William stand and face them, the cry of defeat as silent upon his lips as the cry of victory had been. It was then that I played my small part," he added almost reluctantly, now that the full tale had passed his lips. "With Rowland at his back, his own armor dented and hacked by the blade, William stood firm and then looked to me in the midst of the fray. His eyes were cool, lady, and yet it seemed that he called out to me for something that only I could give."

Ulrich looked seriously into her eyes as if pleading for understanding. "I could but obey him," he said simply.

"With what meager strength I had at that youthful age, I ran to him and threw him a second shield with all my heart behind the throw. God Himself must have aided my arm, for he caught the shield neatly and had it upon his blood-soaked arm before my eye could take it in." He shrugged, as if to dispel the mood he had created. "They were all dead in minutes after that, lady. The villagers huddled behind rocks and trees, watching with wide eyes of fear, for, you see, they knew not if we were of the same caliber as the men we had just bested. We rode out and none did come forward to thank us. To William, it did not matter, for he had done what was right. But lady, it seemed to me that they should have shown us gratitude for the service we did them."

"Yea, Ulrich," Cathryn said softly, her eyes on the ray of light piercing the darkness of the hall, but her mind's eye on that bloody road in that far-off place. "So it also seems to me."

The sight of John crossing the far end of the hall broke the trance that Ulrich's tale had cast upon them. With a grin and a shrug of his shoulders, Ulrich poured William's lady more wine.

"My lord would chastise me strongly if he noted how poorly I had served a lady at table." With an elegant flourish, he presented her the tray of cold meat that he had thinly sliced. "William is much concerned with training me to be a good and chivalrous knight; he believes that too little effort is given by most to the softer side of knighthood and too much to blatant warfare." Ulrich smiled broadly into Cathryn's surprised face. "Those are his words, lady, not mine."

But Ulrich had misread her. She had hoped, even knowing it was foolish, that her husband had told his squire to take special care of his lady. It would have meant a softening, however small. But it was just a part of Ulrich's training for knighthood and had naught to do with her.

A quick nod of her golden head and she affirmed both the groundlessness of her hope and the wisdom of William's training. In truth, she had much to be grateful for: William could have made her humiliation public and he had clearly chosen not to do so. Ulrich had treated her with warmth and respect. If only she could hope for as much from his master.

No, it was folly to think so. Even now, she reasoned as Ulrich kept up his happy chatter, William was surveying the land and determining what was best to be done. She had much to be grateful for; Greneforde and its welfare was of the highest importance to her, and it appeared he felt the same, regardless of what had passed between them. And if he was about the business of Greneforde, it was past time that she was, too.

"Ulrich," she interrupted gently, "I would inspect the bag of seed that Lord William spoke of."

Knowing Ulrich as little as she did, she still knew that he was suddenly very uncomfortable.

She was correct, though Ulrich felt more than simple discomfort. His emotion was closer to stark fear. Those seeds were William's most cherished possession, of far greater value to him than gold or silver or the bag of jewels he carried of equal size.

"Come, Ulrich," she insisted calmly, "they are a part of my portion now that we are wed. 'Twas in the contract."

That was so. And so, very reluctantly, he led her to the small and sheltered room that William had found and where he had placed much of the treasure that had made up his portion. It was below, in the undercroft. Once, it had been filled with sacks of flour and sides of bacon and furs to sell. Once, before her father had robbed himself of all he owned of value to go on pilgrimage. Sitting on a trunk placed against the short wall of the room, Cathryn held the treasured bag on her lap and sifted her hands through the seeds. In her hands lay the end of hunger. It was almost with joy that she examined and experienced the wonder of so many seeds of so many different types, each safely tied in its own small bag within the larger one.

The room was dark and poorly lit—she and Ulrich had but one taper between them—yet she asked him what he knew of the seeds. Unfortunately, he knew little. Some had been gathered before he had joined William; some had been bought in a language he could not comprehend; all were of such value to his lord that no one touched the bag save him. Still, Ulrich did his best to satisfy Lady Cathryn's curiosity, and so it was that they were head-to-head in the most isolated part of the hall when William came upon them.

Ulrich, accustomed to William's silent approaches, knew of his lord's presence before Cathryn and looked up guiltily. He had opened the forbidden bag of seed.

Cathryn, the memory of last night suddenly blazingly bright in her mind and of how she had looked when he left her, naked and spread out upon their bed, also looked up as if she had been caught in mischief. Her discomfort at seeing William again, before she had a chance to prepare herself, was strong.

William saw only that they were both looking inordinately guilty. Knowing what he did about Cathryn, he suspected her of trying to seduce the boy.

And she read the suspicion of adultery in his eyes.

Rising, she held the bag in her hands and faced her lord, her look proud and regal and in no way penitent.

"I am glad you are come," she stated bluntly. "I am eager to know what priceless riches I hold within my hands and would have them named for me. Ulrich has done his best, but he declares that only you have the knowledge I seek."

Again, though he should not have expected less from her by now, he was impressed with her composure. Also, she had gained control of the situation, taking the reins of suspicion from his hands as smoothly as any expert; still, the suspicion remained. Nonetheless, she did impress him. Would there ever come a time when Cathryn of Greneforde would lose control? Yes, he reminded himself, she had lost control when she had fought him last night in their bed. It was not a pleasant reminder.

With a curt nod and a smile to show he was not angered, William dismissed Ulrich. The boy escaped the heavy atmosphere of the room gladly, almost running in his exit. With a clatter of feet, Ulrich was gone and they stood alone in the darkness, man and wife, with two guttering tapers between them. To her credit, she looked him full in the eye. Yes, he was impressed.

She was a beauty, even knowing what he did

about her; it was most probably the cause of her downfall. A woman so lovely, with no parents to protect her, would have her pick of men, though her moral education must have been sadly lacking to be so loose with her body, the house of her soul. Still, watching her in the soft light, the shadows beneath her cheekbones deepened by the dusky light, her eyes black pools, her golden hair gleaming and shooting off warm sparks of light, he could not help wanting her.

"Your hair speaks of Viking blood in your veins," William said softly, catching her off guard.

"My mother's father," she answered after a lengthy pause, "but my forebears' roots in England go as deep as centuries," Cathryn finished proudly.

She watched him watch her and sensed that he was not angry, though he did not trust her. She could hardly blame him. What man expected to find his wife breached before their wedding night? He was a man such as she had never known before: a man hard without being harsh. A man with no cruelty in him. No, there was not such a man, yet . . . he was fair to see, and his words fell softly on her ears. Too softly perhaps; had she not been afraid that this man would have her at his feet with the same amount of effort it took him to breathe? She must beware this man.

"Your external parts speak to me of cold climes and ever-constant war," she said not impolitely, but not warmly either.

William flexed his arm, the muscle bunching for her to see even under the thick wool he wore.

"I am of Normandy and we are ever fractious," he answered pleasantly.

"Perhaps it is the Norse blood," Cathryn said lightly, subtly establishing a bond between them, for her ancestors and his had left the north lands for better conquest elsewhere.

"Perhaps," he answered, "but the world is wide and a man must needs win his place in it."

And just as quickly, he broke the bond she had hoped for.

"And you have won yours," she noted flatly.

"Yea," he said solemnly, his eyes glinting. "Greneforde is mine."

"And what is won cannot be lost?"

"I have no history of losing, lady," he answered coldly, his warning clear. "What I win, I hold."

The urge to strike was strong in her and she yielded to it, if but slightly.

"Yea, le Brouillard, I have learned something of your history, and mayhap you should learn something of mine."

The cold glint of his gray eyes flared for a moment, and he took a step toward her as he spoke, the taper fluttering in his hand.

"I would welcome that," he gritted out, "though it is hours late."

Cathryn jerked as if struck, but she did not back away. Again, he was reluctantly impressed by her strict composure.

"My history *is* one of losing, my lord," she spit out. "All that I had has been lost to me."

"Including Greneforde?"

"Nay," she answered quickly. "Greneforde I give

to you, for she needs a knight and his battle skills to protect her. She has been without a man to defend her for too long."

"But you have not," he choked out, his anger flaring.

Suddenly the Cathryn he had had but a glimpse of—her fire, her fight—was gone, and in her place was the Cathryn of Greneforde that he already knew so well. She stood in cool defiance, her expression blank and her eyes cold. When she spoke, her voice was soft and emotionless.

"The air is stale. I would seek fresher."

She moved to the stair, but he blocked her with his body. He had not meant to fuel this fire of anger and distrust between them. He had never known a man or woman who touched his emotions so strongly; it was a new experience and not a welcome one. Who was this woman he had wed?

Trying for peace, he said, "You asked about the seed."

"And you asked about my ancestry," she replied coolly, her breath frosting the air. "At least you are satisfied."

"I am far from satisfied!" William burst out, angry again despite his resolve.

"Then you may share the state with me, for I have grown quite lonely and could do with a partner," she answered, backing up to stare at him as she planted the barb.

"I would say you have been too well partnered and too often!" William shouted.

"So you say, and therefore it must be," she answered with cool sweetness. "You are, I have been told, the lord of Greneforde."

"And of all within its walls," he added severely, his dark eyes narrowed.

"That is so," she politely agreed.

And his senses, in which he put such well-earned trust, told him that she meant it. He could not fathom her; she seemed to resent him personally, but not his lordship of her inheritance. He could make no sense of her attitude. It could not be that she had a dislike for men in general; no, he knew well enough it could not be that! Opening his mouth for another pass in this battle they fought, he was stopped by Ulrich rushing down the stairs.

"William! Rowland has sighted a doe on the edges of the wood and he calls for a hunt! Hurry, my lord, hurry! I can taste the meat on my starved tongue and my stomach cries out its delight."

William turned to where Cathryn had been standing. She was no longer there, but had returned to the trunk and was carefully brushing off the seeds that clung to her fingers so that they fell with graceful precision into the bag that sheltered them. With sure fingers, she pulled tight the strings of the bag.

Turning to face Ulrich, she said pleasantly, "Fear not, Ulrich, le Brouillard will encompass the doe and we shall all taste meat at today's table."

"You are confident in my skills, lady. Whence does this confidence come?" William asked, surprised.

Cathryn walked calmly to the doorway, urging Ulrich to precede her. When she turned back, the taper lit her face with an uneven glow, turning the scar upon her brow suddenly bright pink. She said with a small smile, "From your own lips, my lord. Are you not the man who has no history of losing?"

"Good shot, William!" Kendall shouted joyfully.

"Your lady was right," Ulrich chimed in with a laugh. "You have succeeded as you always do."

"What is this?" Kendall demanded playfully. "What said Lady Cathryn to William? I demand a full and complete telling of this tale, Ulrich, with no poetic additions."

Ulrich fought a blush at that and hurried to answer. "It is just that Lady Cathryn assured me that we would have fresh meat on our table if Lord William was on the hunt."

"Come, there is more to it than that," Rowland pressed, looking askance at William, who was pointedly ignoring them all.

"She gave me her assurance of success, and when William questioned her confidence in his skill, she answered that he had told her from his own lips that he has no history of losing. Is that not just as a wife should look upon her husband? I tell you," Ulrich continued enthusiastically, "I spoke with her this morn and she was most impressed with William's fighting skill."

"What did you do, pup," Kendall said with a laugh, "bore your lady with tales of knightly valor? Know you not that women much prefer to pass the time in hearing of their own skill at engendering love than of a man's skill at hacking flesh?"

Ulrich looked uncertain for a moment and then

rallied. "Nay, she *was* impressed! Why, she could scarce think to eat when I—"

Kendall burst out laughing. "And you require more proof than that?"

Ulrich could not stop the reddening of his cheeks and turned to William in horror.

"What did you tell her, boy, to make her think me so indomitable?" William asked with a rueful smile.

"I cannot think that it was so bad," he stammered, "and she did, in truth, seem caught on every word . . . I but told her of the battle at the village on the Rhine. . . ." Ulrich's voice trailed away.

"No harm was done," William assured him, ignoring Kendall's rising laughter, "but since you were set to tell the Lady Cathryn a story of knightly bravery, could you not have picked a story in which I was not blooded?"

"I thought that it would arouse her womanly sympathies. . . ." He did not dare admit that he had chosen that tale because of the small part that he had played in the victory.

Kendall laughed the harder, bent over and clutching his belly. Ulrich found himself wishing that he would choke for lack of air.

Rowland sidled close to William and, keeping his dark eyes on the laughing Kendall, asked, "Her words seemed more designed to prick than soothe, or am I misreading her?"

"Nay, 'twas her intent, I am certain, but she did not betray herself with either smile or glint of eye. 'Tis only that I have come to know her better that I can more quickly feel the bite of that smooth tongue she keeps so well guarded. Yet, also, she seemed sincere." William sighed noisily. "I must admit to being perplexed by her."

Rowland smiled slowly and looked at the dirt at his feet. "I do believe that God designed women to be perplexing to men, else we would bore and stray away."

Kendall had stopped laughing and called to William, "A man of Greneforde informed me that the forests have never been short of game, but they have tasted little of it since Cathryn's father left, and none at all for the last few months." Smiling broadly, he added, "You are the master of a lazy bunch, William."

William answered automatically, "No man is lazy in filling his own stomach, man." He pondered this news of meat that was not taken and not eaten though it was within arrow shot of Greneforde's walls.

William did not ponder alone. Rowland scowled, his eyes trained on the dirt, his mind engaged in heavy speculation. William knew that look—knew that it meant Rowland knew something that he did not.

"What is it?"

Rowland looked up at William, his brown eyes serious. "I cannot say. I have nothing but a sense of it." Clasping William's upper arm, he assured him, "I will come to you before the day is done and give you something more substantial."

William nodded and put the matter from his mind. Rowland was and had ever been as good as his word.

The serfs of Geneforder had finished loading the

deer onto Father Godfrey's mule, the carcass quickly stiffening in the cold winter air. The gutting and bloodletting would wait until they were within Greneforde's walls, which were close.

The news of their success must have preceded them, for the whole of Greneforde was there to greet them as they passed through the gate. Eager hands pulled the carcass from the mule and laid it upon the chill ground. Truly they could not delay much longer or the beast would be frozen and impossible to handle. William watched the people of Greneforde as they handled the deer, more closely than he had yet done.

Their movements were furtive, especially when close to William and his knights, and he thought of Rowland's words that they were a beaten lot. Yet the farther they were from him and his men, the more comfortable they appeared, and when they were with John the Steward, their manner was actually easy. They looked to John before making any move, and William saw that John could direct them with just a shifting of his eyes.

And to a man, they were still filthy.

William looked at Rowland, and Rowland turned immediately to meet his eye. With a glance, he indicated John and then looked down again at the carcass, but not before he had seen Rowland's nod of understanding. John would be carefully watched.

Cathryn appeared in the shadow of the stair tower and all activity slowed, all chatter ceased. William noted it, as did Rowland, and they shared the look of experienced warriors facing an unknown enemy. She was the anchor of this place, the hub of the wheel on which all of them sped, and she had betrayed his trust. He could not trust her, and if they all looked to her for guidance, then he could not trust them. It was a coil. How could he be lord here in such a state of perpetual suspicion and imminent betrayal? He could not be. He had voiced both the problem and the solution: Cathryn was the hub. He had but to best her, subdue her, and all would fall into line behind her.

The sun struggled through just then and lit her hair to vibrant gold with filigreed strands of silver running through it. William no longer thought of John or Rowland or strategy; he thought only of his wife and how she looked to him just then. She stood for a moment in the portal and then proceeded gracefully, her movements almost fluid, to stand closer to the cause of the excitement. Long before she reached the deer, William had reached her, though he had no memory of deciding to go to her.

"History need not be rewritten," Cathryn said lightly, to eyeing the deer carcass. Her manner was pleasant, as was her expression, yet she did not smile.

"Would you like it to be?" he asked impulsively.

Cathryn's pleasant demeanor vanished and her guard was fully in place before she answered her husband's unlikely question.

"Would not every man like the chance to rewrite even a small portion of history?"

"And every woman?" he pursued.

With a curt nod, she answered, "Just so."

Her answer soothed him. Perhaps, he thought, she regretted the ill-conceived choices of her youth and would change them if she could. Waywardness was not the sole domain of men, he reasoned. If she felt guilt, if she could but repent . . . Eyeing her, his black brows drawn close over his glinting eyes, he was perplexed by her, mayhap bewitched. For all her warm beauty, she was chilly in her actions, and the contradiction drew him on, despite his better judgment. Then the memory choked him. He was not the first man to be bewitched by her, and if not the first, then perhaps not the last. She had spoken of wanting to rewrite history, and he had jumped to the conclusion that she would rewrite her own; it was more likely, knowing her as he did, that she would choose to rewrite the portion that included *him*.

Past caring if he was subtle, he asked, "What portion of your history would you alter, had you the means?"

Cathryn folded her hands neatly and would not look at him, yet her answer, when it came, was softly spoken.

"I have not the means so 'tis pointless to think upon."

And with his lightning changes of mood, unknown to him before he entered Greneforde just yesterday, William turned her answer back upon her, his own momentary vulnerability well shielded.

"You speak true," he said with gentle fierceness. "The history of Greneforde will record my possession of it."

"That is so," she responded simply, not meeting his eyes.

"And my holding it," he pressed, leaning over her.

"So you have said," she agreed, as cool to him as she had ever been.

"You do not argue the point," he could not help noting.

"To what purpose, when we have readily agreed that history cannot be altered?"

William writhed on the hook he had set and baited for her. He was brewing for a fight, would have loved to clear the air between them and know her thoughts, no matter how bitter. But she was as cool as mist and as hard to strike.

Yet he gave it one further effort.

"Yea, we are agreed," he said, his voice throaty in its intensity. Gripping her chin between his thumb and finger, he added, "The past cannot be changed, just as a vessel that is broken cannot be made whole again."

This time she could not hide the fact that he had struck, and struck true and hard. Cathryn paled and seemed almost to shrink in stature, appearing less a woman and more a child. Yet he had been pushed so far that he could not feel pity for her.

John, as well as the entire population of the enclosure, had heard the exchange of verbal blows between the lord and lady of Greneforde. John moved to stand with his lady—to stand as her shield before her husband, if need be. Rowland had understood only the charged and warlike atmosphere between the newly wedded pair. He did not fathom the cause. He did not need to. If William had a quarrel with his wife, his cause was just, and William would not be hindered in his treatment of her. He would see to it. He marked John's intent and placed his hand upon his sword hilt, his look heavy with meaning. John paused, considering whether there was not another way.

"Just so," Cathryn managed to whisper in answer, her carriage erect even after that mortal blow. "It is also true of broken vows," she parried, trying to remind him of the vow of love and protection he had made to her so recently.

"And broken trust," he coldly added, the light of victory flickering in his gray eyes.

John moved toward his lady, uncaring of the consequences, as Rowland moved to slide his sword free of restraint.

Father Godfrey hurried into the midst of them, his frock pulling at his feet.

"Burned fields and broken homes I have noted here, not broken vows or broken trust," he said to William, stepping to stand beside Cathryn. "Can you do aught to heal Greneforde?"

William heard Father Godfrey's words and knew that he sought to turn him from his path. He answered him in truth, but he did not take his eyes from Cathryn of Greneforde.

"Greneforde I can heal, with men and seed and God's good will. Greneforde will have my care."

Cathryn met his look, her dark eyes of brown absorbing the cold gray metal of his and responding as little as the changeless earth when a sword is thrust into it. Lifting her chin, she said curtly, " 'Tis well, for 'tis Greneforde that needs it."

John stood on her other side and gently touched her arm, ignoring both Rowland and William.

"Lady Cathryn," he said in a voice of profound respect, "I ask that you supervise the quartering of the venison."

"Nay," William cut in, " 'tis my right, as mine was the killing shaft."

"As you will, Lord William," Cathryn quickly and softly agreed, her eyes holding his. " 'Tis bloody work, and you are welcome to it."

"Yea, lady," he answered as she turned to walk away, still protected between Godfrey and John, "you have said it aright, and bloody work requires water. Heat water, lady; there will be many baths taken before the day is done."

Cathryn paused, but did not look back. She nodded once, firmly, and continued on.

William did not hesitate in his task; he looked forward to it with relish. If he could not take out his anger and frustration on his icy wife, then he would find release on the carcass of an already defeated foe. Taking up his knife, he slit the skin from neck to tail. The entrails spilled out upon the ground in a red, steamy mass, and he reached in to cut out the heart and lungs and liver before he cut the neck to allow the blood to drain.

He looked up, his arms and chest and legs coated and spattered with blood, to find that Cathryn had paused on the threshold to the stair tower. He had known she was watching him somehow, and so there was no surprise in his eyes as he looked at her.

The look he gave her was chilling, and Cathryn read his thoughts easily, which was his wish: he stood covered in the blood of the deer as he had not been covered in hers. And he never would be.

Chapter Eight

Cathryn walked up the stairs calmly, though she wanted to surge up them and into the relative privacy of her own chamber as the tide wanted to rush upon the shore. Her husband might not have drawn her virgin's blood, but he had drawn the blood of her heart during their most recent exchange of words. Verily, William le Brouillard wielded words as adeptly and as ruthlessly as he ever did a sword. Did his reputation extend beyond the standard weapons of warfare to include the slicing he did with his tongue? Or was she the only one to have felt its razor edge? It was hardly something she could ask Ulrich.

So deep in thought was she that when Marie softly appeared out of the shadow that hid the entrance to the hall, she almost gasped in surprise. As it was, she nearly lost her footing, and so her immediate response to Marie was a trifle harsh.

"Marie! You should be hidden away at this hour. The tower is overrun with men."

"Yea, Lady Cathryn, I do know it, but I had heard that a deer had been slain by Lord William and I wanted to know the truth of it. Is it true, lady? Will we eat fresh venison this day?" she asked eagerly, her blue eyes alight with hope.

An image of William, his hands covered in blood, his eyes as cold as stone-sharpened steel, flooded her thoughts. Again she felt that she was losing her footing, yet both feet were planted firmly upon the stone.

"Yea," she answered simply, her mind drowning in the ice of William's eyes.

"Oh, lady, you spoke true when you declared that a knight would bring life to Greneforde!"

Marie's words almost made her laugh. Again she saw him as she had last seen him, and the vision was as welcome as a sword thrust. How long would it be before she could escape the picture in her mind of le Brouillard standing over the dead animal, covered in its life-giving blood?

But there was no time to answer. There was a wild clattering on the step, and then Ulrich burst upon them, intent upon some errand for his lord. He rushed against Cathryn, who jostled Marie, who softly cried out in shock and fear and what else, Cathryn could not say. But Marie had been seen. And by William's squire.

In a swirl of frenzied skirts, Marie was gone, disappearing much more silently than Ulrich had arrived. But Ulrich, his eye ever trained to find and pursue available women, had not missed her. He had seen her clearly enough to be enchanted by her vivid blue eyes and her ample bosom. He was as a hound on the scent and he would not easily be put off, though Cathryn did try.

"Ulrich," she called sharply as he made to move past her in the direction in which Marie had fled. "For what purpose do you career through the stair tower?" And when that failed to gain his attention, "Has your lord sent you on some errand of urgency?"

At the mention of William, Ulrich paused and breathed out heavily. Whether it was in frustration or anticipation, Cathryn could not determine.

"Yea, Lady Cathryn. Lord William asked that I find a special soap that was made for him in Flanders; it has a most pleasing aroma, and he is eager to wash the scent of blood from his body."

Cathryn tried to resist the urge to comment on William's fastidiousness, but she could not help the raising of her eyebrows or the look of amusement that entered her eyes. And since it was not William himself whom she faced, she did not much try.

"Your lord seems to be ever about his bath, Ulrich. Is this penchant common amongst the knights of France?"

"Nay, lady," he said in exasperation. "My lord alone, of all the knights I have known, is determined to be clean and to have those around him clean as well."

"Yea, it has come to my attention," she said dryly.

"And, lady, do you know he requires me to bathe once every week?" he blurted out, wanting to share the scandalous news with anyone who would sympathize with him.

"Truly, your knight's training is most rigorous," Cathryn murmured with a half-swallowed smile.

"It is something that he learned of in the land of our Savior, and the practice appealed to him so strongly, and, I do confess, to many other of our Christian knights, but in none so religiously as my lord, that he will bathe near every day. . . ."

"And so today," she reminded him, certain that Marie was once again well hidden.

"Yea, lady," he said in a rush, "and I must find that soap or he will have my head! Your pardon."

And, with a bound of youthful speed, he was gone.

Cathryn, suspecting that Ulrich had made for the lord's chamber, changed direction and proceeded to the kitchen, carefully avoiding the knot of people who surrounded the now unrecognizable deer. But it was William she wanted to avoid.

John was there, and Alys and Lan and half a dozen others. It was clear that they had been waiting for her.

"Hot water has been requested by the lord of Greneforde," she informed them calmly.

Of course, she had not said anything of which they were not aware. Indeed, she was beginning to wonder if there was a fortified dwelling anywhere between London and Damascus that had not been treated to William le Brouillard's fascination with water and soap. But what the people of Greneforde did not know was what Cathryn wanted them to do about his repeated requests—nay, demands—that they all bathe.

"As he is lord, his will must be acceded to in all things," she said pleasantly. "John, please be certain that enough water has been heated for my lord."

"And for ourselves, lady?" he asked.

Cathryn smiled warmly, eagerly anticipating her small revenge. Her brown eyes sparkling, she answered, "Lord William has proven his hunting skill this day and brought down a fat doe. Will it not take most of your time to prepare this splendid bounty so that we may indulge our appetites at dinner?"

John smiled, as did the others. "Yea, Lady Cathryn," John said, "our day is most full."

"Just so," Cathryn replied, and left them to their work.

The knot of helpers who had ringed the deer were gone, as was William, when she passed again. The blood had been drained and saved and the organs removed to form the basis for special, savory dishes. Today would have been better planned as her wedding feast, but without le Brouillard's skill there would have been no venison, and without the wedding, there would have been no le Brouillard. Cathryn sighed. Still, he was proving his worth to Greneforde. And more than his worth, he was proving his willingness, mayhap eagerness, to provide for Greneforde's needs. She had been accurate when she told Marie that a husband would be a good thing for Greneforde. And Marie had been correct when she worried that a husband would not be good for Cathryn.

Fie! What was wrong with her today? She and le

Brouillard could not be friends, but they might progress past enemies. Greneforde had a strong lord to protect her. And though her husband looked on her unkindly, he was not ungentle; that in itself was enough to commend him. Many a man would have killed her where she lay upon finding her unvirginal. He could also have annulled the vows and gone his way, and Greneforde would have been in the same sad straits she had been in before his arrival.

Truly, she had much to be thankful for, even if her husband was too handsome for comfort, too compelling with his silver eyes ringed with long black lashes; even if his mouth was too firm and his cheek too finely drawn. His look was so different from one whose eyes were of palest blue. A roiling in the pit of her stomach put a welcome end to that line of thought as she hurried across the enclosure to the shelter of the great tower.

It had begun to rain again. The blood-soaked earth where the deer had been riven was being cleansed even as she watched. In an hour, none would know that blood had been spilt there. Suddenly soul-weary, Cathryn ducked into the stairway.

As silent as Ulrich had been loud, William descended the stair in a rush. Dried blood covered his hands, arms, and legs, and his curling hair shone darkly with sweat-soaked ringlets. Cathryn sucked in her breath at sight of him and pressed her back against the wall—to keep herself from being thrown down the stair, she told herself. Her heart hammered but it was not in fear. William le Brouillard was a devastating man to the eye.

Knowing what he sought, she spoke before he did. "The water is on the boil, my lord, and will be carried to your chamber shortly."

"You anticipate my needs, lady, and most rightly."

" 'Tis not so difficult." She could not help smiling.

"Nay?" He smiled in return. "Then it would please me if you would share your talent with Ulrich. I sent him for—"

"Soap," she supplied. "A special blend you commissioned in Flanders, I believe?"

" 'Tis as I thought," William grumbled good-naturedly. "The boy has time to talk of the deed but not the time to perform it. I left him headfirst in my chest looking for it. If he has not found it by the time I return, his feet may join his head and he will miss the coming meal, no matter how his stomach protests."

Cathryn smiled more fully. She understood the man better than she had yesterday. He would do no harm to the boy, no matter the provocation. Who knew that better than she?

William watched her, lost in the brightness of her smile and trying desperately not to be. The sharp words of just minutes ago seemed to have been forgotten by both of them. He did not relish spending his days in verbal combat with his wife, and it appeared that she was as eager as he to start again on more cordial grounds. This light mood of hers surprised him. He had hardly thought she had it in her. It was a most pleasant surprise.

On impulse, he asked, " 'Twould please me to have you attend me at bath, Cathryn." His gray eyes shifted and glimmered like a well-polished shield turning in the sun.

But for all the warmth in his eyes, she froze.

"But Ulrich awaits," she whispered, her eyes locked with his.

"He is my squire, Cathryn; you are my wife."

His wife. Cathryn's thoughts flickered as wildly as his silver eyes. They would be alone in their chamber. She would pull the clothes from his sweat-drenched body and the man would be revealed to her. His arms would bulge, the muscles twisting as he lowered himself into the bath. The cloth would be in her hands and she would touch him with it and feel the silk of his skin and the raw strength that lay just beneath. The steam would rise and match the color of his eyes.

Yea, the steam would rise.

Impossibly, they shared the same thought, the same image. He could see it in her eyes. And she could see it in his.

" 'Tis a small request," he said under his breath, his voice low and compelling.

"That is so," she whispered, her gaze caught and held by his. And the image did not fade before her eyes; rather with William sharing it with her, it grew until she began to quake from the center of her soul. She could not feel such for him; she could not. There was no room in her heart for what he called forth from her. There was no room for him, for he was not a man to share her heart; he would want the whole of it, and that she could not—would not—give him. The voice of that other one—with his blue-white eyes—invaded her thoughts, and her tremors increased.

Lan, coming heavily up the stairs and sloshing out as much water as he sought to bring, broke the moment and William's hold on her.

"Please excuse me," Cathryn said in a rush. "There is much that needs my attention."

She flew down and away, her golden hair swinging out behind her before she was gone completely. Lan lost his footing and sloshed water on William's foot. He apologized quickly and continued his climb, his back to William. It was essential, to hide his smile of satisfaction.

William hardly noticed. His eyes marked the spot where Cathryn had stood, his brows drawn low in displeasure that only increased as the minutes passed. He had read the image that she had held of him, naked and covered with naught but water, and he had seen the seed of desire send forth its roots in the deep brown of her eyes. But it was not desire that had flourished within her; it had been fear.

Turning, he ascended the stair, and with each step he called himself a dozen kinds of fool. He reached his chamber before he had exhausted his list.

Lan had been but the first of a long and steady stream of men who carried water to the chamber William had shared last night with the Lady of Greneforde, although Lan was the only one of them to be so clumsy as to spill the contents of his bucket. Ulrich had found the Flanders soap he had been searching for and was ready with a large square of linen to dry William. William stood to one side of the chamber, his arms crossed over his chest, and watched the procession of men through his room. They shared one characteristic besides their common filth, and that was nervousness. There was not one fellow of them all who behaved with anything approaching ease.

Ulrich approached and helped him out of his tunic and hose; when William looked up again it was to find a half a dozen dirty men staring at him, agape. With a final slosh of water into his bath, they disappeared at a pace just shy of a run. It was peculiar, but then there was much that was peculiar in Greneforde Tower.

Lowering himself into the hot water with a sigh, William closed his eyes and enjoyed the penetrating heat of his bath.

"Ulrich," he questioned as he began to scrub his torso, "what can you tell me of the Greneforde folk? How seem they to you?"

It was a logical question. The common folk might be reacting badly to him and even to Rowland because they were knights. He had seen for himself how different was their manner with John the Steward. Ulrich was but a squire, and young.

"I find them as skittish as an untried warhorse," was Ulrich's blunt reply to William's question.

William looked askance at his squire. There was more emotion in that answer than the question warranted. It appeared that Ulrich was having his own defeats in Greneforde's courtyard.

"You have finished here," William announced unexpectedly and to Ulrich's profound pleasure. "I would have you locate the Lady Cathryn and quickly. I desire a tour of Greneforde before we partake of the coming meal, and I ask her courteously for her guidance."

Ulrich rolled his eyes. William's request of Lady Cathryn might have been couched in words that fertilized the flower of chivalry, but it was a command nonetheless. Who knew that better than he?

As he made to leave, William stopped him with another "request."

"When you have found her and delivered my message, I want you to spend the next few hours in the vicinity of the kitchen. Most all of Greneforde will be there preparing the meal, I suspect, and I would have you in the thick of them. Now, Ulrich, here is the crux of my purpose: by whatever subtle means at your disposal, find out what you can of the events at Greneforde preceding our arrival."

Cool silver eyes took his measure, and Ulrich stood the straighter for the slow scrutiny.

" 'Tis a man's mission," William said seriously.

"I have been squire to you for three years, William," Ulrich said proudly. "I am eager to serve and will not disappoint."

With a nod, he was dismissed. Ulrich all but flew out of the room. He was eager to prove his worth . . . and to find the girl with the eyes of sapphire blue.

It did not begin well. Ulrich was having little success in finding Lady Cathryn, and she had been the easy part of his mission.

Not knowing that she was sought, Cathryn was

in deep conversation with Father Godfrey. William would not have been pleased, had he known. Fortunately, he did not know.

"Then we are agreed," she said softly, her eyes luminous. "The mass will be read at dusk."

Godfrey searched her eyes with compassion, understanding her eagerness.

"Yea," he answered simply, "we are agreed, but may I ask, have you spoken of . . ." He paused uncomfortably.

"Nay, I have not," she said, mercifully breaking the silence of his discomfort. "I do not see the need." And she turned away to shield her face from the priest's eyes.

"William wants to know."

Cathryn clenched her hands into a tight and compact knot.

"He said so?"

"He said as much," Godfrey answered. "With the knowing would come understanding and pity for your time of hardship," he finished diplomatically.

Cathryn turned at that, the skirt of her green bliaut swirling in an angry tide at her feet.

"I do not seek his pity," she said forcefully, each word distinct and clear. "I did not know William le Brouillard during Greneforde's hard year, nor the years before. I do not see that he has the right or the need to know the private details of my life before the day he entered it. Indeed, in that it was a time of poverty and hunger and war, I would prefer to forget it."

Godfrey crossed the space that separated them, space she had deliberately created, and took her hand in his. It was like the moment, even to the hour of the day, when he had taken her hand to place it in the larger and much stronger hand of William le Brouillard. It was a reminder and they both knew it.

"You are bound to William now, your life to his."

"My life as it began yesterday and not one hour before," she argued coolly.

Godfrey was gathering breath to answer her, to explain that life was not cut into segments, but was a continuous thread that began in the womb and ended in the grave, when man was resurrected to a new life. Cathryn did not give him the chance. She turned and left, as cool and erect and as hurried as Godfrey had ever seen her. Truly, William's wife was not hampered by an excess of emotion.

For the third time that day, Cathryn was nearly run down on the stairwell, and for the second time, Ulrich was the juggernaut.

"Lady Cathryn!" He gasped, his cheeks pink with exertion. "Lord William asks that you be ready to show him Greneforde, all of Greneforde, so that he may be better able to understand her strengths and weaknesses and provide for her in either case."

"You have delivered your message," she answered. "I will be waiting for Lord William in the great hall. But Ulrich," she added, her eyes as serious as she could make them, "you will cease to run this stair as if pursued. Someday, someone, likely me, will be knocked to her death while you are on yet another mad charge to accomplish your lord's bidding."

"Yea, lady," he readily agreed, and then charged

off down the stair, the ringing of his shoes echoing against the stone.

Cathryn shook her head with rueful humor. Ulrich was a likable youth, and she found herself closer to laughing than she had been in many a day. Or month.

Reaching the hall, which was quiet just now, Cathryn considered the possible, plausible excuses she could offer William. Yes, she had accepted Ulrich's message, but she had no intention of fulfilling the request. Why be coy? It was a command, no matter the wording.

There was the matter of the venison, on the fire even now, and the attendant meal that would accompany such a feast of fresh meat, yet she had used the cooking and serving of meals often in her efforts to elude her husband's company. It might come about that he believed the people of Greneforde to be inept, and that she must avoid. Perhaps the care and storing of the bounty he had brought into the marriage would serve her purpose, for such wealth must be well cared for and well guarded. In truth, none of the Greneforde folk would meddle with it, but of his own men, she had no such certainty. There was no sickness to which she must attend and no injury and she could not ask her people to feign, for they would risk rude disclosure if le Brouillard chose to become involved.

She was still pondering when John appeared. John, ever at her side and ever quick in the exercising of his mind; he would have a solution.

"John!" she called softly.

Cathryn had been his goal upon entering the hall, and he was soon at her side.

"Yea, lady, how may I serve?"

"John, the lord has required that I lead him about Greneforde, explaining as we go every blade of grass and the setting of every stone. I would spend my hours in other pursuits."

John considered this for but a moment. Lord William's request was not unusual; rather, it spoke well of the man who would lead the folk within Greneforde's walls. Also, it was not burdensome toil he required of his bride, though he knew she did not see it so. In any other circumstance, Cathryn, who loved the stone of Greneforde as much as honor, would have been joyous over walking every step of her home with a man who was prepared to love it just as much as she. It was not the request; it was the man who rankled her. And because John loved her as a daughter, he would help her.

Before he had the chance to speak his plan, William le Brouillard appeared as suddenly and as silently at her elbow as the Lord Christ had appeared in the midst of his disciples.

"Thank you for waiting, lady," William said pleasantly, his hair still damp and tightly curled from his bath. "I would not have had you endure my company in my former state, and since I would have a most thorough tour of our home, I think we will be fully occupied for what remains of the day."

Cathryn whirled at his first words and held his look most politely. When he had finished, she looked toward John with hope carefully masked.

"Your pardon, lord," John bowed. "Greneforde's

last mare has turned her leg, and Tybon has requested Lady Cathryn's aid in soothing her while he applies the dressing."

Cathryn was already nodding and moving away from William, a smile just kept in check at John's cleverness, when she felt le Brouillard's fingers close on her elbow.

"This is sad news, John," William said sympathetically, but Cathryn felt his fingers tightening as she edged away, and she was not deceived into believing his sympathy genuine. "Tybon requires help in the bandaging of a mare? Would that be the ancient mare I noted standing solitary in the stable when I arrived yesterday? And how ancient is this Tybon that he requires aid when dealing with such a remnant of horseflesh?"

John had no answer. He merely looked at Cathryn, his wise eyes resigned.

Cathryn did not relent so quickly.

"Tybon is not ancient and he is not inept, nor is he incapable of tending to the ails of our mare. 'Tis just that he understands that the animal would be more soothed were I present." Cathryn stopped and gave William a measuring look. "The beast, her comfort and care, is more important than Tybon's pride, is she not?" she finished chillingly.

William smiled, but his eyes did not, and his hand slid more firmly upon her arm, his hold sure.

"Nay, Cathryn, the mare does not take precedence over you, and since the animal is so skittish and unpredictable in her behavior, I would have you well away and far from possible injury."

Wrapping his free arm around her waist, he

guided her to the stair tower, looking for all the world like a besotted husband when she and everyone else in Greneforde Tower knew that he was not.

"John," he said over his shoulder, "there must be someone else who can stand in Lady Cathryn's stead in this matter?"

"Yea, Lord William," he answered calmly. "I will see to it myself."

William smiled and then they were gone, down the stairs to begin their tour of Greneforde from the ground up. But John was not distressed by this turn of the tide, though he well knew that Lady Cathryn was. This William le Brouillard was a man—and a man of strength sheathed in control. It was not the control of Cathryn, achieved and maintained at high cost and at the loss of all other emotion; his was the control of a warrior accustomed to his own strength and comfortable in dispensing it. In whatever degree required, no more and no less. And something else: William had the strength of kindness.

And now John smiled as he stood in the quiet hall. This man who had come as stranger and lord to Greneforde just yesterday was no longer an enemy to be swiftly outmaneuvered. On that point John was in swift retreat. No longer would he stand as a shield of protection between Cathryn and her husband, whether Lady Cathryn liked it or not.

At that moment the lady in question was standing with her husband in the chill winter rain, his grip upon her arm as firm as if he held a battle-ax. She liked it not.

"And this is English rain," she said crisply.

155

To her surprise and irritation, William laughed and slowly released her arm to the care of its proper owner. He looked her over, from top to toe and back again, his gaze lingering the longest on her face. She did not avert her eyes. She only masked them from behind, leaving him nothing to see but his own distorted reflection.

"You are a cool one, lady wife." He chuckled warmly, his voice deep and throaty. "Yet not so cool as I first believed."

She knew then, though she did not understand how, that she had lost ground to him. She must lose no more.

" 'Tis a raw day to be standing abroad, my lord. I am, indeed, quite cool," she responded cryptically.

"Yea, Cathryn"—he smiled—"I give you no argument. 'Tis a raw day."

Turning away from the amusement she saw on his sculpted face, Cathryn ambled away from him. He ambled with her, his long stride easily matching hers.

She was miserable in her discomfort, and he knew it was more than the weather that had her in such a state. She was miserable because she was with him, and it annoyed him. Why should it not? Yet she amused him and he could not fathom why. It would be foolish to enjoy her company, that he knew well; others had enjoyed his wife's company before him.

Cathryn could not be trusted and he did not trust her, nor would he ever. She had betrayed him before she had ever laid eyes upon him. She had given herself to another man, accepting his arms around

her golden slenderness and his seed within her hot
sheath. No, he would never trust her, but they were
lord and lady here, and she was best suited to give
him answers.

He would simply have to try to smother the pleasure he felt in her company.

"The hall, I was told," he began politely, "was begun in the reign of Henry the first?"

"Yea," she answered, and stopped her forward
motion, "on the foundations of a bailey built in
Saxon times. 'Tis an old place, with ancient memories," she supplied in a soft voice, her eyes taking
in the line of the rampart.

"A well-chosen site," he offered in compliment.

"Yea. And much desired . . . in years past," Cathryn finished a little rapidly, not wanting his
thoughts to be led in that direction.

"And present," he added gallantly.

Choosing not to respond directly, she continued,
" 'Twas rebuilt of stone by my father's father during
the reign of Henry, and my father built the tower
gate before he left on pilgrimage."

Cathryn and William stood in the center of the
courtyard, and he held his tongue as he looked
about him. Cathryn saw what he saw. The orchard
was small; three trees had died of disease in recent
years, and she was unsure if they had checked its
spread to the rest. The stable, its roof sagging, was
empty of fine horses, unless one counted the many
that William had brought with him as his portion.
The tower gate was strong, but the wooden wall that
surrounded Greneforde Tower was not stone, as
was the current fashion. Greneforde had not ful-

filled the promise of its youth, begun so long ago in the time of her grandfather. Like a proud mother, Cathryn rose to her home's defense.

"Before my father left, the buildings were in good repair and we had food aplenty. He had even ordered glass for the wind holes in the hall."

William did not stop her. He turned to look at her, her gaze focused on a time when her home had been strong and vibrant, and he saw the longing for those days in her dark eyes. Nay, he did not stop her. He knew what it was to lose a home, in whatever manner.

"The hall was hung with six tapestries of excellent workmanship and glowing with brilliant thread," she said softly. "My father's bed was thick with coverlets of fur and silk, and the curtains were of damask—a most fine, warm bed. He had contracted for the painting of the ceiling beams in colors of red and yellow when . . ." Her voice faded, and she stared at the muddy ground at her feet.

William dared not disturb her progress through time. This was his first glimpse of the woman beneath the ice of control that sheathed her, and he did not want this flickering of emotion to die. He knew without knowing how that the cold would be intensified in its wake.

She looked up again, this time not at the hall but at the tower her father had built.

"The tower was already more than half-completed when my mother died. My father allowed it to be finished, but his heart was no longer here. His heart and soul were on his pilgrimage, and he would not rest until he set out to touch the sand that had borne the weight of our Savior. He died there," she whispered. "I believe he knew he would."

Clasping her hands tightly together, Cathryn said flatly, "And pilgrimages do not come cheaply. Nay, the cost is dear."

After a lengthy silence, and only when he was certain she would not volunteer more, William asked, "How many years has it been since he left?"

Cathryn did not look at him, nor did she give any indication that she had heard him speak until she finally answered, "It has been six."

William reeled inside himself at that. Six years she had been alone, bearing the sole responsibility for Greneforde and all its people. Six years of intense civil disorder and mayhem. Six years, and she but a child of twelve at the onset. He looked at her with compassion. Truly, her burden had been heavy and cast upon her at too tender an age.

"You have done well, Cathryn," he praised, his voice warm.

She jerked slightly and looked at him with wide eyes, as if she had forgotten that he existed or that he stood but a pace from her side.

"Nay. I have not," she said coldly, and looked away.

And he could not argue the point with her. Greneforde was near starving. The fields were overgrown. The village had been sacked and burned. She had been no virgin when he claimed her. She had not, by God's Holy Writ, done well.

But his compassion would not die so easily.

She had whet his appetite for information, and

159

he would have that appetite appeased with news from Rowland and Ulrich. And John the Steward. Yes, John would soon receive a lengthy visit from the Lord of Greneforde. William would know the history of Greneforde, and he would know it to the full before he lay again with Cathryn in their spartan bed.

"The seed I have carried with me cries out for land to be buried in," he offered pleasantly, turning them both from their black thoughts. "Will it thrive in Greneforde soil?"

"Yea, it will take root and grow and flourish here, if you can keep it safe from warhorses and thieves and roguish knights," she answered mildly.

William smiled and offered Cathryn his arm. "Show me your fertile fields, Cathryn, from the height of the curtain walk, that we may best determine the proper siting of the crops."

Cathryn laid her hand upon his arm the barest degree, unwilling to slight him when he was being so cordial, yet uncomfortable at the contact. Carefully restricting his stride to hers, William escorted Cathryn to the walk and they looked down upon the bare destruction of the fields.

"They are war-ravaged," she supplied by way of apology.

"As is all England," he agreed with courtesy.

"Greneforde has had need of you, William le Brouillard," Cathryn said impulsively, keeping her eyes on the horizon, unwilling to reveal the deep truth of those words to this near-stranger.

"I am here," he said solemnly, looking at her profile, so golden and delicate in the gray chill of the day. "Greneforde's needs shall be met in me."

She had no answer, no response to that. She could not think of one with her heart beating so full against her ribs and the air suddenly so chill, for were her hands not as cold as new-fallen snow? It had been said time and again that she and Greneforde were one. Did he include her in his promise? For the first time, she wished it to be so. If such was the case, then her dual identity with Greneforde would not be so heavy a weight to bear, however lovingly she bore it.

Breaking the heavy stillness in the air between them, William said lightly, "In truth, I have been much in need of Greneforde. Those seeds of mine have traveled far in search of a home, as have I."

There was so much truth in those casually spoken words, and she sensed it, even if she had not known that he had lost his family lands as a youth.

Seeking to aid William in easing the weight of emotion between them, Cathryn spoke also of the seeds he cherished. It was one topic that was not a potentially volatile one and in which they both had a genuine interest.

"You are an unusual knight to be so interested in farming when making war is both pastime and profession for one of your station," she offered with a slight smile.

"It is not so unusual to become fascinated with the production of food when you have spent years searching for it with an empty belly," he answered with a smile that made her forget the light rain that veiled them.

Truly, he was fair of face and limb, and truly, she

161

had not been cursed with him as husband.

"Walking the Way of the Cross has changed you much, I vow," Cathryn remarked.

"And how, lady, do you think me changed when you knew me not at all before and but little after?" William challenged softly. It was not the softness of gentleness; nay, it was the expectant quiet before thunder.

"I . . ." she stammered, confused as to his abrupt change of mood, "you, you do not seem an average knight, my lord."

Again she had blundered, but she could not fathom how or in what fashion to extricate herself.

William's voice was as cool as the rain, his eyes as sharp and cold as the sword. "Lady, do you indulge in wifely flattery or are you speaking from a storeroom of experience?"

Cathryn closed her eyes against the pain. *So.* She had her answer. He suspected her of wild fornication, and he had a fine and unassailable foundation for his belief. The worst of it was that she could not fault him for the accusation, as his proof was so damning. She been caught unprepared for his assault. That was most foolish of her. No matter; it would not happen again.

Standing in frigid isolation before the heat of his anger and suspicion, Cathryn drew her dignity about her. It did not warm her as well as a cloak, but it covered her just as completely.

"Neither, my lord."

She would offer nothing more; indeed, she had given him more of herself than she intended when he had taken her from the hall. Moving with fluid grace, Cathryn descended the stair and crossed the courtyard to reenter the great tower.

William made no move to detain her or to accompany her. He did not want to be anywhere near her in his present anger.

And, though he was loath to admit it, he enjoyed watching her move.

Such would it ever be with her. They could reach neutral ground and sue for peace, yet they would not attain it, for he could not forget that she was a woman who had accepted his vow and his touch when she knew that she was impure. That she had known the most intimate touch of another man, mayhap many men, the bonding that was reserved for a man and a woman pledged before God, rankled him more with each hour that he knew her. Yet he would not relinquish Greneforde, though the cost was high and rising as he came to know her better.

Her heart was not with him, was clearly sheltered against him in favor of another. To spend his lifetime with such a woman . . . Yet he had learned something from their most recent exchange of verbal blows: Cathryn was not as coolly unemotional as she pretended. He was beginning to believe that her admirable composure was the result of practiced effort.

He was a motherless dog if he did not like her the better for it.

Chapter Nine

Dinner had just begun, the first course but barely served, when Rowland entered the hall. He was back from his search for details concerning the history of Greneforde . . . and Cathryn. This William knew. Ulrich had come to him earlier, just before the meal, to relate that he could make no inroads into the Greneforde mind. The people were cordial to him, easier with him than they had been with men who had achieved the accolade, but they had revealed nothing. Wisely, Ulrich had not pressed, not wanting to give away his purpose, no matter how earnestly he sought to prove his worth to William. For that wisdom, he had been sincerely praised. It would serve no good purpose for the people of Greneforde to think that their lord was not dealing from an open hand. But Rowland had a gift for understanding more than was said. Rowland would have news.

Cathryn and William, sitting in polite animosity and together for the first time since their conversation earlier that day on the wall, watched as he strode toward them. In truth, Cathryn had never seen Rowland look so grim. Nor had William.

Rowland seated himself next to Cathryn, his rightful place as William's closest friend, and began to eat. He did not appear to be enjoying his meal. In truth, he looked as though he would choke on each and every bite. His looks, dark as they were, were only for William; for Cathryn he spared not a glance. It was as if she were only air, of no substance. Or as if he would make her so if he but could. In such a strained atmosphere, Cathryn lost her taste for food. She reached for her wine-filled goblet.

Cathryn endured the first two courses in silence. By the time Ulrich had filled her goblet for the third time and the venison was being carried in by John, she summoned breath to speak.

"Rowland," she said, "my lord and his knights have earned the gratitude of all Greneforde this day. It has been long since we tasted of fresh meat. I give you my thanks."

Rowland, as skilled in diplomacy and chivalry as William, did the impossible: he said nothing. He did not acknowledge her words, her thanks, or even her presence. Rowland stared at William, his dark eyes shimmering with an inner fire.

William's mood worsened.

Cathryn reached again for the wine.

William's hand upon her arm stopped her. With a reluctance he could feel, she rested her hand upon the linen cloth, her goblet just out of reach. She would not use that means of escape again. Not today. Not when he was using all his warrior's strength, skill, and discipline to fight the desire to lay her beneath him again.

It tormented him that he wanted her so. She was a beauty—he could admit it—but she was as sly and deceitful as a serpent. Untrustworthy. Impure. Undisciplined. He could not want one such as she, yet the delicate line of her nose, the slender column of her throat, the fine, golden smoothness of her hair told him she was none of those things. To look at her, he could believe that she was pure and worthy and innocent. When he looked at her, he wanted to possess her and protect her in the same instant. When he lay between her harlot's legs, he wanted to shout his betrayal to God and have God take His vengeance upon her. That he yearned still to lie with her was his agony.

Greneforde was the object of his yearning and had been for so many years that he could not recall a time when he had not pursued her, though he had not known the name of his future home until just days ago. Greneforde was home and legacy. Greneforde would be his children's heritage and their birthright. Children . . . to lie with Cathryn . . .

Nay! Greneforde was the object of his desire, only Greneforde. He had not sought a wife, and certainly not a ruined wife. Ruined as she lay in the arms of . . . whom?

William gulped his wine in silence. Cathryn, whose arm lay entrapped by his mighty hand still, did not watch him, though she could feel the waves of his anger until they washed over her in a crimson tide. Her husband's anger was a quiet thing—as quiet as the slice of sword through flesh, and just as fatal to her heart. This she knew, though she did not know how. Perhaps his anger was the deadlier of the two, for with a sword thrust, there was warning. With William, there was just the strike.

As his anger and his torment rose, so did the chill from the center of her heart, until he pounded against the rock-hard walls of ice that she had called forth to shield her. If his anger, the cause of which she did not know, rebounded against her, it would strike walls of thickest ice, and she would be safe within their innermost core.

It would be so. There was no other course for her, and it was a familiar path.

Father Godfrey, seated at William's other side, understood the present situation. Knowing William as he did, he knew that his unease at his marriage had grown since last evening, and that he must have sent Rowland to cover his flank. It was always so between them. Their friendship went back years and was beyond question or doubt. Rowland would have beaten the ground itself for information in his effort to protect William. Rowland knew what had occurred in Greneforde. That knowledge was written on his face, and it was knowledge he was desperate to impart to William.

Godfrey sighed and sipped his wine. In truth, he was also eager for William to know what had befallen Greneforde and Greneforde's lady during the past years. The words would be bitter to hear, yet he believed that William would be able to come to terms with the truth; he would never be at peace grappling with the suspicions that plagued him now. And, as much as Cathryn objected, he also believed her husband's discovery of the truth would do her no lasting harm. No, it would be of benefit to her, if her husband understood the desperate times that Greneforde had barely survived.

"Rowland," Godfrey interjected into the oppressive silence of the high table. "Lord William will not enjoy his meal, a meal so long awaited by all, until he hears the words crowding your tongue. Go. I will stay with the Lady Cathryn and entertain her with stories of battle until your return."

Rowland rose without a word, his entire manner bespeaking ready eagerness, his dark eyes urging William to follow him from the hall. William rose also, yet he was not so urgent. He had sent Rowland out to learn what he could concerning Cathryn and Greneforde, but there was a part of him that shrank from what he suspected he would hear. And still he was drawn to her. It mattered not; he would know what there was to know. There was no other path.

Gazing at Cathryn, he said, "Enjoy your meal, Cathryn." He added softly, his smoky eyes not leaving hers, "Ulrich, no more wine for my lady; I fear it blunts her appetites."

She had naught to say to that and watched in puzzlement as William and Rowland left the hall. William le Brouillard was an unexpected man; anger rolled through him as well as desire, and both swirled in the same current. He was definitely an unexpected man. His anger she could understand; his desire in the wake of his carnal knowledge of her was not what she had expected. Not after his heartfelt proclamation that he cared nothing for her as she lay naked upon his bed.

Father Godfrey moved to Rowland's place and seated himself next to her. Her usually calm expression was replaced by one of mild confusion. Wanting to comfort her without betraying the confidence William had placed in him, Godfrey offered, "Rowland has information regarding the well-being of Greneforde that is of supreme importance to William. They should rejoin us soon."

Cathryn nodded, her brown eyes fixed upon her plate, the food scarcely touched.

"The bond between them is strong," she commented, lacking anything of substance to say, her mind on William's remark regarding her appetites.

Godfrey smiled. "Yea, a bond unbreakable they share."

Cathryn lifted her eyes from her plate, her interest aroused. Godfrey's smile widened. He had achieved his purpose: to draw her thoughts off herself and onto another.

"It takes time to forge such a bond," she said.

"Time and much heat," he supplied.

"And hammering?" she asked.

"Yea, they have had their share of hammer blows in this world," Godfrey agreed, "but they are the stronger for it. So it is that God causes good to come of evil."

Cathryn's eyes turned again to her plate, her expression almost wistful.

"Does He?" she asked softly.

"Yea, Cathryn, He does. Though 'tis hard to give Him thanks when obstacles litter the path He has chosen for us, but thank Him we should."

"And William," she challenged, "did he thank God when his family lands were lost to him?"

Godfrey's eyes did not reflect censure nor even surprise. He only said, "So you know something of William's long fight for Greneforde? I wonder, do you know the whole of it?"

Before Cathryn could answer, he said, "Nay, for how could you when no man knows the full tale of another, though he hear it word for word. 'Tis in traveling the same path that the true tale is known, and each man travels his life path alone, save for the knowledge of God he carries in his heart."

Godfrey suspected that Cathryn would adjust herself more readily to her husband if she knew the long travail his life had been, yet he did not want to be the one to share it with her. That should come from William, and from William she should seek it.

"Rowland and William met in Damascus, did you know?" he asked.

"Yea, Ulrich told me a pretty tale of valor beneath the blazing sun and the shadow of the wall," she answered with a smile.

"A pretty tale and true," Godfrey informed her. "There has been naught that could separate them since that day, not even Rowland's grief."

He let that lie between them, understanding women better than many another priest of God.

When Cathryn could no longer bite back the words, she asked, "And what caused Rowland's grief?"

Godfrey settled into his seat, fingering the tassels on his cushion, before he began what Cathryn prophesied would be a long and sad tale.

"If you know of Damascus, you must also know that Rowland d'Albret is of France, but not of Normandy, as is William. Rowland is of Aquitaine." Godfrey sighed and took a sip of wine. Cathryn waited for him to continue.

"Lubias was his wife."

Cathryn's eyes widened. She had not suspected that Rowland was married, or had been married.

"Rowland has been long from his wife," Cathryn said.

"Nay, his wife has never left him," Godfrey contradicted, his voice heavy with emotion. "The journey to the lands of our Savior is a long one, and Rowland was not eager to go, though he is a worthy and earnest soldier of Christ; 'twas his love for Lubias that hindered his going. But go he must, for is there a man alive that does not hunger for war and a chance to wet his blade on God's behalf? Lubias, loving Rowland, understood his quandary and solved it for him. Lubias rode at Rowland's side when they left Aquitaine."

Cathryn had heard of such. It seemed there were wives, loving God as deeply as their husbands, who also followed the Way of the Cross and willingly endured the certain privations that came with such a journey. Few, even the hardiest of men, survived

171

such a trek; Cathryn knew by Father Godfrey's tone that Rowland's wife had not survived.

"She was not at his side when he left Damascus," she said quietly.

Father Godfrey looked at her lingeringly and said sadly, "Nay, for William rode at his shoulder then."

"Was the road Rowland and his Lubias shared a long one?"

"Rowland would answer nay, but she was no flower to wither at the first frost. Lubias rode with her husband the breadth of France to Verdun. She bathed in the waters of the Rhine and the Danube and they entered Vienna together."

"Did she ever see Damascus?"

"Nay," he answered, "she traveled as far as Philippopolis, a noble Latin town. There the Germans—" Godfrey frowned—"in ungodly fashion, turned the market into a brawling mass, which was their usual practice."

"To what purpose is such an ill-advised practice?"

"None but a German could tell you, and I doubt even he, for they act without thought, moved by impulse and not by reason. In this instance they charged ahead, not allowing the French to inspect and buy the goods we all so earnestly needed; they were intent only on filling their own needs with no thought of those others who traveled with them. As a result, a brawl broke out, and French and German rained blows and shouted insults upon each other in equal measure. The French managed to break free of the market with their newly acquired goods, and this enraged the Germans. Seizing their arms, they pursued their allies in the cause of Christ. The

French took up their own arms and put up a stiff resistance against the rage of the German horde. It ended only when God caused night to fall."

Godfrey looked into his goblet, now empty, for many moments.

"What of Lubias?" Cathryn whispered, knowing the answer.

Godfrey looked up, his eyes weary.

"Lubias." He sighed. "Lubias was with Rowland in the market that disgraceful day. A German knight faced him and they fought with swords ringing, the sound clanging like a dissonant bell. Rowland slipped and fell to one knee. 'Twas not a mortal fall, and I am certain he would have recovered swiftly, but Lubias would not take such a chance."

Cathryn edged forward on her seat, certain of what was to come and recoiling from that certainty.

"She rushed to Rowland's assistance, striking a blow upon the helm of the German. Striking from behind."

Godfrey breathed deeply and set his goblet down, his eyes closed against the memory.

"The German whirled and struck her down. He did not know his attacker was a woman. 'Twas over more quickly than words can tell it," he finished grimly, "and Lubias lay lifeless upon the stone."

"And the German?"

"His blood joined hers at the next strike of Rowland's sword. Then Rowland carried her away; he would not have her soiled by the Germans even in death."

Cathryn closed her eyes and clasped her hands. She would never have suspected that Rowland carried a memory of such sorrow. Then she remembered Father Godfrey's words.

"He carries her still," she said, opening her eyes to seek out the priest's.

Godfrey looked at Cathryn appraisingly. She understood much.

"Yea, he carries her still, and though his burden is heavy, he will not relinquish her."

"You have advised him to?"

Godfrey smiled ruefully. "He would kill the man who spoke such words to him of his Lubias, priest or no."

Cathryn sat silent, as did Godfrey, in the high-ceilinged hall, their food forgotten. She wondered, in the most hidden corner of her heart, if it were truly possible for a man to love a woman as Rowland loved his Lubias.

They stood near the stable, the smell of the hay pleasant, the heat emitted by the horses comforting. They stood far from the great tower to insure their privacy.

"Greneforde Castle had a neighbor," Rowland began, his dark eyes as bleak as death. "Lambert of Brent. He occupied a motte and bailey fortification to the east of here."

William waited, knowing there was more, knowing that Rowland had searched until all that had been hidden was revealed. He ignored the twist in his gut at hearing of Lambert, so close to Greneforde, so close to Cathryn.

"His holding was not impressive," Rowland continued, "and was destroyed by mercenary knights not a year ago. He and his men—" Rowland swallowed heavily—"lived at Greneforde for a few months."

William was silent, waiting for all of it, knowing he had not heard the worst.

"They left," Rowland continued slowly, "upon hearing of Henry and Eleanor's coronation. They left hurriedly after they had delayed as long as possible."

William waited, his eyes the color of heavy fog.

"Lambert was ever in the company of Lady Cathryn."

He had a name now for the man who occupied his wife's heart, a heart she kept carefully defended against him. A name for the man who had taken what rightfully belonged to him; the virgin blood that should have covered him had covered another. Lambert of Brent.

William le Brouillard turned away from Rowland and faced the tower, rising solidly in the darkness and the rain. His eyes were as impenetrable as the fog that lay shroudlike above the chapel. With steps quiet and quick, William moved toward Greneforde Tower.

Rowland, despite his loyalty to William, found himself pitying Cathryn of Greneforde.

William sought not Cathryn, not yet. He would give her every chance, though he could in no way imagine what could save her after what he had just learned. She had consorted with Lambert for months, breaking off the sordid pairing only when Henry took the throne, he who was vocal in his intent of restoring order to a wildly chaotic land.

William sought John the Steward—John who knew all that occurred within Greneforde's walls and would have access to information that perhaps Rowland had not. If there were words to save her, John would have them, but William would have the truth, whether it saved or damned her. He would know all before he faced her again. He found John on his way to the kitchen.

John was caught completely off guard when the lord of Greneford clasped him on the shoulder with a heavy hand. Turning quickly, knowing who accosted him by the very strength of the grip, he faced a solemn William with black-eyed Rowland at his back. Tremors gripped him and rolled unevenly through his innards. This was to be a confrontation; he had no doubt of it.

"You have been steward of Greneforde long, John," William said quietly, with no sign of emotion. "There is much I would know of Greneforde's history. You will tell me."

It was a command and nothing less. John responded in the only way he could: he obeyed.

"Yea, Lord William."

William nodded his acceptance of John's capitulation and asked, "Greneforde has a neighbor, Lambert of Brent."

John's wide eyes and indrawn breath were all William needed in the way of confirmation.

"Lambert's holding was destroyed."

"Yea," John agreed.

"He came to Greneforde. He resided here, in my

lady's company, for many months," William intoned, his gray eyes icy.

"Yea, he came—" John began.

"She sheltered him," William charged, his voice a heavy monotone, his manner as cold as that of an executioner.

John could see that the facts were lined up against his lady. Despite his fear of William's manner, John could not allow such an indictment to stand against Cathryn.

"Lord," he said urgently, "Lambert was not invited to Greneforde."

"Yet he stayed for many months," William softly contradicted.

"Yea, he stayed," John agreed, all thoughts of caution quickly evaporating in angry defense of his lady, "for there was none to make him go!"

"Lady Cathryn could have—" William began.

"Nay, not Cathryn," John argued, his voice hoarse with suppressed emotion. "Not she. She could do naught against him, though she did try."

William's black brows lowered in a scowl, his gray eyes appearing even stormier than before.

"She did not send him away."

"Lord, listen and believe what I will tell you, though I break the confidence my lady placed in me and whose honor I hold dearer than life," John beseeched. "Lord Lambert appeared at our walls with Lord Philip, Lady Cathryn's brother, in his grasp."

"I was told of no brother," William cut in, frowning furiously.

"Nay, none were told, and that was his sister's doing. Upon the death of her mother, Philip grew ill and was thought close to death. He was long in recovering his strength. It was at this same time that Lord Walter, lord of Greneforde, departed for the Holy Land. My lady knew her situation was dangerous: a young woman and a younger heir, left with a prize that many would covet. Philip was sent to Blythe Tower in greatest secrecy, his survival depending upon all thinking him already dead. So they separated for their very lives, with only a few knowing the truth of Lord Philip's whereabouts."

"And Lambert found him," William commented, not at all convinced of the veracity of the tale.

"Yea, through the duplicity of Greneforde's priest," John spit out.

"Holy God," Rowland murmured in horror.

"Lambert appeared with Philip in tow and all his knights with him, calling for Greneforde to open her gates to him. To surrender. There was no fight, though what remained of Greneforde's knights wished differently. Cathryn would in no way put her brother's life at risk. The gates were opened and Lambert came in. By nightfall, Greneforde's knights lay dead," John said harshly, his wise face stark in the dim light.

"Go on," William commanded.

"Lambert is no honorable lord," John continued flatly.

"Such things are done by knights," William argued. "Greneforde is not the first great tower to have been taken by treachery."

"Nay," John all but shouted, "such things are not done by knights sworn to uphold Christ's holy standard." His brown eyes wide, he croaked, "Lambert took my lady! With savage brutality he took her. Do you comprehend? He took her and beat her when she fought him. Have you not marked the scar that slices her brow? Lambert did that, the first time."

"It cannot be," William argued in a whisper, unholy images rising to curdle his thoughts with their poison.

John ignored him, his eyes filled with unshed tears, and said, "When Philip heard her cries, he rushed to aid her. Before her eyes, Lambert killed him."

"Nay," William said under his breath. It was all he could think to say. He believed it not. It was but a tale to turn his wrath from his wife, and spoken by one who openly confessed to unshakable loyalty. It could not be. It was too much like . . .

John saw the doubt on William's face hardening to disbelief. He had gone far, broken a sacred vow to give William the information he now possessed; he took a new vow that it would not be for naught.

He beckoned into the shadow of the kitchen wall and waited. "Come," he urged.

With slow steps a girl—nay, a woman—stepped away from the sheltering darkness into the relative light of the rain-wet yard. It was Marie.

William and Rowland looked her over in surprise. She was of Greneforde, her very cowering proclaimed her so, yet they had not seen her, and each had looked over the folk of Greneforde most carefully.

"You have heard," John stated baldly.

"Aye," she all but stuttered.

"They believe Lady Cathryn welcomed Lambert

179

into Greneforde." John paused, as if reluctant to continue. When he did, his tone was gentle though his words were not.

"They believe she welcomed him into her body."

"*Nay!*" Marie cried in horror, her lovely eyes filling with swift tears.

"You must tell them what you saw and heard, Marie. He is her husband and must know the truth concerning his wife."

When she hesitated still, the fear a livid mask riding her features, John urged, "You will do her no hurt if you but tell the truth."

Marie searched John's face and gulped heavily, wiping at her eyes with reddened hands.

"She loved her brother," Marie began simply, struggling to find her way through the painful memories. "Lambert used Philip to gain entrance. Once inside, he discarded the boy and searched for my lady. She was not hiding; he found her quick enough."

Lifting her eyes to stare into William's, she stammered, "I . . . I was with her . . . in the bedchamber. We heard him on the stair. She pushed me into the chest and bade me say not a word, to make no sound. Lambert found her, dragged her to her bed by . . . by . . . by the length of her hair." A small sob rushed out of her open lips; she gulped it down and continued: "I could not see, but I could hear. I heard her fight him, the sound of flesh meeting flesh, and then he struck her with his ringed hand and caused her blood to flow from a wound on her brow. This I know because I tended the gash myself when he had left," Marie asserted.

"And still she . . . she did not submit, and he told her . . . he told her"—Marie sobbed—"he told her that all the women of Greneforde would be taken as she was being taken if she resisted him, and that he would kill them, kill us . . . kill us . . . if she did not submit."

The sobs racked her shoulders, and she wound her arms around her waist to still the heaving of her stomach. She would have stopped if John had not commanded, "Finish."

"Philip rushed in to defend her, but . . . but . . . he could not. Lambert killed him. Killed him with his dagger or his sword, I know not. Lambert kicked Lord Philip's body from the chamber." Marie pressed her fists against her eyes as if she would grind out the memory.

"I next heard . . . he said that . . . that he had lost his lands and that he had taken Greneforde and that she . . . *she*," Marie cried hoarsely through her tears, "was part of Greneforde and his by right of conquest."

Marie's cries mingled with the lightly falling mist and soared to the gates of heaven itself. She could hardly stand, sobbing from the depth of her soul the pain she had felt and still felt for Cathryn. She leaned into the welcome embrace of John. He let her rest; she had told what she knew. There was naught else to say regarding Lambert and his taking of Greneforde.

William stood rooted to the rain-soaked ground, his face as white as a summer cloud. He had heard—heard every pain-filled word, and the pain had filled his own heart until he wondered how he stood to face it. His thoughts were filled with visions of his dark-haired Margret and then of Cathryn until the two merged and the pain was multiplied by more than two.

So much of what he had observed of Greneforde was clear to him now: the skulking of the servants, the distrust, the lack of food. And of Cathryn. She wore her strict composure as armor, and as armor it protected her. She was not a woman of no emotion; she was a woman shielding herself against pain—against a pain, both of the body and of the mind, that had killed many a woman of lesser strength. *Margret* . . .

Cathryn, taken as spoils of war. And had he not said much the same to her himself? Yesterday. On their wedding day.

Rage, guilt, and sorrow twined as one and rose to choke him. He could not breathe. There was a blackness before his eyes that was heavier than any darkness of night. A dull roaring filled his ears.

He saw a vision of Margret, the blood pumping with rhythmic precision from between her legs to soak her favorite yellow bliaut. Her maidenhead had been ripped from her unwilling body and he had known it not, had known nothing, not until the life flowed from her in a brilliant pool. He had been powerless to help her; he had come to her too late. He had failed to protect her, to save her, when it was his sworn obligation to do just that. He had found the man, the knight, who had fallen so far as to take a damsel against her will, and killed him at a blow, but his Margret had bled to death, her life softly pulsing away in ever-slower beats until her skin was white and cool beneath his hand. His sister. Dead at fifteen.

An image of Cathryn as she had been last night rose in his thoughts to take precedence. He saw again her terror at coupling with him ripping her self-composure to rags. He watched with new vision her mute struggle in the face of a force greater than she, and the blankly staring eyes that had unmanned him. He had held her arms above her head so that she could not thwart him, while he forced himself into her unready warmth. . . . She had been unwilling, as Margret had been unwilling, and though he had the lawful right to couple with his wife, he remembered only that Cathryn had been fighting him and unwilling. And he had forced her.

Rowland was gripping his shoulders, shaking him, but the roaring was there and he could not hear. The roaring faded slowly; Rowland was calling his name, shouting. . . .

"William!"

"Aye," he answered, his voice hoarse and low.

Rowland released him, but slowly. John and Marie were gazing at him in stark fear. He cared not.

He had wronged her. Oh, how simple were the words and how heinous was the deed! He had wronged her? Was it not more than wrong to take an unwilling wife of tender years and shame her on a point of such vulnerability? Yes, it was more than wrong. He had flayed her spirit and raged at her in his heart, and did the Lord not read the heart of a man and judge him accordingly? And he had wondered at her coolness and self-control. If only he had displayed more of those attributes himself, he

183

would not have spoken the words that must have seemed to her to ring with the same force as nails upon her coffin.

Thoughts of Margret again came to him. If she had survived, would her husband have welcomed the gift of her life joined to his or would he have beaten her for her loss of virtue at the brutish hands of another?

And what had Cathryn of Greneforde faced and endured from him upon her marriage bed? She had borne her pain, her loss, as privately as she could, but what was her bridal gift from the one man who would of necessity share in that secret pain? The man who had just hours before sworn to love and honor her throughout this life though the cost be his own?

Margret and Cathryn. So similar. Yet Cathryn had survived—survived to be abused by her sworn lord and husband. He would not tell Cathryn of Margret's pain, not when her own pain rode her so fiercely—pain he had increased by his own thoughtless pride.

His gray eyes crystal shards of ice, William looked deeply into Rowland's eyes before turning away, communicating his anguish and guilt and repentance to him in a way that he could not articulate, not even in the tortured blackness of his soul. He made for the tower, his motion silent, as he had been silent since the beginning of Marie's sobbed confession.

They watched him as he went, looking like nothing more substantial than a dark wraith on a wet night. Marie shivered with chill foreboding and burrowed into John's warmth.

William le Brouillard mounted the stair to the hall as silently as rising mist, seeking out his wife.

Chapter Ten

Kendall had seated himself on the other side of Lady Cathryn, and between him and Father Godfrey, had helped disguise the emptiness of William's chair. Dinner had long since been finished. Men sat in scattered groups throughout the hall, some playing chess and backgammon, others in quiet conversation. It was a warm and homey scene, yet an undercurrent of uneasiness ran over them all. William was closeted with Rowland, and that boded ill.

Rowland had been a very specter of doom since he had first sat to sup. That he was informing William of some dire circumstance was without question. How it would affect them was the only mystery, and would be clear only when William returned, for it was as unlike William to conceal his intent as it was unlike Rowland to reveal it.

"Lady Cathryn," an unfamiliar voice began. Kendall looked up and beheld a man of Greneforde, he was unsure exactly whom, fondling the floppy ear of a large brown dog. "Lady Cathryn," he said again, the attention of all who sat at high table upon him now, "would you please sing for us?"

Kendall smothered the urge to chuckle. Cathryn to sing? And how could any verse strung on pretty notes come to life if sung by a woman as bloodless and chill of heart as the Lady Cathryn? The man must be truly desperate for song to ask it of such a woman, beautiful though she was.

William's wife lacked the sensibility to blush and avert her gaze. It would not be beyond possibility that William would send away for a good French-woman to teach his lady the most basic course in chivalric love. It would be only out of love for her, else he would not care if she disgraced herself with her lack of manners.

"Nay, Tybon," she declined, "though you are most kind to think of me when you think of song."

Kendall smiled at her answer, given prettily enough. It was to her credit that she embraced her shortcomings. Truly, it did not hurt her in his esti-mation. She was modest. It was most becoming.

"So long has it been since you have entertained us with song," Tybon argued politely, "that I would ask again, speaking for more than myself. Please, lady, a song from you would make the night warmer."

Kendall fiddled with his goblet. The freemen were more chivalrous than their lady. It was most odd.

Cathryn looked down at the hands folded compactly upon her lap, her wedding ring glistening in the flickering light. She could not help noting that the faded green she wore was not flattering to her skin, making the slender veins in her hands take on a greenish cast and masking the desired blue. The very thought disturbed her. Never before had she taken such an interest in her appearance. She was acting most unlike herself to put such thought into the color of her gown and the unfashionable golden hue of her skin. Cathryn let Tybon's request hang upon the air like a cloud; it was only after the passage of minutes that she answered.

"I would not disappoint you, nor those for whom you speak," she said with a hesitant smile. "I will sing."

Kendall watched as she stood and called for neither harp nor lute; he sighed lightly. It would be a singularly lackluster performance without accompaniment, yet those familiar with her singing edged closer to her in respectful silence. But then, he thought with another sigh, they were far from France and its sophistication. It was ignorance, nothing more.

"Once, there were fields, fruiting at my touch," Cathryn began, her singing voice a warm, full alto with husky undertones.

"Once, there were flowers, hungry for my breath. . . .
Once, there were birds, eager for my hand. . . .
Once, God blessed me, but no more.
No more."

Kendall, his urbane sophistication forgotten, felt her words pull at him, twine around him. The melody was simple and suffused with melancholy. Slowly the words of the song were sung, as if each were wrung from the singer's grasp to float upon the air with quivering resonance. The song was becoming a part of him.

He did not know it now, but he would carry it to his death.

"I hope for the dawning of this endless night.
I hope for the yielding of the fruitless earth.
I hope for the releasing of my burdened heart.
I hope for forgiveness . . . no more.
No more."

William stood on the threshold, unnoticed in the absolute silence of the great hall, listening to the pathos of his wife's song. He had heard all of it, from the moment of Tybon's request to this final syllable; he knew enough of his wife now to know that there would be no uplifting final stanza. Two of his knights were frozen over their chess game, their strategy forgotten. There was no movement of arm or leg, no shifting of weight, scarce sign of breathing in all that large room.

She had caught them. Caught them with the eloquent hopelessness and loss of her song. Each man in that room had felt such loss, such abandonment; Cathryn had put that pain into words for them, made that ache a tangible thing to be held and remembered. But for her it was not remembering. For her it was the pain she carried.

In her song, he heard the emotion and pain she kept under such close guard. He heard the slow and smothered breaking of her heart. He felt more than a longing to heal her; he felt a compulsion to do so. She was his wife, a part of him now, and he had sworn a vow to lift her before God as holy and blameless. That he would do. He would heal her because he had vowed it, and if that vow was easier to face now because he knew of her past, he thanked God for His mercy in allowing him such ease. He had no more doubts about Cathryn. She was his wife and would remain his wife. He counted himself well and truly blessed in her. Now there but remained the healing of her heart, and that he was confident he could accomplish with his complete acceptance of her. No longer would he prod her, doubt her, distrust her, and she would see the difference in him and be at peace. He would heal her by wanting her wholeheartedly.

Pushing back the curtain, William entered the hall. All eyes turned to him, though no one spoke. He did not note it. He looked at Cathryn and Cathryn alone, as he always had and now knew he always would.

Crossing the wide expanse of board silently, he approached her as swiftly as incoming fog from off the sea. She could not look away from the dazzling silver of his eyes, and she did not try. She watched him come and knew that she was eager for his nearness, but she could comprehend it not. Something had changed.

He was coming, and she could give no thought to

any but him. He charged the very air about him as did an impending storm.

He was closer, his hair a shining blackness against the paleness of his face . . . his lips so full, his eyes so luminous.

He was near upon her. The air quivered between them. In all that space, there was but the two of them, or so it seemed to her.

And so it seemed to them all. There was something binding the lord of Greneforde to his lady, something almost visible shifting in the air between them. Something was very different.

He drew near, so very near and yet not near enough. She drew a breath with difficulty and fleetingly wondered what ailed her so.

He was so very beautiful. It was her only thought, and it circled in her mind like a falcon seeking its master's hand. He was so very beautiful and he was looking at her—nay, into her, as he had not yet done. He was . . . touching her with his eyes. Touching her in that place she had kept for herself. What frightened her was not only that he had touched her there, but that she had allowed him to.

And the stillness, that welcome stillness, rose from within her to sheathe her in its chill. She would be safe. She would be distant. She would be.

Father Godfrey saw with utter clarity that William knew the truth about his wife and that all would be well between them. The truth, as Christ had promised, would set her free, as it had set William free.

Touching her gently on the hand, he murmured

comfortingly, "Today your marriage begins in truth, Cathryn."

Those words, combined as they were with the intensity of William's eyes, told her one thing and one thing only: William meant to bed her again.

She folded her hands into a strangling knot to still their trembling and stood to meet her husband.

And then Father Godfrey was forgotten. William stood before her and all else faded into shadow.

"The lady of Greneforde sings beautifully, if sadly," he said, leaning over her intimately.

"Not sadly," she argued, lifting her chin. "I do not sing to crush the hearts of those who listen. I but sing of—"

"Loss," William interrupted. "Irretrievable, inconsolable loss."

"Yea," she admitted after a pause. " 'Tis so."

"I would join you when you choose to sing again."

"The song is mine," she argued. She had no intention of sharing anything so intimate with this man. "The words are mine. You could not sing it with me."

"I could." He smiled and leaned even closer, his chest nearly touching hers. "For my heart has known such melancholy, or I could compose my own words and our songs could blend and join," he whispered throatily, "perhaps becoming a new song entirely."

He had her off balance, this le Brouillard. His mood was an unfamiliar one, a very tender one, and she sensed an underlying message behind his words, though she could not understand it clearly.

"Two voices joined would create a harmony that

a solitary voice lacks," William encouraged. "Shall we join and create a stirring song that will cause the people of our hall to sigh and weep?"

With a jolt, Cathryn remembered that they stood in front of all their people. She felt that she had suddenly been found undressed before them all.

Eager to end their conversation, she said quickly, "Yea. Perhaps."

"Then let us go to a private place where we may compose a composition that declares the twining of our hearts." And at her alarmed look, he added with a boyish grin, "In song."

He was well named. Hardly had she suspected that they might be engaged in battle when he had won with quiet efficiency and was escorting her from the hall, her compliance affirmed by her own lips. He was le Brouillard in name and act, for he had surrounded her and overwhelmed her as thickly and with as little warning as the fog shrouded the wood. She was enshrouded. Enshrouded now by his hand upon her arm as he propelled her from the familiar faces of the hall. Those faces were raised in good-natured laughter and well wishes at their departure; why, even John the Steward was smiling in his quiet way!

He was light of step upon the stair, though he all but carried her with him. It was when he led her to his chamber that the fog began to break.

"*This* is the private place?"

"Is there any more private or more suited to the joining of . . ." he began suggestively, his gray eyes the color of a smoky fire.

Claudia Dain

"Words! You spoke of words!" she cried out in rising alarm.

"Yea," he acceded mildly, a smile hovering at the corners of his mouth. "Thoughts and hearts were also mentioned. But it still holds that we must go to a private place for joining."

He was stubborn. She had not understood that with such clarity yesterday.

"I am much fatigued," Cathryn maneuvered. "I will be fresher on the morrow."

"There is much of myself I would share with you. I would not wait," he said, "though on the morrow there will be more sharing still."

That sounded to her ears like a threat. His smile did not dissuade her from the conclusion.

"How long do you think it will take for us to compose a simple song for the people of Greneforde?" she argued suspiciously.

"I was not thinking of a simple song, but one of many variations connected by a single theme. Verily—" he smiled, his eyes darkening—"it could take us years to perfect."

"Verily," she bit back, "if it will take years, there is no rush. I will retire."

"In truth, since it will take years, we must not waste a moment and must strike while the mood is upon us."

"The mood is not upon me," she spit out.

"But it is upon me," he said with thick politeness; he had not thought her so obtuse.

"Then follow its dictates as I will follow mine."

" 'Tis a mood that must be shared, and, as your husband, I would share it with you."

"As your wife, I would follow my own course."

"As my wife—" he smiled fully—"I must ask that you follow mine."

And so they had reached a stalemate. She could think of no retort to his latest high-handedness, and stopped to look about her. He had maneuvered her again and most effectively; during their verbal sparring, he had edged her into his chamber and now stood between her and the door. Only the fire was lit. The room was full of shadow, but she could plainly see the white of his smile as he leaned against the heavy door and closed it.

There was no doubt now what was coming, though she could not credit it. He had told her clearly just twenty-four hours ago that he cared only for Greneforde and would not seek her out. They had spent the better part of their time together this day in verbal sparring. Such was not the behavior of a man seeking a woman. She had taken much comfort in that.

There was no comfort to be taken in the way William was behaving now.

He moved from the door, and she backed up a step and another and another until she finally stood at the foot of the bed. Logic told her that she should not stand so near the bed, that she should move to some far-off corner. Logic also said that any defensive move she might make was hopeless. Logic was a cold ally.

"Your movements are as fluid as the most delicate of waterfalls, Cathryn," William softly complimented. "I discover that I could watch you in motion for hours and not tire of the sight."

She stood rooted to the floor planks at the foot of the bed, all desire to move away stolen by his words.

William smiled. "And now you do not move, but await me at the place where we will lie together. You are a most accommodating wife."

"What need we to lie when composing song? 'Tis a most unusual habit," Cathryn challenged.

"Certain compositions cannot attain their full measure in any other fashion, I assure you." And when she looked at him with brown eyes brimming with suspicion and hostility, he amended, "Nay, I will teach you."

With liquid grace rare in one so muscular, William skimmed through the darkness toward her. She could see him, but it was more that she felt his coming nearness and jerked away instinctively. He had changed toward her; she could feel it. She could not account for it.

His touch featherlight, William caught one beribboned plait, catching her as if by a leash. He began to loose the binding, murmuring as he did so.

"Your hair is a rich bounty, Cathryn, with both moon and sun caught and held within its strands. I watch it move as I watch you move, and it seems a thing alive and separate, willingly giving its heavy beauty to generously enhance the fragile loveliness of your slender perfection."

He had released her hair, and now it fell in a heavy and shimmering mass to the back of her knees.

" 'Tis hair," she said curtly. "All of God's creations have it in one manner or another."

William smiled and lifted the weight of it in his hands, forcing her to face him.

"He was most generous in His manner with you, lady, and I am grateful and appreciative of His generosity."

His eyes were the color of wood smoke and burned as hot. She would swear an oath before Father Godfrey that his eyes were burning her flesh and causing a licking unease to flit about within her. How else to explain the sudden heat of her skin and the tremors rippling from her throat to her stomach? Something was not right within her; she knew that with certainty. She must escape this room and this man, if only for a time, to gather her composure more firmly about her. She said the first thing that came to mind, thankful that it was the truth.

"Father Godfrey is prepared to say the evening mass in remembrance of the dead. All has been arranged after much planning. I would not miss it."

William slowly released his gentle hold upon her hair, studying the petite features of his wife. What she said was true, and he knew now for whom the mass was to be read; it was no light matter to be cast aside. Her burden for her brother's death was heavy—that he understood full well—but he also understood something he had not even an hour before. His wife at her coldest was Cathryn at her most vulnerable; her rigid composure and lack of emotion were her final defensive barriers.

Cathryn was now as cold as he had ever seen her. Her back was straight, her chin high, her hands folded, and her eyes blank. But within the blank brown she turned to him, he was certain he detected the spark of passion. It was that passion he was intent on fueling.

"Tomorrow will serve just as well," he said gently, and when she made to argue, added, "for the dead have all eternity where one thousand years is as a day."

She could say no more, that much was clear. He was a man set upon sating his own desires, and none knew better than she that a man in such a state was beyond reason or courtesy or compassion. And so she prepared herself for the assault that she knew was fast coming.

He reached again for her and she did not pull away, to her credit. Though his touch was gentleness itself, she could not subdue the shiver that passed down her spine.

"Come, Cathryn, you are chilled. I will build the fire and warm you."

Because of his words, she did not expect his next action. He pulled her full against him and released the strings that held her faded gown together at the back. With a single tug, she stood in but her well-worn linen shift, the length of her golden hair more of a covering than the cloth.

Large hands caressed the skin of her back, skin both hot and cold together, until they wandered to the full mounds where back and leg were joined. These they cupped and stroked, the fingers dipping between them more than once. And all the while, with her downturned face buried in his chest, William breathed his words of seduction.

"Your skin is as the rarest silk from the East; it is

so soft beneath my hand, and the color is of a finer and more luminous gold than any man could fashion. You are as late summer grass, golden and moving with effortless grace beneath the waning sun, illuminated as you are touched by its fire."

His hands traced the curve of buttock and hip and waist and shoulder until they rested momentarily beneath the slight weight of her bosom. His mouth brushed her hairline, leaving light kisses at ear, temple, and brow. Cathryn stood unmoving and unmoved.

"When first I saw you as you stood in the great yard of Greneforde," William whispered, dropping kisses upon her face as quickly as spring rain fell upon the earth, "I thought you looked as splendid as a golden candlestick that graces the finest church in any land. I thought you the most beautiful of women, Cathryn."

His mouth teased the corner of hers, and she trembled deep within herself. William felt her trembling.

"You are beautiful, Cathryn." And his mouth possessed hers.

So slowly and so gently he had moved with her, and so still she had been. So wrong he had been about the passion he had seen struggling to life within her, for it was not passion awakening but panic suppressed. His kiss, with his hands upon her breasts, urging her nipples to plump life, caused panic to surge within her.

Wriggling free of his grasp, Cathryn gave him her back and stood facing the fire.

"Men want a wife pleasing to the eye," she said

with bite. "That you are so easily pleased gives me cause for thanksgiving, for a man not pleased with his wife's face is a man hard to please in all things."

It was not the reaction that he had been hoping for, and he was no fool to follow a strategy that was a proven failure. His acceptance of her, his desire, his approval, were not enough, it seemed, to warm her heart. He was not persuaded that she had no heart beating within her breast, though he knew that was what she wished him and all others to think. There was hope in that.

Pulling a stool closer to the fire, he made no attempt to answer her. They held their positions for a score of heartbeats, Cathryn staring into the flames, her dark eyes black voids framed by silvery hair, and William sitting with the light caressing his black curls and catching the molten glow of his gray eyes. With one hand, he reached out to clasp her wrist and encourage her onto his lap. She came reluctantly. But she came. William rubbed her back with slow strokes, much as one would stroke a dog. They both calmed with each measured stoke, their eyes upon the fire.

His hand grew warm with the friction and he welcomed it, for he was remembering his time with her last night, and the friction that memory caused within his soul was not welcome. He had done little better than rape her, married or not. It would have done little to endear him to her, especially as she had a history of nightly rape to strangle the natural desire that God gave all women. The thought gave him fresh hope to feed the struggling hope within him; God had designed Cathryn to receive pleasure at her husband's touch, and with God, all things were possible. This night was not over yet.

"It has been a full day that we are one in the sight of God," William observed quietly.

Cathryn had cautiously lowered herself so that she leaned slightly against William's chest; she found his touch on her skin strangely comforting. His words caused her to jerk upright.

William ignored her physical reaction and continued to rub her back.

"We became one the moment that we pledged our union before God and Father Godfrey, Cathryn," he clarified. "It is our words that bind us; our bodily union only bears the testimony of what our words have accomplished."

She sat silent, unsure of what he expected of her, unsure of where he was leading, as she ever was with le Brouillard.

"You may rest in my guidance on this, wife," he joked, "for Father Godfrey is of the opinion that God's inspired word is for all conversation, not just for the mass, and I have traveled the breadth of a continent with him. He is a talkative man," he finished with a melodramatic sigh.

Cathryn again held her tongue, but she could not stop the smile that tickled the corners of her mouth. Luckily her back was to William, so he would not note her loss of composure.

"We pledged before God and man that we would live out our lives as one, and God takes our pledges very seriously, lady. I am sworn to love you as I love my own body, and this I do," he vowed. "We are one flesh, Cathryn."

And suddenly she knew the purpose of le Brouillard.

"You know," said she with suppressed horror.

He debated lying to her, but he could not, especially with his words of being one so warm upon his lips.

"I have learned more of the history of Greneforde," he said delicately.

Waves of humiliation, worse than the night when he had taken his unvirgin bride, washed over her, and she struggled to be free of him. Before, she had almost taken comfort in his ignorance. He would know she was not virginal, but he would not be privy to the wrenching details that preyed upon her thoughts whenever she relaxed her mental vigilance. Her degradation, in its privacy, was manageable; this knowledge of his was brutal. In some strange manner, it raped her spirit as Lambert had raped her body. William would not release her. He held her firmly upon his lap, his arms closed around her, until she gave up her struggle and sat, resolved to bolt at the first opportunity. Sensing this, William did not relax his hold. No words were spoken as they sat staring at the ever-constant, ever-shifting fire.

William had ceased his stroking with her struggle, and now he fingered a lock of her shining hair. She did not fight him. She was still beneath his hand. It was a small victory, but it cheered him.

"God and king have given you to me, Cathryn," William said with quiet force. "I accept the gift, and gladly."

She did not believe him.

He knew well that she did not.

"You are beautiful," William said feelingly.

"Nay," she finally said. "I am . . ." The word *dirty* almost passed her lips.

"Guiltless," William finished.

And in spite of all the heavy weight of the moment, or perhaps because of it, he caused her to see humor when she had so recently believed she never would again.

"Can anyone be both beautiful and guiltless?" Cathryn said with a hesitant smile.

"There is only one, and you are she," he answered with tender solemnity, and kissed the tip of her nose.

He was an odd man, this le Brouillard, and she could not help smiling even as she shook her head. William took no offense but merely tucked her head beneath his chin while he played with the length of her hair. And stealing over her with all the natural silence of clouds in a summer sky was a feeling of comfort and safety. And something she had never thought to experience again: the sense of being loved.

What William felt was mounting arousal.

She was light upon his lap, and the soft weight of her pressed delightfully against him. The firm mounds of her derriere were deliciously full, and he could feel his manhood rising to nestle between them. His hand slid from her hip in a smooth glide to her breast, his fingers seeking her dormant nipple.

Cathryn stiffened immediately.

"You are my wife," he said into her hair. "I desire a proper wedding night."

The warmth she had felt blossoming within, the sense of peace, retreated from the chill that was fast covering her.

"Can we not just stay as we are?" she tried, speaking from her heart. "It is . . . nice."

His other hand swept up to capture her breast, and her nipples rose in mutiny to her will, eagerly giving themselves into his care.

"I desire more than 'nice.' I desire you, Cathryn."

Her back curled away from his touch, even as her nipples reached for him.

"William, please," she pleaded.

"Do not beg me not to take you; 'twould hurt my pride," he teased, answering the silent call of her distended nipples and rolling them between his thumb and forefinger. "Have you not heard of the Frankish man's expertise in matters of love? We are renowned for it."

"Nay—" she smiled in spite of herself—"I have heard only of their penchant for warfare."

"Night must fall in due course every day," he explained with a straight face, "and a man must needs keep busy."

He had his first taste of victory; Cathryn was accepting his touch and was in the first stages of arousal, though he doubted that she knew it. He stroked her hair as she leaned gently into his hand. And sometimes his hand went just a bit astray and he touched her abdomen or her inner thigh or the roundness of her breast. Her nipples, beneath their linen covering, grew tighter and darker in hue. He urged himself not to hurry.

She followed his hand now with her body, anticipating the location of his next touch and arching to meet it. Her dark eyes still stared into the fire, but they were no longer eyes of suspicion and hostility.

He touched her knee in a light caress that dragged upward, taking the linen with it. She did not protest. The cool air felt good against her heated skin, but there was a prickling uneasiness that was nudging aside the pleasant languor she was feeling. She ought not to feel this way. She should not enjoy his touch, husband though he was. Her control, so familiar a friend, was slipping away from her and she must call it back. But . . . but . . . she did not want this to end.

When his fingers brushed against the apex of her thighs, she sighed and opened to him, her eyes closed against the light of the blaze. With one hand he rolled a nipple with gentle roughness, and with the other he traced the portal that would soon admit him. And she did not turn from him, did not fight him; she submitted to each and every touch, murmuring softly in her throat for yet more.

William's fingers were slick with the milk of her readiness. The shift was bunched up under her arms, revealing all of her to his eyes and his touch. His hand upon her breast became as light as mist, and she moaned with a whisper on an expelled breath and arched her back to find him. He came down upon the other breast and she sighed her satisfaction, a shiver of pleasure shaking her. He widened the angle of his thighs, and her thighs, resting atop, followed his unresistingly. She was as open to him as an unmanned tower gate. He circled her tiny erection with his fingertip and she gasped. When he flicked it with all the swiftness of a falcon taking flight, her hands clasped his thighs in a grip to do a warrior proud.

And his own warrior throbbed and burned, eager to bury itself in wetter warmth than the globes of her derriere offered.

Lifting her, William carried her to the bed and laid her upon it. Her dark eyes opened at the movement, looking with dull confusion at her change of position, but not closing her legs against his weight.

"You are near to purring, Cat," William said in a seductive growl as he entered her wetness.

Cathryn went stone cold.

His orgasm came quickly, but it was several moments before he realized that he was alone in his pleasure. After a few more strokes, he stopped, resting between her splayed thighs.

"We but need practice," he offered.

"I have 'practiced' aplenty."

For the second time in this bed, William felt icy rage and profound hurt descend upon him. This time he controlled it. He pulled out of her and she immediately turned away from him.

"But not with me," he said softly.

"Are you truly so different?" she asked, curled into a ball on her side.

"Am I truly not?"

That gave her pause, for had she not noted repeatedly that he was an oddity in her experience?

The Holding

"You are different," she finally relented.

"Different how?"

This required more thought and greater effort. How to put into words what it was that was so different about William le Brouillard? She did not think his passion for the bath was what he wanted to hear at the moment. His humor? That was a goodly part of it. He caused her to smile at the most unexpected moments and was not so proud that he would not be the source of the joke. But what lay beneath all was his gentleness, displayed so clearly on their bridal bed, and even now, when she had hurt his pride with spitefully spoken words, William treated her with kindness.

"You are gentle," she finally said, "and have a care for me."

"I am your husband, Cathryn, and God has said that I must love you as I love myself. This I do."

Cathryn turned to face him, only his eyes visible in the darkness.

"Is it that simple?"

"I have vowed it at our wedding ceremony," he answered. "I do not give my word lightly."

"Nor do I," she said, bristling.

"I am relieved to hear it," William answered, his teeth shining white as he smiled.

And again, she could not help but smile with him.

"I have sworn to be your wife, William le Brouillard, and I shall be," she affirmed, the resolve unmistakable in her voice.

William considered her for a moment and then asked, "In all ways?"

To her credit, she hesitated for less than a moment before answering his challenge.

"In all ways."

"Without hesitation?"

"Yea."

"With an eager will?" he added, a humorous lilt to his voice.

"You do ask much, le Brouillard," Cathryn retorted.

"No more than I ask of myself," he explained, his voice once again serious, "for are you not 'bone of my bone and flesh of my flesh'?"

"From whence comes that metaphor?"

" 'Tis no metaphor, but fact, Cathryn. I but quote Adam when he first beheld his Eve."

"She who was the downfall of all mankind, according to our priest," Cathryn said wryly.

"She who was created from and for Adam by God's own hand," William rejoined. "Should we believe that God was off His stride when He did fashion her?"

" 'Tis blasphemy you speak!" she said, shocked, and also amused. It was sinful the way he made her smile over matters of eternal seriousness.

"Nay," he argued. "Eve should not be flayed for Adam's folly."

"What folly was his?" she asked when her curiosity overtook her.

"He listened overmuch to his wife's counsel," William answered with lazy seriousness.

Laughter, so long repressed, so long missed, burst from within her to rock the walls of William's chamber. Cathryn could scarce remember the last

Thrill to the most sensual, adventure-filled Historical Romances on the market today…

FROM  LEISURE BOOKS

As a home subscriber to the Leisure Historical Romance Book Club, you'll enjoy the best in today's BRAND-NEW Historical Romance fiction. For over twenty-five years, Leisure Books has brought you the award-winning, high-quality authors you know and love to read. Each Leisure Historical Romance will sweep you away to a world of high adventure…and intimate romance. Discover for yourself all the passion and excitement millions of readers thrill to each and every month.

SAVE AT LEAST *$5.00* EACH TIME YOU BUY!

Each month, the Leisure Historical Romance Book Club brings you four brand-new titles from Leisure Books, America's foremost publisher of Historical Romances. EACH PACKAGE WILL SAVE YOU AT LEAST $5.00 FROM THE BOOKSTORE PRICE! And you'll never miss a new title with our convenient home delivery service.

Here's how we do it. Each package will carry a 10-DAY EXAMINATION privilege. At the end of that time, if you decide to keep your books, simply pay the low invoice price of $16.96 ($17.75 US in Canada), no shipping or handling charges added*. HOME DELIVERY IS ALWAYS FREE*. With today's top Historical Romance novels selling for $5.99 and higher, our price SAVES YOU AT LEAST $5.00 with each shipment.

AND YOUR FIRST FOUR-BOOK SHIPMENT IS TOTALLY FREE!*

IT'S A BARGAIN YOU CAN'T BEAT! A Super $21.96 Value!

LEISURE BOOKS A Division of Dorchester Publishing Co., Inc.

GET YOUR 4 FREE* BOOKS NOW— A $21.96 VALUE!

Mail the Free* Book
Certificate
Today!

4 FREE* BOOKS & A $21.96 VALUE

Free *Books* *Certificate*

YES! I want to subscribe to the Leisure Historical Romance Book Club. Please send me my 4 FREE* BOOKS. Then each month I'll receive the four newest Leisure Historical Romance selections to Preview for 10 days. If I decide to keep them, I will pay the Special Member's Only discounted price of just $4.24 each, a total of $16.96 ($17.75 US in Canada). This is a SAVINGS OF AT LEAST $5.00 off the bookstore price. There are no shipping, handling, or other charges*. There is no minimum number of books I must buy and I may cancel the program at any time. In any case, the 4 FREE* BOOKS are mine to keep—A BIG $21.96 Value!

*In Canada, add $5.00 shipping and handling per order for first shipment. For all subsequent shipments to Canada, the cost of membership is $17.75 US, which includes $7.75 shipping and handling per month.[All payments must be made in US dollars]

Name _____

Address _____

City _____

State _____ *Country* _____ *Zip* _____

Telephone _____

Signature _____

If under 18, Parent or Guardian must sign. Terms, prices and conditions subject to change. Subscription subject to acceptance. Leisure Books reserves the right to reject any order or cancel any subscription.

(Tear Here and Mail Your FREE* Book Card Today!)

Get Four Books Totally
F R E E* —
A $21.96 Value!

(Tear Here and Mail Your FREE* Book Card Today!)

PLEASE RUSH
MY FOUR FREE*
BOOKS TO ME
RIGHT AWAY!

Leisure Historical Romance Book Club
P.O. Box 6613
Edison, NJ 08818-6613

time she had laughed even the smallest titter. That her husband could entice the kind of breathless hilarity that shook her now almost shocked her. And over matters spiritual!

William had once more worked his silent magic. Cathryn had all but forgotten that they lay near to nakedness in the same bed. She was relaxed. There were no walls between them, at least for the present.

Touching her cheek when her laughter had finished, William nestled her against his warmth, his hand resting upon the curve of her waist.

"Sleep, wife," he gently commanded.

And to her surprise, she did.

Chapter Eleven

Dawn came quietly, scarce able to break through the rain-filled clouds. In infinitesimal increments, the light increased in William's chamber. With each passing moment, Cathryn's face was more clearly revealed to William's searching gaze.

She faced him, her hand beneath her cheek, her hair tangled around her throat. Even in the darkness, her glorious hair glowed gold and silver like an angel's nimbus. A little more light and he could see the delicacy of her upturned nose and the well-defined rim of her jaw. And then he watched as the scar upon her brow cast its own small shadow upon her silken skin: the testimony of her rape.

She was asleep and very near him; he could indulge his fury at Lambert of Brent but little. Cathryn would never know the fury of his rage for any cause. He would not release the blinding, roaring anger that pounded at his temples at the thought of what that man had wrought upon his wife.

She was a broken vessel—not in body, as he had first believed, but in spirit—and the breaking was the worse for that. What she had been before, he would never know, not unless he could heal the scars that maimed her, and that he was determined to do. Cathryn was his second chance; what he had failed to do for his sister, Margret, he would do for her. God was most merciful in giving second chances. If he could heal the scars upon his wife— and he vowed very quietly before God that he would—mayhap the pain and guilt that had ridden him so hard since Margret's death would ease. Mayhap . . . if God was merciful.

Cathryn did not trust him. She had erected wall upon wall against him, against all, and though he had made ground last night, proving she was not impregnable, he still had far to go in his campaign to have her vulnerable before him. For such was the way between a man and his wife. There must be no barriers between those who were one, else they were not one at all and their marriage was a travesty of God's law.

He would win her trust and turn her fear and hatred of their physical union into the mutual desire that God in His wisdom had intended. It would take time and patience—he did not delude himself—but he would succeed. He was a man who had no history of losing.

Cathryn awakened slowly, reluctantly. He knew she was awake long before she first opened her eyes. William had the sense that this was her normal way, that wakefulness did not come swiftly to her.

William had been watching her while she slept, she was sure of it, and the knowledge made her stomach roll uneasily. Asleep, she was her most vulnerable. Had she spoken? She was sometimes known to speak out loud as she slept most deeply. Had her mouth been agape? Ah, there was a pretty thought. Such was the price one paid when sleeping in someone else's bed.

With a quick and uncomfortable smile, she hurried from the bed, the floor cold upon her bare feet. Her shift slid down to cover her to the knee as she searched for her lost bliaut. She found it upon the floor before the dead fire and remembered in a rush the events of the previous night as she'd sat upon her husband's lap enjoying more than the heat of the blaze.

"Good morrow, Cathryn," William said with cheer, seeming to ignore the haste with which his wife had left his bed.

"Good morrow," she mumbled, stepping into the dusty bliaut that had seen much hard duty the day before.

"You are eager to be at your morning prayers, I see," he commented, not moving from the warmth of the bed.

She turned from him, pretending in her heart that he was not in the room as she struggled with her laces.

"Cathryn?" he prompted.

"Yea, I am eager to be about the tasks of the day."

" 'Tis early."

" 'Tis past the dawning!"

He did not argue with her, but watched, his back against the wood, as she tugged at her strings, or those she could reach.

"You have another gown?" he finally asked.

"Yea," she said with a huff.

"And where is it?"

Le Brouillard was talkative today and it pleased her not.

Turning to him, she answered, "In my chamber."

"*This* is your chamber, wife," he answered, his voice both pleasant and firm. "Have your possessions moved."

And when she did not answer and only turned to face him in silent mutiny, he added, "Today."

William spent no more time on that matter, having settled it to his satisfaction. He rose from the bed, as naked as the day his mother presented him to the world. Cathryn spun around as wildly as any top and gave him her back again.

He was glorious.

She could not survive glorious.

In her turning, William had caught a flying skein of her hair and now gave it a gentle tug.

"Do I shame you?" he asked, his voice as light as a sparrow on the wing. "I am as God made me."

She knew that well, and it was a burning draft to admit that she liked what God had wrought that day—and liked it well. He was magnificent, with his silver eyes and shining hair. His nose, so straight, pointed a direct line to lips both firm and finely molded. Black brows sweeping as gracefully as swans, sheltered the beauty of those glinting gray eyes.

Muscular arms, broad shoulders, narrow hips—he was beautiful in his masculinity.

"I like greatly the way in which God fashioned your parts on the day *you* were conceived," he said, giving her hair another tug. And when she would not answer, he cajoled, "Are you so little pleased?"

Cathryn knew enough of William to know that there was true uncertainty in his mind. Oddly, the knowledge gave her a tickle of pleasure.

Turning slightly, she smiled. "Is this another point on which rests Frankish pride?"

William shrugged casually and smiled back. "We are known to be a handsome race."

Cathryn faced him fully, her eyes shining as she used her fingers to tick off her points. "Let us review the traits of Frankish men: fractious, warlike, lovers of women, and lovers of self. I note humility is absent."

"To every great people a fatal flaw is given, else we would think ourselves equal to God. And with my race, lack of humility in the face of such superior attributes is surely understandable." William crossed his arms across his massive chest and smiled in victory. "God has given us a flaw, which I find most logical."

"You think to know the mind of God?" she asked on a gasp.

"Nay." He shook his head as he unfolded his arms. "I would but know your mind. Does my form please you so little?" he asked again, his voice more serious than he had intended.

Cathryn turned from him and gave him a splendid view of her back before answering, "I am not little pleased."

Because her back was turned, she could not see the scowl that crossed his features at her ambiguous reply. Did she truly find him disagreeable? If so, she was the first, but the English were not like other nations; it was something the whole world knew. Yet could her words, so carefully imprecise, not also mean that she *was* pleased, and not a little? It could be so. And then he smiled, for clearly Cathryn felt free to tease him, and a woman frozen with fear would not.

The sounds of the morning drifted up to them: the call of Kendall to his squire, the ring of hammer on iron, Ulrich pounding up the stair.

William threw his mantle over his nakedness, easing Cathryn's discomfort; it was assuredly not for Ulrich, who had seen him naked countless times. He had just done so when Ulrich rushed into the room, talking as he entered.

" 'Tis a fine day for hawking, William—oh, good morrow, Lady Cathryn—as there is no sun to blind us, and I thought that we could go and return with a fine catch to present to the people of Greneforde. My lord?"

William paid Ulrich scant attention. He watched as Cathryn hurried past him, using the unbound length of her hair to disguise the fact that her gown was unfastened, and the chatter of his squire to hide her escape. When she was at the portal, he simply said, "Today."

She paused but briefly and nodded, hardly an acknowledgment.

"Cathryn."

This time she stopped completely, but still she did not turn.

"There is something else that will be done today. Baths for one and all. Today, wife," he ordered to the back of her head.

And now she turned to give him a clear view of her profile. He could see that she was smiling, and then she nodded and was gone, but not before she heard Ulrich whine, "But William, I bathed but a week ago!"

Chapter Twelve

When William entered the great hall, Rowland was awaiting him at the hearth, a mug of ale in his hands. He handed William the ale.

"When do you hunt Lambert?" he asked softly.

It was a question entirely expected. Lambert and the meting out of his punishment had been prowling the corners of his thoughts since he first learned of the man's existence and his relationship to his wife.

"I know not," William answered just as softly. "Cathryn could better answer you, for I will not leave Greneforde until the scars on her soul are healed. She takes precedence over my revenge." William indulged in a healthy swallow of ale before continuing: "I will have justice, though it may come more slowly than I would choose."

Gray eyes met darkest brown in mutual understanding and agreement. William and Rowland were ever of the same mind.

" 'Tis a wise course you follow, William, and mayhap Lambert will find his judgment more bitter for believing he has escaped it."

They studied the fire in silence, each plotting the various ways Lambert could be repaid for his villainy.

"There is something I would have you do for me," William began.

"Name it," Rowland vowed, his hand going to his sword hilt.

"Track Lambert so that I may know where to find him when I am ready."

"Done."

"Mayhap you should take Kendall with you and travel to the king, for I would inform him that the marriage he blessed has occurred and Greneforde is mine. Have a care," William added, his hand upon Rowland's arm. "Be circumspect in your actions. I would not have Lambert aware that we know of him. He could well be lingering in the area, plotting some means by which he can regain Greneforde."

But William no longer looked at Rowland; his eyes were upon Cathryn, who had entered the hall and was engaged in quiet conversation with John.

"I would not be quick to abandon such a prize," William finished.

"Your will and mine are one, William. Kendall and I will leave at next dawning."

They left the hall then, to wander where there

were fewer ears to hear their plans. They left the
hall to Cathryn and John.

"The water is on the boil, lady, though some of our
people have already bathed."

For a moment she was shocked speechless. It was
not what she'd expected to hear. A way out of this
latest and so familiar command was what she had
been seeking of John, not compliance.

John saw her shock and understood it, but he understood something else as well, and this he voiced
to his lady.

"William is not Lambert."

"Obviously he is not," she blurted. "Yet what—"

"Marie is moving your belongings to the lord's
chamber even now," John interrupted to add.

It was not welcome news.

"John," Cathryn accused, her eyes large in her
delicate face, "you have turned your loyalty to the
other side."

"Lady—" he smiled gently, his brown eyes crin-
kling at the corners—" 'tis not possible. You and
William are married. Your sides are the same."

And he left her standing in a corner of the hall,
quite bemused.

But only for a time. With renewed resolve, Cathryn made her way to her old chamber, the one she
had shared with her brother. After her father had
left on pilgrimage, she had taken the lord's chamber
as her own. It was a logical choice and one expected
of her. But with the coming of Lambert she had
retreated to her old room. She saw the coming of
William in no different light.

Entering, she found it empty of all her possessions. Her chest remained, but what it had held, her meager clothing and her comb, were gone. She was afraid she knew where. She was even more afraid that Marie had turned against her as John had.

She hurried into William's chamber, certain that he was not in it, as she had observed him leave the hall after a serious discussion with Rowland. During that talk William's eyes had strayed again and again to her, their silver intensity piercing her even at that distance. Not that she had looked. It was with profound surprise that she found his chamber inhabited—by Ulrich and Marie.

"Is it that someone else has claimed you for his own, Marie? Is that why you will not encourage me?"

Marie said nothing, but she did not cower. In fact, she smiled and hid part of her face with a pretty bit of cloth, moving away just a step.

"He must have told you that your eyes are beautiful," Ulrich gushed, "but did he tell you that they are color of the sky over Damascus, as blue and unending as the cap of heaven? Did he tell you that they shine as sapphires worn in the crown of a king, and that the most beautiful of women, Queen Eleanor, would give up her throne to have eyes such as yours?"

Cathryn waited for Marie to run or at least deny her involvement with another. She waited in vain, for Marie denied nothing.

"Nay," she said, smiling behind her cloth, "he did not tell me that."

"Then he must be a churl and unworthy of you,

Marie. You must scorn him and take me as your love," Ulrich declared.

"Must I?" Marie giggled and moved another step, watching carefully as Ulrich followed her yet again.

"Yea, you must, or I shall battle him for your favor, and God shall decide who should win your regard."

"It may be that God will decide in the end, but I would decide at the start," Marie flirted. She seemed to be enjoying herself immensely.

Ulrich darted in front of her, allowing Marie no further movement away from him. She stopped prettily and with no sign of alarm.

"Then decide, but be forewarned that I will accept no answer but that you will have me, and if the wooing takes a hundred years, then I am ready," Ulrich stated with characteristic drama.

Cathryn watched, her irritation mounting with each moment. If things did not turn around—and quickly—William and his horde would break through every last one of Greneforde's defenses, for if Marie could be turned . . . It was not that she bore Ulrich any ill will—in fact, he was a charming lad and had coaxed a smile from Cathryn himself—but Marie was different. Marie had come to her for succor, an orphan in a world ripped apart by war, and Cathryn had supplied it in full measure. Freeborn and alone, Marie had been welcomed into Greneforde, a safe haven in a world dark with uncertainty; even when Lambert had come, Cathryn had kept her safe. Marie needed her.

Cathryn coughed and the two spun to face her, alarmed at being caught in their lord's chamber.

"I am quite certain that your lord wants you, Ulrich," Cathryn announced.

Ulrich left quickly enough at hearing that, but not before he had looked meaningfully at Marie, who blushed and lowered her eyes. In truth, Cathryn had never known Ulrich to leave a room so slowly.

When he was gone and clattering down the stairs, she looked at Marie, who was just getting her blush under control.

"I worry for you, Marie," Cathryn said gently, entering the room more fully. "Ulrich—"

"You need not worry for me, lady," Marie interrupted with a wide smile, her coyness vanishing like the mist at morning. "Ulrich cannot be taken seriously, not with all his gay talk and his broad shoulders; this I know." Her eyes fixed on a point in the space between them and grew dreamy. "But, lady—" she grinned, suddenly aware of Cathryn again—"I am having a gay time not being serious with him!"

And she all but skipped out of the room.

In all her life, Cathryn had never felt quite so . . . unneeded. It was a singularly odd sensation.

Descending the stair to the great hall, not quite sure what she was going to do with the rest of her day, Cathryn almost bumped into William.

"Cathryn." William smiled, clearly glad to see her. She smiled weakly back, feeling that even in so small a gesture, she was losing ground to him. "Rowland and I are off to hunt. If all goes well, there will be fresh meat at today's meal."

"And who will accompany you, my lord, besides Rowland?"

William frowned for a moment and answered, "Why, no one. As I said, 'twill be just Rowland and I. Do you doubt that I can provide for the table?" he teased.

"Nay, my lord." She sighed. "I know well that you will not return with an empty hand."

It was just that she looked for a reason to get Ulrich out of the keep and away from Marie, but she could not say so to William.

William also had left certain things unsaid with Cathryn. When he and Rowland left, they did not head for the wood on the Greneforde side of the river Brent. Instead, they made for Lambert's former holding.

The clouds of dawn had fulfilled their promise. The day was full of rain. It came down gently but steadily, soaking the already wet earth and swelling the brooks, flooding the banks of the river Brent. Yet they had crossed it easily, perhaps because they had no thought of being dissuaded by mere water, and now sat mounted on their shivering horses, surveying Lambert's legacy.

It was a motte and bailey fortification, or had been, the walls all of wood. One wall was ashes now, long since cold. The roof was half gone; fractured timbers, charred and black, struck into the gray sky.

It was naught but a ruin.

Lambert would claim it not, not with Greneforde and her stone walls so near at hand.

Rowland and William shared the thought, though not the words.

Movement and a heavy grunting in what was

once a cultivated field caused both heads to turn toward the sound and hands to go to swords. It was no man, but a boar of immense size rooting for food in that deserted place. William smiled with cold satisfaction. He would have his meat for Cathryn and he had not had to hunt for it; it had come to him handily.

Pulling forth his spear, William took aim with a steady hand and let fly. It struck the beast in the shoulder. Enraged, the beast charged, his eyes red, the blood running in a stream down his leg to the rain-soaked earth underneath his feet. It was a sight to strike fear in any man, for only the bravest hunted the wild boar. He was a ruthless and fearless killer, striking with his sharp tusks whatever was at hand, and could rip the bowels out of a man with but a few slashing cuts.

William le Brouillard faced his quarry with a cool eye; if the beast had been blessed with more reason, he would have stopped his headlong charge and reconsidered his adversary. But he had no such reason. He was a wild beast, nothing more.

In one motion, William dismounted and pulled his sword free, the metal glinting dully in the heavy air. He stood his ground as the very earth shook with the pounding of five hundred pounds of blood-maddened animal. William's eyes glinted, matching the deathly glimmer of his blade. He waited.

The beast was upon him, and with a swift turn William sliced downward at the base of the neck, breaking it with the force of his blow. The boar dropped at his feet, dead in an instant.

William raised his sword again to the sky, the

rain mixing with the blood and coursing down the blade in ever-widening rivulets of red. With a mighty hack, he separated the head from the body and kicked it away. It rolled into the debris that was all that remained of Lambert's bailey.

Rowland watched all in silence—amused silence.

"You did not miss with your throw."

"Nay," William agreed.

"You could have killed him cleanly had you aimed for the lung."

"Yea, 'tis so."

Rowland watched as William quickly slit the carcass and blooded the animal, staining the thick mud at his feet a richer shade of brown.

"Boar's head is fine eating," Rowland remarked casually. "You have thrown the best away."

"Nay, he was too ugly to eat," William disagreed, cleaning the blood from his sword on the wet grass a few paces away from the killing site. "We must make do with the body."

"You are covered in blood," Rowland observed as William remounted. "You will most likely want a bath when we return to Greneforde."

A vision of Cathryn bending over his body, the heat of the water dampening the hair that framed her face, rose before him. He and his wife had shared the image of such a scene before and it had rocked her composure; how much better might be the reality of her touching him? All of him.

William smiled and urged his horse into a canter.

"I most certainly will."

Chapter Thirteen

Again Cathryn was in the storeroom in the under-croft, as she had been at the same time the day before. This day she did not spend her time on the precious seed that William had brought as part of his bride price. This day she studied the cloth. It could not stay long in such damp surroundings or it would molder. It was only sensible of her to inspect and tally what had been gifted to her through marriage and to determine where it would be stored on a permanent basis.

Though Greneforde had once been prosperous, she could not remember a day when they had possessed cloth such as this. It was most fine. The fabrics were rolled and stored in a large chest, glistening richly even in the dim light of the storeroom. Cathryn did not dare hold her taper near them for fear that a falling ember would burn a hole. Setting the taper in a holder on the wall, she cautiously drew near the open chest, afraid to touch the splendor at her fingertips, yet helpless not to. There were silks and sarcenets and baldachins and they were cool to the touch.

Gathering her resolve, she lifted a brilliant azure from the pile. Even the summer sky did not have such a hue. With it came a rich acajou, rivaling the lush brown of freshly turned fields, and then a shimmering aureate. She let it cascade against the azure and it looked like nothing less than the sun against a cloudless sky. Beneath the aureate was ebon, and she thought how well the color matched her husband's hair; it might make a fine tunic, though it was an unusual color for such a choice. Then cordwain followed by burnet and then bure; all shades of brown from deepest red to yellow. All beautiful. And then she saw, at the bottom of the pile, a rich scarlet silk with golden thread. It was in her hands and at her cheek before she realized what she intended.

" 'Tis called acca, from the city of Acre," Father Godfrey said.

"Your pardon," Cathryn said quickly, dropping the cloth.

"Silk woven with gold thread—'tis called acca," he repeated, misunderstanding her.

" 'Tis most fine," she said calmly. " 'Twould make a kingly mantle for William, would it not?"

"It would," he agreed pleasantly.

"Your pardon, Father, for having to delay the reading of the funeral mass."

"There is no need to apologize, Cathryn. It can

just as easily be performed after today's meal." Godfrey smiled into her solemn face. "Have not the dead all eternity, where a thousand years is as a day?"

" 'Tis odd." She frowned, absently fingering the scarlet acca so near her hand. "William said much the same to me."

Godfrey smiled broadly and approached the chest, smoothing the cloth with his hand.

"It pleases me that some of God's Holy Word has penetrated William's skull after so much effort."

"You have been with him long?" she asked almost shyly.

"Many years, though not until he had departed Damascus. I have known Rowland longer."

"Then you did not know him as a child," she said, a little disappointed.

"Nay, I did not, but I know of his childhood, short as it was."

Her expression was so hopeful and so wistful as she stood there caressing the scarlet cloth that Godfrey decided to tell her what he knew of William le Brouillard without betraying any trust. Knowing more of her husband might help her to soften toward him; that she was curious he took as an excellent portent.

"His father lost his lands to Matilda's man, he of Anjou, and died in the process," Godfrey began. "William, just a lad of less than ten and two, began his knight's training while his mother and sister traveled the land, staying with first one relation and then another, staying long enough for hospitality to sour."

"I did not know he had a sister," Cathryn murmured.

"Yea, and he loved her much, though he did not see her often, for he had his obligations to uphold. In time, the wandering from home to home weakened his mother to the point of death." After a pause, he added, "She died before William could return."

"How sad," Cathryn said softly.

"Yea, sad for them both, for William felt driven to earn his accolade at an early age so that he could support his sister with his knightly feats."

"And did he?"

"Oh, aye, he won his spurs before the age of ten and eight, in part because the knight he squired under was a harsh man and prodded those he trained with a steel tip."

"Please continue," Cathryn prompted when Father Godfrey had been silent for many minutes, seemingly lost in his own thoughts.

"He rode as swiftly as angels about God's will to his sister's side . . . but too late."

"Why too late?"

Father Godfrey blinked and swallowed before answering, and his tone was reluctant.

"She died just hours after his arrival, lying near death even as he rode through the gate. She died in his arms."

Cathryn absorbed that. Truly, her husband had known sorrow in this world. He had known sorrow, yet his spirit had not been dulled.

"Her name?"

Godfrey looked deeply into Cathryn's eyes,

pleased with the compassion he saw there.

"Margret."

Cathryn nodded. Margret would be included in the mass.

" 'Twas after burying her that William departed for Damascus."

Where he could so easily have died. After all, what had he to live for? Why, he had lived to find a home. He had lived for Greneforde.

Father Godfrey noted that Cathryn had not stopped fingering the scarlet acca, though she seemed unaware of it.

"The cloth would flatter you, Cathryn," he observed quietly.

Again, with a start, Cathryn dropped the fabric.

" 'Tis an odd remark for a priest to make," she said.

Godfrey smiled and replaced a bolt of vivid cloth.

"God did not see fit to take my eyesight when I gave Him my vows, and for that I am grateful."

"You are an unusual priest," Cathryn pointed out, helping him to reorder the bolts.

"And you are not the first to remark upon it," he answered. "The scarlet suits you, Cathryn. William would be pleased to see you in it."

All the cloth had been replaced, all except the scarlet acca. She dropped it as if burned.

Father Godfrey smiled again and left as softly as he had come. When he was gone, Cathryn again picked up the scarlet. She could not seem to stop herself, and if Father Godfrey was correct, she might not need to try.

She touched just a corner and then an arm's

length. It was not long before the fabric was unrolled and draped over her shoulders. Cathryn looked down longingly at its vivid color and blazing warmth, and twirled to catch a glimpse of it spinning out behind her.

Would William like her in the scarlet? It was hardly possible that she could look less appealing than with the faded castor gray she now wore. In the scarlet, she felt . . . she felt . . .

Cathryn dropped the cloth into the chest and hurriedly closed it before rushing from the room in search of Marie. She would probably find her in the company of Ulrich. With a vision of herself swathed in the glimmering red, Cathryn hurried on. She needed an excuse to keep Marie away from Ulrich anyway.

It was the sound of giggling that alerted her, coming from the corner where the kitchen wall met the wooden wall of the enclosure. It was a well-shaded spot and nearly black on a day such as this. The rain had stopped, but looked ready to return again before dusk. It was a dreary day—hardly a day to be standing in the mud, giggling.

Rounding the corner, Cathryn was taken aback at the sight that met her eyes.

A buxom young woman with bright blue eyes and glossy brown hair was trapped, so very willingly trapped, within the outstretched arms of Ulrich. *Marie!* He had her pinned within the corner, her back against the wall, his arms planted on either wall to hold her in a very warm cage. And she was laughing! Marie, washed and wearing clean clothes, had been transformed into a pleasing-looking woman. And under Ulrich's appreciative eye and glib tongue, her manner had been transformed as well. The timid girl was gone. A coquette had supplanted her.

"Ulrich!" Cathryn began, and had the satisfaction of seeing him drop his arms and spin to face her, a blush rushing up from his throat. "You have time to waste, it seems, for this is the second time today that I have caught you idle. If your lord does not have enough tasks to keep you busy, then mayhap he will lend your strong back to me. Under my eye you will find the day passes quickly, and you will yearn for the rest the night brings."

"Lady, your pardon," Ulrich answered, "but time spent with Marie is not time wasted. Indeed, it is the reason for my rising each day and the curse of my sleeping at night, for then I must be absent from her and only await the dawning—"

"Yea, Ulrich, I understand," Cathryn interrupted. "You like Marie."

"Ah, lady." He sighed, casting his eyes to the smiling object of his discourse. "Do I 'like' to breathe? Does the hawk 'like' to hunt? Does a knight 'like' to battle? Nay, she is the reason for my existence, and without a smile from her, my day is as black as if there were no sun in the sky to light our way."

"You have little reason to worry that there will be no sun," Cathryn noted, fighting a smile, "as Marie smiles often when you are near. But begone; I have a greater need of her than you," she commanded.

"Yea, Lady Cathryn," he acquiesced, moving off. He looked backward at the object of his affection so often that Cathryn wondered that he did not fall facedown in the mud. As lovestruck as he was, he most likely would not notice if he did.

"Now, Marie," she said when they were alone, "I have decided to make use of one of the bolts that my lord brought to our marriage. I need your help."

"Yea, lady, I will help, and gladly," Marie answered eagerly.

With brisk steps, they were at the chest in the storeroom. When Cathryn lifted the heavy lid and Marie saw the shining scarlet in the flickering light, she gasped in pleasure.

"Oh, lady, 'twill make you glow as bright as fire flame!"

"You think it not too bold for me?" Cathryn asked, suddenly unsure of her course. She had never worn anything brighter than citron all the years of her life.

"Oh, nay, nay," Marie argued, " 'tis all the fashion for ladies of rank to wear colors bright and bold."

Cathryn smiled in amusement, "And how is it that you know more of fashion than I? We who have not left the walls of Greneforde for endless seasons?"

Marie blushed lightly and answered, " 'Tis Ulrich who told me."

"Believe all Ulrich tells you and you plot your own heartbreak."

"I do not believe *all* he tells me, only, why should he prevaricate upon the subject of women's fashion?"

Cathryn chuckled and began to gather the cloth in her hands.

233

"I do not know as to that, but I will say that it is wise to consider the 'whys' of whatever he whispers in your ear."

"Or proclaims to his lord's lady?"

Cathryn stopped in surprise. Marie? Parrying words with her? Truly a transformation had been achieved, and with a few kind words from a romantic squire.

"I am learning that I do not need to counsel you, Marie." Cathryn laughed lightly as Marie closed the chest. "Mayhap you should counsel me? The cloth," she specified, "how shall we fashion it?"

The upward climb to the solar was achieved on light feet as they discussed how the cloth should be cut and sewn.

"Ulrich has told me that fashion is running to long and slender for ladies of the French nobility," Marie said, sitting on a stool in the well-lit room and running loving fingers over the scarlet acca. "Perfect for you, Lady Cathryn."

"In what manner do they fashion the sleeve? Or did Ulrich forget to mention that particular?" Cathryn teased, enjoying herself immensely despite the butterflies fluttering in her stomach.

"Aye, lady, he told me, for 'tis different than the English sleeve. It is worn so long that the ends must be knotted to keep them from dragging on the floor, and also the width is cut fuller."

"And better?"

Marie blushed. "He did imply so."

"It is queenly fabric and should be worked to its own best advantage, but I am English and will wear an English sleeve," Cathryn stated, ending all talk of sleeves.

"What will you use as mantle, Lady Cathryn?"

"I had given it little thought," she admitted. "Let us begin with the acca and move to the subject of the mantle as we are ready."

Cathryn had just laid out the fabric to determine the line of cut when Kendall requested admittance to the solar. He showed his breeding. A man did not enter the solar except by express invitation of the ladies present. Cathryn quickly stood in front of the flaming fabric and bade him enter. For reasons unknown to her, she did not want all within the walls of Greneforde to know she was fashioning a new garment for herself. And out of William's cloth.

"Lady Cathryn! William and Rowland have returned from the hunt lugging a large boar between them!"

There was naught to say to that. Boar was a vicious adversary and therefore rarely was its taste enjoyed. The three rushed from the room and down the stairs, eager to witness such a glad homecoming.

William was dismounting as they hurried from the stair tower. He was covered in blood and grinning from ear to ear.

"Our lord had gone a-hunting and come back heavier than when he set out!" Tybon joked loudly amid the general noise.

"Would you have him come back the lighter?" Alys laughed.

"Nay, for that would make us all the lighter! In our stomachs!" Lan supplied, and his remark brought gales of laughter from the crowd for his saucy wit.

"His person should not look lighter, as with one who has expended great effort," Rowland said with a rare smile, and loudly enough for all to hear, "for he did but little to bring down the beast, which was rooting peaceably in a field."

"Little, you say? Why, is he not a monstrous big beast and am I not covered in blood?" William demanded good-naturedly.

"Aye to both, but the most strenuous work done by you this day was in the carting of him back to Greneforde!"

"Spoken by the man who did none of the first and little of the second." William laughed, pointing his finger at Rowland accusingly.

"And so they bicker," Lan said with a smile to show his true intent, "while the heaviest work is yet to come."

"The heaviest work?" William laughed. "You make light of my accomplishment? To face down an enraged boar, for I assure you, he did not welcome the spear that pierced him, is no light encounter."

"Nay, you with your mail armor and spears and sword and warhorse against one of God's dumb beasts . . . nay, I can see you were sore outadvantaged."

The crowd tittered and looked to see if Lord William was enraged by their joking. He was not. He was noble and they were not; the gap between them was wide, yet they lived in close proximity within the narrow walls of Greneforde curtain. The sense of being of one family came to each of them in time. Cathryn's father, Lord Walter, had been a warm man, and they had taken their cue from him. It was difficult to cast off the patterns of a lifetime, and they were hardly eager to. Lady Cathryn, alone in her leadership since her kin were all dead, had welcomed the teasing warmth of those around her, though they were hardly her equals. Lambert had been avoided and looked upon by them as a rabid dog. William, so new to Greneforde, was proving his worth, and they were grateful for his coming, but would the gap be wide that separated lord from freeman? Only Lord William could decide it, and they looked to him now.

William looked with face aghast at Rowland, who sat laughing in silent mirth until the tears ran down his nose.

"And so, my newest adversary," William challenged, "what is the heaviest work regarding the boar?"

"Why, the gutting and skinning of him, my lord, as any one of us can tell you."

Cathryn watched them all with a smile she was not aware she wore. When had they accepted him? She did not know, but accept him they had.

"My lady"—William turned to her—"do you tell me so as well?"

Cathryn shrugged delicately. " 'Tis tiresome work, to be sure, but which is the heavier task, the killing or the skinning, I could not say, not having done both."

"And so she proves her blood by not taking sides

against her husband," Ulrich proclaimed, adding his own eager voice to the throng.

William did not turn to comment on Ulrich's statement; he would not turn from Cathryn's smiling face, a smile reflected on his own face in full.

"John!" William called, his eyes holding his wife's. "Heat water! Ulrich, see to my horse!" And holding her so forcefully with the power of his pewter eyes that she felt physically touched, William spoke his final command: "My wife will attend me at my bath."

At his words, the lively butterflies in her stomach fell dead at her feet.

The last bucketful of heated water dropped into the tub with a heavy splash, and then the servant disappeared. It seemed to her that all the servants had been overly quick in both the filling of the tub and the leaving of William's chamber. The sounds of descending footsteps faded quickly, very quickly, and then were gone. The quiet in the great tower was unnatural, or it seemed so to her. The pounding of her pulse was the only sound to be heard. It was unnatural.

She looked up. William stood in all his bloodsoaked glory, his smile still bright, waiting for her to disrobe him. And so she should, so she should; if only she could take a breath, she might be able to move.

He would not prompt her. She would get no push from him. She would proceed or not, on her own and at her own pace; he determined that that would be the best for her composure. She was a woman who preferred to hold the reins of her own mount, and so he would let her and he would wait. In time, she would come to trust him. She must.

Slowly, paralyzingly slowly, she approached him. Never did the width of this chamber seem so wide. She was a fool. To touch blood-soaked garments, to undress a body longing for the bath, it was not so great a deed that she should quake in fear and hesitate, praying with all the fervor of her soul that the Lord of Hosts would split the sky and spirit her to heaven with the rest of the saints. No, it was a simple bath. And for bathing one must needs remove the clothes.

Fie! She was a coward! And for what cause? She had seen his unclothed body before. Aye, she muttered to herself, and that was the source of her cowardice.

William said nothing. He waited patiently. And when she finally touched him to remove his tunic, he did not flinch or start or in any way change. And he ignored the trembling of her hand.

It was not so difficult to render her husband ready for the bath. It would be wise of her if she could become well used to it, for he was ever about his bath, and she suspected that he would ever want her assistance. And so she would assist him. She had faced more daunting specters, she silently assured herself.

He moved in silent assistance, dipping a shoulder here, bending his head there. He did not sigh when her hair brushed against his thigh. He did not groan when her hand skipped lightly over his buttocks. He was practicing patience, but he believed he deserved another holding for the battle he waged against his desire.

And so he was ready for his bath. Finally. Never had she thought it could take so long to strip a body of its garments. Yet, she supposed, with so large a body . . . And she made the mistake of looking up and seeing what she had so recently uncovered.

No man should look as he did. God, in His mercy, should have given him some flaw, some blemish, or mortal man would be tempted to worship William le Brouillard as divine, so perfect was his face and form.

And as she stared at him, he felt his manhood rise, though he had beaten back the traitor with every method he knew. There was no method strong enough for the look Cathryn was giving him now. Turning swiftly, he stepped into his bath; the cooling water calmed the traitor.

He must be bathed, she reasoned within herself. Yes, he must. There should be no terror in that thought, and there was not. There was not!

Picking up the soap, of such a lovely scent, she lathered her hands. It would be better not to face him; yes, there was sense in that. She began at his back, rubbing his shoulders with pretended efficiency and moving briskly down his back. But the briskness did not last, and what had begun as a soaping ending as a caressing.

Nay, nay, nay! It was no caress but a thorough job of washing! That was all. What sort of wife was she to shirk a duty that all wives shared? Not such a wife as that!

The front must be done. She moved forward and

put her lathered hands to muscle covered with soft, black hair. The feel of him intrigued her, the softness and the strength beneath; it was not unlike the nature of the man God had gifted her with. And so he must be cleansed of the blood that covered him— and cleansed well. The broad line of his shoulder received her care. The curve of his back, so wide for so small a tub, and so smooth when compared to the fur of his chest, needed her touch. And the angle of his jaw was particularly fine; was there not a spot of dirt there that resisted the power of the soap? So it must be, for she found her hand there again and yet again.

Her hand slowed to a stop and she stared at the beautiful symmetry of his face. His eyes were downcast, as if he were studying the pattern of the soap trails on the surface of the water. His eyes were downcast, but she could see a silvery gleam from beneath his long fringe of black lashes.

He could feel her awakening desire, and he dared do nothing. But he would rather have been scourged than face its struggling heat and remain as passive as a newborn babe. When she touched him, her fingers caressing the skin that sheathed his face, she robbed him of his control.

William le Brouillard looked up at her, his eyes as hot and shimmering as molten silver, and Cathryn jerked at the stark desire she saw mirrored there.

"He is a mighty boar, Lord William," Ulrich enthused as he burst, unannounced, into the room. "He will make good eating, if he is not too tough with age!" And he laughed at his own jest. He laughed alone.

Cathryn, desperate to escape, whirled to the door, glad for once that Ulrich was so impetuous in his comings and goings.

"The killing of that boar must have been very dirty work, my lord"—Ulrich laughed—"for I have never known even you to take such a great length of time with your bath."

"Your lord is cleansed and ready for robing," Cathryn said in cool tones to her husband's squire, darting from the room with unaccustomed haste.

He did not stop her. He was practicing patience with her and her smothered desire, was he not? But Ulrich was another matter and not so fragile a creature as his wife.

Turning cool gray eyes to his squire, William said dryly, "I must pay more attention to your training, boy, for you are much lacking in knightly courtesy."

"I?" Ulrich asked in exaggerated affront. "I? Lacking in courtesy? Nay, Lord William, it is my greatest wish to be a knight renowned for his gallantry, and I have spent much effort on—"

"On bursting through a door that had been firmly closed to ensure privacy and into your lord's chamber where he and his wife were alone and where you knew your lord to be undressed?"

"My lord, I . . . I ask your pardon," Ulrich stammered, red-faced.

William did not answer either to accept or reject his squire's apology. He merely grunted and rose from his cold bath. Ulrich could suffer the pangs of regret for his indiscretion a mite longer, as William was suffering the loss of Cathryn in his chamber.

When William entered the great hall, he stopped in the portal, amazed. Men and women were laying the cloth upon the board and hurrying with cutlery and goblet, yet they were folk he scarcely recognized. The men were strong of limb and straight of back, their hair glossy and well cut. The women were younger than he thought the women of Greneforde to be and more comely. And they all wore smiles of goodwill and vigor.

They definitely smelled better.

Father Godfrey approached, and William entered the room more fully to meet him.

"You see now why they were not quick to wash," Godfrey said in greeting.

William pondered that. The Greneforde folk he had met when first arriving had seemed a sickly lot, aged and weak and stinking of neglect. They now appeared as they were in fact: healthy and strong.

"This was her doing," he mused aloud, "to shield them."

"Yea," Godfrey agreed, "and it was effective. Lambert saw what you saw and did not give them a second look or thought." Godfrey looked at Cathryn as she stood in conversation with John the Steward. "She stood as a brightly polished shield between his people and hers. They will love her unto death for that."

"So they should," William said with so much emotion that it changed the texture of his voice.

He watched her, her yellow hair glimmering like

rubbed gold as she went about her tasks. She had used the means available to her to spare the people in her care the awful weight of complete defeat. She had borne the weight of Lambert's hacking blows and been badly battered as a result. She was a wife about which songs could be written.

And then Ulrich crossed his line of vision, angling after some young maid of bounteous bosom. Whence came a woman of fewer years than his Cathryn? He in no way recognized this smiling wench as the same woman who had, with hunch-backed sobs, told him of Cathryn's rape. William chuckled. *Leave it to Ulrich to find a young and un-married girl with which to slake his thirst for ro-mance.*

"Are there any more such as that one?" William asked Godfrey with the slightest indication of his head.

Godfrey looked at Marie and laughed. "Only Marie. She serves Cathryn."

William watched Ulrich's pursuit and shook his head in amusement.

" 'Tis just as well there is only the one. Ulrich can but just manage her."

"Young Marie would argue the point with you, if she dared; she is much afeared of men," Godfrey informed.

"Perhaps someone should tell her Ulrich is fast becoming one."

Godfrey smiled. "For Ulrich, she would make an exception."

William saw that it was so, for Ulrich had captured the girl's hand and passionately kissed it. It was telling that no slap followed such gallant aggression. If only he were covering such ground—and as swiftly—with his wife.

And then he thought of a way.

He beckoned John with a gesture of his hand, calling him to his side, and when he came, instructed, "I would have you prepare a fresh bath for my lady. Collar Ulrich and have him fetch for you the bag with the rose design embroidered upon it. Add its contents to the water until the scent of summer assails your nostrils. Do you comprehend, John?"

"Yea, lord"—John smiled—"I comprehend. The bath will be hot when she seeks it, this I assure you."

"Thank you, John. 'Twill be on the heels of the mass."

As John returned to the supervision of the laying of the board, Godfrey turned to William and teased, "You have remembered that the mass will be read tonight?"

"Yea," William answered with a mock scowl, "and do not prick me about it, priest. I had to search my mind as thoroughly as a hound the marsh to find a plausible reason we might miss it without suffering penance."

Godfrey made no reply except to nod his head and swallow a grin, which William did not miss.

"She told you," he said with sudden surety.

"Yea," Godfrey admitted, "and I told her some things."

"About me."

"Yea, for she would know the man she married,"

Godfrey explained, sensing a change in William's mood.

"As I would know her, but the time for advisers and intermediaries is done. Whatever we learn now, we learn firsthand."

"That is wise," Godfrey conceded. "I will but offer one thing more: remember that this mass is for her brother and that he died in her defense."

"I am little likely to forget it."

"I but caution you to use tender care in your dealings with your wife tonight; her grief will be fresh."

"Father," William said, his voice deep within his chest, "your concern for my wife is misplaced, though sincere. Do you imagine that I am ever less than tender with her?"

"Nay, but—"

"Nay, say no more," William commanded. "Trust me as you know me. I believe that I know Cathryn better than you. What is more, I believe that God will use me to heal her."

Godfrey knew he had reached the end of William's patience, perhaps even trod one step beyond. He held his peace and did not question William's belief, but he could not help thinking that God, in the intricacy of His eternal plan and with magnificent efficiency, would also use Cathryn to banish the specters that haunted William.

Dinner had been laid upon the cloth. All was in readiness. Father Godfrey and William walked to the table, but William did not sit. He stood, as he had that first day, waiting for Cathryn to join him.

Again, as on that first occasion, Cathryn stood in hurried conversation with John, supervising the last details of the meal. Again she felt the intensity of William's eyes upon her. Would it ever be so? Would she always find herself rushing through her duties to attend him at his whim?

Would he never cease being able to touch her with his eyes?

Turning slowly, she walked to where he stood upon the dais. Though she walked of her own will, with calm dignity and grace, she could not disavow the sensation that he directed her steps, and that her steps would always lead to him. The hall quieted as she neared him; his cool eyes glinted with all the shine of sun reflecting on water.

Demurely she allowed him to seat her before he sat himself. With their sitting, the hubbub of the room rose again to its normal pitch.

"You need not wait on me," Cathryn said gently, her irritation well buried, though she did not look at him as she spoke the words.

"Lady," he said, watching her profile, "a well-trained man waits."

She smiled at John as he set the trencher between them and took a small sip of wine before speaking again.

"I commend you on chivalric lessons well learned, but I have duties and I would not have your stomach rumble on my account."

"I am in control of my body, not it in control of me," he stated. "I will wait."

Fie on the man for his chivalry! She would be running through her whole life if he did not loose his hand upon the reins that held her.

"To know that makes me feel harried and anxious," Cathryn said bluntly, honestly, her own attempts at courtly banter exhausted. "I would not be rushed."

"Then do not be rushed," he assured her with a full smile. "I but wait upon your pleasure." And he brushed the knuckles of his hand against the sensitive skin on the inside of her wrist. " 'Tis my wish that you take your pleasure ere I take mine."

Again, with this le Brouillard, this fog, Cathryn had the feeling that the topic under discussion had subtly shifted, as wind shifted the fog, but she was helpless to tell in which direction.

"Yet another point of honor for your race?" she asked with just the barest bite. "Verily, you have traveled very far in culture from your Viking roots."

William watched her as she drank deeply of her wine, watched the rhythmic movements of her throat as it pushed the drink down, watched the flutter of her dark lashes against the pale gold of her skin, watched the glistening of the jeweled gold band that marked her as his.

"Not so very far," he murmured throatily, his gray eyes glittering sharply.

Her stomach rolled against her ribs and the butterflies were set to new life, they that had so recently fallen lifeless. It was the wine, no doubt; she had consumed it too fast, or else it was a new cask that was stronger than the one before. It was not William who summoned such emotion from within the iron cage that sheathed her heart. No, it could not be.

The serenity and solemnity of icy control called to her familiarly, and she turned to it as to an old friend, yet something called her to reconsider her path. Something that had William's voice and William's eyes and William's touch; what he offered was not easy to turn away from, even though she could not put a name to it.

"And how comes the composition?" Kendall called to them cheerfully, ignoring Rowland's elbow cutting into his ribs. "Must we still wait to hear the sweet blending of your voices?"

"Yea," William answered for them both, his eyes merry, "you must wait. My lady and I are still training our voices to merge harmoniously."

"And will the wait be long, William?" Kendall asked again, pushing away Rowland's arm and dodging the hand that moved to cuff him.

William looked at Cathryn before answering. It was a brief look, yet full of hidden meaning. "Nay, the wait will not be burdensome."

"Where did you learn music?" Cathryn asked, wanting the conversation to move to ground she was familiar with.

"Where I learned anything and everything of value, or so he would tell you—from Father Godfrey."

"I would be a poor teacher if I did not believe I had instructed you in matters of merit, would I not?" Godfrey joked.

"Oh, aye, your logic is most reasonable," William answered.

"Cathryn," Godfrey directed, turning away from William, "I was pleased to hear your song and would ask who taught you musical form?"

"Greneforde's priest instructed me, but I was

taught that only one voice could be raised in song, so I am confused as to this talk of many voices uniting."

"Two is not so many," William interjected.

"Nay, William, cease," Godfrey commanded, "for she speaks of monophonic music, and such must have been taught by her priest. And it is beautiful," he said to Cathryn, "but there is a way that has been developed in which the cantus firmus is accompanied by another melody."

"And how is this done? Do the two melodies parallel each other?" Cathryn asked, genuinely interested.

"Nay, Cathryn," William answered, turning her attention again to him. " 'Tis the way it started," he admitted, "but now each voice may have a linear design of its own, uniting in combination most intimate."

The ground shifted and she was cast off balance again, unsure of the deeper meaning beneath William's words, yet sure there was more by the look in his black-lashed eyes.

"Come," Godfrey said, standing and ending her discomfort, " 'tis time for the mass."

Happily, Cathryn left the table and its multilayered conversation for the peace of the chapel and the long-awaited funeral mass.

So long awaited and so soon done. The memory of Philip rose before her eyes; so blond was he and so exuberant of spirit. The years spent in enforced exile at far-off Blythe Tower had not dulled his warmth, nor had being the captive of an unscrupulous knight. He had expected nothing more than the taking of Greneforde, and she suspected that he had felt some measure of relief at having their deception uncovered, for it meant the end of their separation.

She had always loved him, as he had loved her. Sending him away had been the most difficult decision of her life, but she had known it was the right decision. Philip could not have known what sort of man Lambert was. But she had known. When first she saw him from the high wall, holding Philip as hostage, she had known. His eyes were blue without a hint of warmth, and they had looked at her in a way that she had not understood then. She had learned what that look meant. He had taught her well, and she had not forgotten. The truth was that there was no stopping a man when his desire was raging.

Were all men, in truth, the same? She had believed so. But William le Brouillard was not like other men. She could run from that knowledge no longer. Aye, he was a man proud and strong, as all men were or strove to be. But . . . his strength did not bruise and his pride was perhaps justified, though such would never pass her lips to tickle William's ear. His Frankish vanity would rise up to unimaginable heights.

John the Steward was right: William was not Lambert.

Emotion, so long repressed, so long denied, and coming at her from all quarters, rose within her. William, his hand strong upon her arm, urged her to lean against him, to draw from his strength, but she could not. She dared not. Her emotions had been plucked many times today. She had gone weeks without feeling anything, and these new sensations were uncomfortable. It was like the cracking of ice before the thaw. She liked it not.

And she, she who had faced Lambert, was afraid to release the powerful emotions that surged within her—afraid that if she did, their very strength would overwhelm her. She knew this. She could admit her fear, and so she pressed the harder to contain her feelings.

The mass ended and, in a fog of her own turmoil, she allowed William to escort her to his chamber—no, *their* chamber now, for were not all of her things neatly in their place? It was not so large a chamber that she could fail to notice the tub full of scented water before the fire. It was a sweet scent for a man, but then, he was French.

"Will you bathe twice in one day, lord? To my eye, eating did not dirty you noticeably."

William smiled at her jibe and answered, "Nay, for I have known since swaddling how to direct the food to my mouth and avoid my other parts. Nay, wife"—he grinned—"the water is for you. It is my turn to play attendant."

"Nay!" she protested, loudly. "I bathed mere days ago!"

"And have been avoiding bathing again because you know it to be of importance to me?"

Cathryn gulped nervously. It was unlike William to be so direct in his responses; it boded ill—for her. Especially as he had seen the truth of her actions.

"Your will is mine, my lord," she said calmly, changing tactics entirely. "If you say that I am filthy, then I will send for Marie and she can attend me, as she did when last I bathed. Just days ago," she added pointedly.

"I did not call you 'filthy,' " William argued politely as he moved toward the tub, shepherding her ahead of him, "though the word brings to mind the people who inhabit Greneforde. They are a fine-looking lot. Where have you been hiding them?"

There was no answer to that—none that she could use—so she ignored it entirely.

"Filthy or no, I can bathe myself," she said flatly, drawing herself up to what she hoped was a dignified height.

"Nay, Cathryn, you will not," William contradicted. "I will simply do for you what you have so recently done for me."

And that was exactly what she feared. William's hands stroking her slick skin . . . his large, gentle hands on her naked body, caressing her . . . She felt a rolling in her middle just contemplating it. No, it could not be borne.

"It has been a tiring day," she tried, hoping for pity. "The mass . . . and I would prefer to bathe alone, in solitude, to gather my composure."

She could not have said anything that would have so strengthened his resolve to remain.

"I would be a poor husband if I allowed my wife to minister to me and did not do the same for her," he said with a cheery smile.

"Allowed?" she burst out, abandoning her search for pity. "You compelled me to attend you!"

"And you obeyed," he said, "against your own inclination?"

And so he sprang his trap. She could not admit so, not after having sworn to be a willing wife to him in all ways. It would make her look sullen and childish, and though she felt so at the moment, it would not do to appear so.

"Come, Cathryn," he urged, " 'tis no more than Christ did when he washed the feet of the twelve."

"You compare this to that?" she trilled. "There is more of seduction in this than of cleansing!"

"Truly?" He smiled wolfishly.

And so she had trapped herself. She had admitted that she would find his touch arousing, as she had found touching him.

Drawing herself to her full height, Cathryn commanded herself to stop this game of wits and manuevering with le Brouillard. It was impossible to win with him; he ever shifted until he had his way, and he would have his way in this. It would disgrace her to twist any further in escaping his will, but she would have her way in one regard: he would not disrobe her. That humiliation she would not allow, and she communicated such to him with a flash of her eyes as she reached for the tie holding her mantle. It was a small victory, and he allowed her to have it. In moments she stood naked before him, unbent and unashamed. She stepped into the tub with all the dignity of a queen stepping into her cart.

Her very serenity and supreme composure were bright signal fires that her emotions were raging just beneath her cool surface; so much he understood of her. He would move slowly, seducing her with such measured steps that she would be caught unawares. That he was already highly aroused by the sight of her slender nudity, her golden cloak of hair both hiding and revealing at once, was inconvenient, but the traitor between his legs would obey him, and his face would remain calmly impassive. They would, for he was le Brouillard and he did not relinquish his control when in battle. And this was battle.

She would not look upon his face, but stared fixedly at the blazing fire when he approached—a defensive posture. He was not so dulled in the head by sword blows that he did not see this as a good sign; she was defensive because she felt the need to be. She was not indifferent to him. That was good. It was better than good.

He dipped his hands into the hot water and lifted them high above her skin, letting the heat trickle over her. Only water would touch her at first.

The feel of the dribbling water against the skin of her breasts was startling. She had expected his hands to touch her. His hands she was prepared for; this gentle drizzle she was not. It was most unnerving, particularly as he did not touch her. What a thought! It was simply an odd way to bathe. No wonder le Brouillard was ever about his bath, if this was the method of his washing.

Again his hands were raised above her, and again he let the streams of water run between his fingers to caress her skin. The water was uncomfortably hot, or it felt so as it fell and traced pathways over her. Her skin was unbearably sensitive to the touch of the water; mayhap the soap was irritating to her. That would explain the prickling she felt just beneath her skin and the uneasy feeling in her stomach.

Again he raised his hands to release his waterfall. How long would he bathe her in this fashion? It was most irritating. Probably some Frankish habit, and all the fashion there. If she complained, he would again sing the praises of his people and ask that she sing the chorus. He was an impossible man. This was no bath such as she had ever taken, and despite what he thought of her sanitary habits, she was accustomed to taking quite a few in the course of a month.

Fie! If again she felt just water, hot and scented though it was, touching her skin, she would run shrieking from the room. And most likely bump into Ulrich on the stair tower.

William watched her nipples rise and her breathing quicken, but still he did not touch her with aught but water. When she asked for more, then she would receive it.

"This is an odd bathing," she bit out finally. "I shall be shriveled to look three times my age before you deem me clean at this pace."

William said nothing, merely smiled and added more of the scent to the water. He swirled it in with the fingers of one hand, but none came near to touching her.

"Is it soap you add, and will it clean my skin by just mingling with the water?"

A log falling on the fire was her answer, and the sparks it sent up seemed to mirror the light, burning sensation flickering just beneath her skin.

"I cannot be properly clean if you refuse to touch

my skin with water and soap!" she burst out, her dark eyes snapping with as much heat as the flames.

William did not smile as he looked into her eyes, though the urge was there.

"You ask for my touch?"

"To cleanse me, yea," she answered swiftly, her composure badly shaken.

"My touch *will* cleanse you, Cathryn," he affirmed softly.

He spoke words that seemed to her to have two meanings, as was his wont, and she cursed the ways of Frankish knights in the quiet turmoil of her heart.

To her surprise, he reached beneath the scented water and lifted a foot out for his scrutiny. The soap made his hands slick, and if his touch had not been so firm, she would have laughed at his tickling. But his touch *was* firm as he stroked the curves and hills that comprised her foot. Never did she know that the human foot could be so sensitive to touch, used as it was to walk upon cold stone or rough wood. She sighed, sinking deeper into the water as he lifted her foot higher; never did she know that a man's touch upon her foot could be so . . . pleasurable.

The word *erotic* had sprung to mind, but she cast it out. It was a simple bath and his touch was not unpleasant. There could be nothing sensuous about her foot! And so she relaxed against the back of the wooden tub, her hair falling in a curtain to lie upon the floor.

William had not looked at her directly. He concentrated upon the cleanliness of her feet and did not allow his thoughts to stray to what lay within easy reach of his hand just beneath the water. No, he did not look, but he felt the muscles of her leg relax and the full weight of her foot rest upon his hand, and he knew that he had broken through another one of her defenses.

Unable to deny the urge any longer, he allowed himself a quick look at her face, his eyes glittering like polished steel. Her look was one of heavy languor, her limbs relaxed, her eyes closed. It was going well. William quickly lowered his gaze again; it would not do for her to know his own state of arousal, and he did not dare look upon her longer or else he would become impatient for his prize and rush headlong, defeating himself.

William released his hold upon her foot, having ventured no farther than her ankle in his northward movement. His hands next caught and held her hand, rubbing with his thumbs along the line of her pulse and the muscled joint between thumb and fingers.

Could the touching of hands be so intimate? She would never have thought so, but now she was unsure. He had declared that he would bathe her, and she had imagined his hands upon her breasts and hips, and mayhap his mouth . . . but there was none of that in this. It was as he had said: a washing such as Christ had given his disciples; yet they had all been clothed for that cleansing, and though William was dressed even out to his mantle, she was completely nude, covered only by the darkened water. And why did that realization, that he was clothed and she was nude, cause her pulse to jump and her eyes to flutter open? There could be no further denying of the word. It was erotic.

Slowly, ever slowly, he moved his hand to the hollow of her elbow and caressed the tender skin there. He was dangerously close to her bosom, yet his hand did not stray and she found herself wondering why, relieved and puzzled at once.

He moved to her shoulders, a hand upon each one, and gently massaged them. She moved her head to give him greater access, a cascade of golden ripples trickling to the floor with the motion.

"There is a small mark of dirt upon your breast," he whispered near her ear. "May I cleanse you there?"

"Yea," she answered in a like whisper, her eyes closed against his nearness. Her heart pounded in expectation.

She knew that he would touch her there. She expected his touch there. Still, he moved slowly from her shoulder down to her breast and massaged gently. Quickly he was finished and moved his hand away. Odd, but it was almost disappointment she felt.

"Your leg has a smudge of wood ash," he said.

"Yea, my legs are dirty," she agreed, waiting for his touch upon her leg.

A soft caress, once, twice, up the length of one leg and he was through. Her extremities began to shake and disturb the stillness of the water.

"You tremble," he observed, his tone husky.

In truth, she did, and from the center of her soul to the outermost parts of her, but she would not admit the cause to be his touch.

"I am chilled. The water has long since lost its heat."

He would not allow such deception from her.

"But you have not." And with his hand he lifted her chin so that she could not escape the penetration of his smoky eyes. "You are as warm to my touch as sun-baked steel."

With no words of warning or intent, William lifted her from the bath and stood her upon the rough floor, the water sheeting off her to soak the boards. Briskly he rubbed her dry, the linen sheet quickly becoming wet through.

She was dizzy from the heat of the water, the proximity to the fire, the length of her time spent soaking . . . or was it the heat of his hands, her proximity to him, the length of him almost rubbing against her upthrust nipples? She could not say, but she could not find the strength to stand.

He caught her against him and then set her back upon her own feet, holding her by the waist and looking deeply into her dark eyes.

"Are you clean, lady?" he asked, his own eyes dark.

The double meaning was there, but this time she understood what he asked of her. He wanted her to be clean—clean of Lambert, clean of guilt.

Hesitantly she answered, "I know not," for it was the truth, and then laughed, turning aside his deeper meaning. "I should be."

His eyes missed nothing as he answered, "And so you are."

He fingered a tendril of her falling hair and she did not fight him; in truth, she leaned toward him, almost eager for his touch. Another lock of hair found its way into his tender hands, and another and yet another, and she allowed him access to it. She wanted his touch upon her hair. She wanted his touch until his hands were buried in the richness of her hair, and when he had achieved it, she reached up for his kiss as he was reaching down and their mouths locked in a kiss that was in no way hesitant or shy. It was a kiss of passion, with tongues and teeth in play and his hands bound within her hair, holding her as she held him.

She wrapped her arms around his neck, lifting on tiptoe to attain a firmer purchase. She rubbed the length of herself against him, her nipples rising and enlarging at the friction. She whimpered into his mouth and thrashed her head.

He did not relinquish his hold upon her hair.

In time, William straightened and pulled away from her.

"What do you want, Cathryn?" he said under his breath, his eyes as bright as any dragon's.

"I . . . I know not." She gasped, hanging on to him for support.

William grinned down at her, "Well, think of something, lady, or my Frankish pride will suffer a near mortal blow."

And then she smiled, catching his mood. "I would see if *you* are clean, Lord le Brouillard."

"Well said and timely, lady," William answered, pulling off his clothing as he spoke. When he was as naked as she, he pulled her against him and kissed her soundly.

But the effects of the bath had cooled and she was

not so heated a partner as she had been just minutes ago. The fire within her required rekindling.

"Touch me, Cathryn," he urged. "Know me."

Obeying him, she touched him, her hands skimming over the planes of his chest in a light flutter that was not quite a caress, enjoying the feel of him, the strength of him. Enjoying the control of touching him and of not having him touch her.

For he did not touch her, though he yearned to. He let her explore the sum total of his skin, and he made no move to explore her in turn. She needed to become familiar with his body as much as she needed to be in control of her own involvement. He would not force her. He would wait until she could wait no longer.

She grew bolder, touching his back with long strokes, watching the play of muscle ripple the ivory of his skin. Moving to his front, Cathryn laid a soft hand against his cheek, her fingertips resting near the long curl of his lashes. The blaze and glitter of his eyes almost seared her.

But she did not pull away her hand.

With one hand on his cheek, she slid the other down the tapering line of chest and waist to hip and paused with her hand upon his naked hip. Amazingly, his skin was almost hairless at that spot, and she stroked it lingeringly, allowing her fingers to graze behind to the hard mound of his buttock.

The faintest growl rumbled in William's throat and she jerked back, startled. She had almost forgotten he was a living man, so enraptured was she with the perfection of his form. Looking back into his steely eyes, she remembered with a start that he was a man very much alive.

Her backward flight was so abrupt and so unplanned that she stumbled and landed on the bed—flat on her back.

William grinned as only a man can grin when a naked woman appears in his bed, and said lazily, "You had but to ask, Cathryn. Of course I will recline with you. Tonight I am in attendance upon you and will follow your inclination."

With those words, her nervousness at her position was replaced with the urge to laugh. Truly, the man would be capable of urging a chuckle from her on her deathbed.

The urge to laugh was soon swallowed by another urge even less familiar to her. His kiss, so delicate, plucked away all thoughts save one: she liked his mouth on hers. With the tip of his tongue, he explored her mouth, stopping now and again to nibble on her lower lip. It was a kiss most sensual. Her flesh seemed afire and she writhed, her movements sensuous in the extreme, though she did not know it.

William did not touch her unless she initiated it by moving her body against his; so it was that her breast nudged his hand, seeking a caress with wordless eloquence, and when he touched her there, his fingers plucking gently at her nipple, she arched beneath his hand.

"I almost expect to hear you purr, Cat, you are so warm," he said softly.

Cathryn reacted like a cat doused with ice water. "Do not call me Cat!" she cried out hoarsely.

It had happened each time before, and at just such a moment. He had thought that it was their physical bonding that caused her to go stiff in his arms. Mayhap it was more than that.

He did not move. He was as still as she. The sound of the fire and of her labored breathing were the only noises, yet William believed that Lambert lurked within their chamber with them.

Taking Cathryn in his arms, he lay down facing her, nestling her against him and stroking her back.

"What is it, Cathryn?" he questioned softly, trying to split the heavy silence that had fallen like a sword between them.

But Cathryn, a master at regaining her composure, would not answer. She pushed against his chest with the palms of her hands in a polite struggle to be released.

" 'Tis a name I do not care for," she said simply, hoping the matter would end there.

William understood. He understood that she had retreated from him, closing all roads between them. He understood that he would need to cause a fire to blaze in her again before she would melt against him. But this time it would not be the fire of passion. This time he would fire her anger.

Picking up a thick strand of her hair, he flicked it casually against her nipples.

"That is strange," he said conversationally. "Cat is a name that suits you well. The way you arch and rub against me, the sleek grace of your form. Yea," he said against her erect nipples, causing them to tighten even more, "you are a most sensual cat."

He cast her hair aside, sweeping it behind her

shoulders so that her breasts were revealed to him without defensive covering. He covered one small mound with the flat of his hand, rubbing the sensitive peak with the callused heel of his hand.

"Cat," he whispered just above her ear, "you are soft. Wrap yourself around me, Cat. Purr your pleasure, Cat, and I will stroke you."

"Do not call me Cat!" she shouted, pushing his hand from her frantically, fighting to escape his touch, shaking violently.

"Why, Cathryn?" he questioned again, his voice as hard as gravel beneath bare feet.

Her arms continued to flail against him, but he was not moved. She could no longer escape the pain that lay like a wolf waiting to destroy her in the black depths of her soul.

Sobs, so long held back, rushed up and now choked her. Wrapping her arms around her torso, trying to keep herself from being torn asunder by the force of those racking sobs, Cathryn rocked herself with the wordless misery of a child.

"Cathryn," he murmured.

"He called me Cat," she said in a sob, the words wet upon her tongue.

She turned away from him and continued her mindless rocking. William reached out his warm hand and rubbed her back, his hand tracing the bumps of her spine.

"He called me Cat," she repeated, her cries almost making her words unrecognizable. "He called me Cat and laughed when he said it. He called me Cat every time . . . every time."

And when her husband touched her and called

her Cat, she saw Lambert, felt Lambert's hands upon her. This he understood. He watched her rocking and felt her sobbing cries as if they were his own. She was so thin, and she had borne so much in Greneforde's name.

He longed to heal her.

He longed to kill Lambert.

"He called me Cat and nothing else," she continued, the words bubbling up from her as from a spring, "in the hearing of his people. And mine."

No man addressed a lady with such casual disregard. To do so was to strip her of her rank and to heap humiliation upon her. This Lambert had done.

"And when I walked in the yard, I would hear the sounds of his men meowing, the high-pitched calls echoing against the walls."

Yes, he could imagine it. The men, following the sordid example of their master, and Cathryn alone against them all. And he knew how she had responded to their base cruelty: with her head held high and with her dignity unconquered. Such was her courage and her pride that, in the depths of profound defeat—the defeat of her lands, her home, her people, and her body—she had sought and achieved a victory. She had let no one witness the evidence of her shame and loss. Until now.

Turning her in his arms, he rocked with her, cradling her as easily as he would a heartsick child, for so she was. She did not turn to him, yet she did not fight him. Eventually her tears stopped. Her rocking did not, and he rocked with her, holding her against his warmth and his strength, willing her to avail herself of both.

Finally she lay still.

"I ask you again," he said with gentle force, holding her against his chest. "Are you clean, lady?"

Cathryn squirmed until she could see his face. With eyes as lifeless and hopeless as those of a corpse, she answered him.

"Nay. I will never be clean."

"You are wrong, Cathryn."

Again he had pricked her anger, though this time it was unintentional.

"Of all matters on earth which man may know," she spit out, "in this one I am expert. I am not clean! His seed stains me inside and out. I am as soiled linen, fit only for the fire."

"Again you are wrong," William argued, his voice low and vibrating. "Did not our Christ's sacrifice wash us whiter than snow? Is there any sin that man can devise that can outpace our Lord? Have you forgotten that you are redeemed, having been washed in Christ's sacrificial blood?"

His eyes were shards that she would have avoided if she could, but he held her firm and forced her to face him and his words.

"Do you not know," he continued more calmly, "that Lambert's relationship with you is as water to blood? I joined my life, my blood, to yours, Cathryn, the moment we were wed. All that has passed before cannot wash away or dilute the blood bond we share."

His words were sweet, and she longed to believe him, but she could not. The stain of her sin was great, greater than even the force of William le Brouillard.

William read her rejection of his words in the darkness of her eyes.

"You are my wife, Cathryn, bound to me throughout this life. You share my blood, which I would shed gladly in defense of you," he stated. "What went before has no part in this; indeed, it is so weak as to be candle flame to bonfire. You are my wife," he repeated with heat. "You have never been so joined. Trust me," he implored. "I would show you the fire so that you will know what a dim candle has lit your world."

His words tore at her, beckoning her from the safe if lonely place she had constructed for herself.

"I would love you, Cathryn," he whispered against her hair, and then his hands moved upon her. They moved as she had yearned for them to move before, but now she was not in control and William would not be stopped.

Both hands in play, he caressed her bosom until both peaks throbbed against his palms. He played upon her nipples till she scarcely could remember a time when he had not had her under his hands.

With kisses deep he smothered anything she would have said to stop him, and, after so little a span of time, she could think of no words to halt his progress. His tongue plunged into her mouth, and he was welcomed. His seduction was both so rapid and so heated that she did not have time to be reluctant. He carried her away on a tide of his own making, and she found no thought in her head to dislike it. In truth, her mind was wiped clean of all thought.

And so William had designed.

She rubbed her hips against his as she arched into his hands, seeking, wanting, needing . . . and more. She had never known such searching.

This, William had known.

"Close your eyes, Cathryn," he ordered softly. "Do not think or reason now. Now is a time for feeling."

She obeyed him, and in the darkness the sensations became so intense that she thought she saw color explode and swirl in her mind's eye.

He flicked his thumbs against her swollen nipples as he flicked her questing tongue, and she groaned into his mouth.

The sound, coming so unexpectedly from her, shocked her into stillness. In truth, she was embarrassed.

"Do not stop yourself," he reprimanded in a whisper, his mouth against her throat. "You must relinquish control over your body."

Cathryn covered his hands with her own, wanting him to stop his erotic torment.

"And give it to whom?"

"To me, of course." He grinned wolfishly before kissing his way to an eager nipple.

With a giggle at his comical expression, she fell back upon the mattress. But the giggle turned quickly to a moan as he feasted upon her, his mouth moving from one small breast to the other until she was twisting and moaning with an abandon that she had not thought possible.

A vision of Lambert hovering over her sprang to her mind, and her eyes flashed open.

She absorbed the sight of William's black hair nestled against her breast. It calmed her.

"Speak to me," she commanded. She needed to hear the sound of his voice, a voice unlike any other she had known. A voice not Lambert's.

And he obeyed her.

"I will speak to you for the rest of my days of things great and small. You are my wife. Our blood, our bodies, our flesh, are one," he began, his words warm against her bosom. "You are beautiful, wife. Your skin is finer than any of the silks I labored to win . . . and so much more pleasurable to clean."

She giggled again, and the movement planted a nipple firmly in his mouth. He suckled at her breast in a way unlike any babe and then moved up to lick the rim of her ear.

"What else would you have me speak of?" he murmured, sending chills down her back.

"Anything," she murmured back, becoming lost in the sensation of his touch again. "Speak of anything; I would but hear your voice."

"And you shall," he promised, "as well as feel the touch of my hand upon your silken flesh."

His hand moved with husbandly authority down over the small swell of her breast to the dip of waist and abdomen and to the protrusion of her hip.

"You are well curved, wife, in the way a husband wants his wife to be curved."

With a fingertip, he explored the folds of her heat as his other hand rolled a nipple almost casually. Cathryn's legs began to tremble when he inserted his thigh between her knees.

"Do you tremble for me? Or because of me?" he

asked softly before covering her mouth with his own in a kiss both deep and quick. Still, his fingers explored the most secret and vulnerable part of her, and the heat in her breast seemed close to a burning fire. His triple attack left her without any thought but the most fluttering kind, and the trembling worsened.

As he had intended.

"And your eyes," he continued, leaving her mouth and kissing his way down past her breasts, "are as dark and unfathomable as the wells of Nicaea, surrounded as they are by the golden sands of the desert, sultry in its heat. Such are you, wife."

And she was hot. He could feel her heat as if he stood on the desert sands at midday, and he burned with her. For her.

Cathryn writhed beneath his hand, moaning intermittently. William stretched her legs wider, positioning his bent knees between her thighs. With one hand he rubbed and teased the nub of desire that now rose against the soft folds of her womanhood. With the other he twisted and rubbed her reddened nipple, and with his mouth he feasted on her breast, nipping and licking in turn.

He would leave no part of his wife unattended. She thrashed beneath his hands, moaning continuously now, and clutching at his dark hair.

William abandoned her breasts. Cathryn opened her eyes slowly. William, without stopping his nether hand, turned her so that she lay upon her stomach.

This was new to her, and a frisson of fear shot through her. Brushing her hair aside, with his fingers ever in play, William kissed the full globes of her derriere.

Cathryn cried out softly and lifted her hips in the direction of her husband's mouth, thereby opening herself to him more fully. His drenched finger took advantage and inserted itself into her full length. Her drawn-out moan of pleasure and desire made him tremble.

With force, William flipped his wife onto her back, spreading her legs to their utmost width and holding her by her ankles. Cathryn, desperate for a handhold on the physical world that was falling away from her, reached up to hold the headboard with both hands and hung on tenaciously.

He watched her, her legs spread and quaking beneath his grip, her nipples red in the firelight, her yellow hair a tangled mat beneath her weight.

"You torment me, wife," he said hoarsely.

"Why . . . why," she choked out through parched lips, "why do you wait?"

Gray eyes of smoke and sword impaled her.

"I wait for thee," he answered in a rough whisper.

And, holding her wide to receive him, he bent to take her with his mouth.

Cathryn lost control quickly at that. She did not know exactly what he did—she did not want to know—but the power of it knocked the breath from her lungs.

She had never been more afraid.

"Nay! Stop! William, please!" she cried, trying to pull his black head from between her legs.

His hands released her ankles and she thought for a moment that he had heeded her, but it was not so. With his broad shoulders he kept her legs apart, and with his arms he pushed her back and held her down, her strength no match for his.

"Follow where I lead you," he commanded. "Release the reins of this horse you are riding and fly!"

His mouth closed on her again and she sobbed out his name, thrashing and jerking beneath his grip.

Her cry did not end, but became a long and unending wail that had nothing of fear in it, only passion—uncontrollable, consuming passion.

She clutched his hair, hanging on to him, unable to bear another moment of his delicious torture and eager for the next touch of his tongue against her, wanting it to end and wanting it to go on so that she thought she would tear herself in two with her conflicting desires.

Something, some weight, was building inside of her, crushing her, and again she sought the reassuring feel of wood beneath her hands.

Her wail increased in pitch. Her legs grew hard and stiff. Something was coming—something like being thrown off a cliff with no bottom, a cliff that faced the stars and was grounded in starlight.

And William would not relent. He increased the tempo of his tongue and brought his hands to her breasts, where, with rapid rhythm, he squeezed and pinched.

With a scream, Cathryn was hurled off the cliff, where she fell . . . and fell . . . and fell . . . with a scream never-ending. A throbbing pounded at the juncture of her legs with a force stronger and more demanding than the beating of her heart. She was certain that she faced her death—death from exquisite pleasure.

William rose up and plunged into her, and her scream, which was lowering, rose again, but this time she did not fall alone. This time she fell with her arms around the strong back of her husband.

When their frenzied thrusting stilled, William lay atop her, his weight a reassuring thing. Cathryn clung to his shoulders to keep him there.

With eyes wide and unblinking, she could only whisper breathlessly, "Oh, God, oh, God, oh, God, oh, God . . ." with each panting breath.

William smiled into the sweetness of her hair and said softly, "You have a way of trammeling my vanity, wife. What you should be saying is, 'Oh, William, oh, William, oh, William.' . . ."

Hugging him closer still, Cathryn laughed as loudly and as long as she had just screamed her pleasure.

The echo of her cry drifted in the air of the great hall below as lightly and as lingeringly as the scent of costly perfume. Kendall looked up from the chessboard to say to his opponent, "Cathryn's part of the song is quite stirring. William is an apt instructor, is he not?"

Rowland reached casually across the board to cuff him.

Chapter Fourteen

The dawning saw Kendall and Rowland ready to depart for the king. It would be no easy matter to find him, for he traveled constantly with his court, making his presence known in all the lands of his domain. It was a wise policy, and one Stephen could have put to better use. In the case of Henry, Rowland was not dismayed that their journey would by necessity be a circuitous one, for that was the main objective. He would cast wide for sign of Lambert, though Kendall would have no knowledge of it, thinking they searched exclusively for King Henry.

"We shall have no gay farewells and wishes of Godspeed, it seems," Kendall remarked with a mischievous smile. " 'Tis unlike William. What think you detains him in his bed this morn?"

"Your head is thick, Kendall," Rowland stated calmly.

" 'Tis well it is for all the pounding you give it with your meaty hand." He chuckled.

"Mayhap the pounding will soften it, much as with tough meat that must be pounded before releasing its juices."

"Ah, and now we speak again of why William remains abed." Kendall smiled. " 'Tis that he must pound his wife so that she will release her own sweet juice."

Rowland's dark eyes tried to mask their shining amusement at Kendall's remark, and to help, he struck his companion a glancing blow upon his neck.

When Kendall rose from the dirt, he was smiling still.

"We had best be off before I am too bruised to begin."

"Yea," Rowland agreed, "and ride not at my side or I will be holding back a temptation that I find I have a little chance of besting."

Kendall laughed as he mounted and kicked his horse into a quick canter away from his traveling companion. They left the walls of Greneforde behind and crossed the river Brent without delay. The day was one of struggling sun, and Kendall's mood ran high; it was highly unlikely that they should encounter the king this day, and he looked forward to a day of roving freedom in woodland and meadow.

Rowland had not much thought to spare for King Henry; his mind was trained upon finding Lambert, and his eye was upon the ground seeking tracks not made by Greneforde folk. If he were Lambert, he would not stray far from Cathryn and what she offered, so finding signs of Lambert's proximity was not unreasonable.

But Rowland was not Lambert and did not think with Lambert's reasoning.

Lambert had not stayed at Greneforde upon hearing of King Henry's coronation; what purpose would that have served? Lambert had made for the king, and with the king he now spoke.

"And so my lands were lost to me, and not through neglect or rebellion against my king," he said with emotion, facing the king and his advisers. "I then made for Greneforde, my closest neighbor, and a holding not unfamiliar to me. There I lived and ruled until that time the anarchy should end."

"Would it not be better said that you enjoyed the hospitality of Greneforde Tower when your own had been destroyed?" one of Henry's councilors asked.

Lambert eyed Edgar of Lisborne with a cold look before answering. "As Lady Cathryn was alone there, I assumed the role of lord, taking the part that God in His wisdom has ordained for man."

Edgar cast his eye toward the king, not liking the way this tale was playing out. He saw that King Henry also liked it little.

"You were welcomed willingly?" the king asked.

"She did open the gate to me when I asked it," Lambert answered with deceptive truth.

"How long did you reside at Greneforde?" Edgar asked suspiciously.

Lambert did not look at Edgar as he answered; he looked at the king. But he did answer.

"For three months I lived and acted as lord of Greneforde, making no war upon my sovereign or his will. When word came that King Stephen was no longer king of England and that King Henry took his rightful place, I hied here to explain my connection to Greneforde and ask that it be given into my hand for the good of all. For my lord, who needs men who will be loyal to his standard; for the Lady Cathryn, who needs a husband; and for myself, one who has lost his holding and has already found another bailey in good repair, joining the two lands as one, under one lord."

Edgar thought how odd it was that Lambert placed himself last when he was certain that, in his secret thoughts, he placed himself first, no matter his words of loyalty to Henry. It was a shame that Lambert of Brent had not lingered at Greneforde; he could have then met face-to-face with Greneforde's new lord and had this conversation with him. William le Brouillard would not have had to play this hand with careful diplomacy as Henry was bound to do.

It was a twisted tale, that much was sure, but what was false and what was true could not be deciphered at such a distance and from such a source as Lambert of Brent. That Lambert was ignorant of William's part in this situation was obvious. Such could not long remain the case.

"There are other donjons that stand empty and that call for loyal men to arm them," Edgar stated, hoping to turn Lambert from his course.

"And many are they which are being dismantled, having been built without the king's license. Greneforde is a lawful tower," Lambert answered.

"You seem much attached to Greneforde Tower, given that you resided there for so brief a span of time," the king commented, his hand stroking the softness of his beard.

Lambert made his final move—the move that would either win Greneforde for him or cause him to lose all, mayhap his life.

" 'Tis so, my lord. I am much attached to Greneforde because I am much attached to the lady who resides there and to whom Greneforde is lawful inheritance."

The king's brows rose in mild surprise, but he said nothing. Edgar knew that gesture did not bode well for Lambert, for Lady Cathryn had already been given to le Brouillard, but he, as well, said nothing. To what purpose when Lambert was doing so well at his own destruction?

"Much attached," Lambert repeated, a band of sweat glistening on his brow as he faced the cold eyes of his king and the king's advisers. "My lord, I must be blunt: I have had carnal knowledge of Cathryn of Greneforde, and on that basis I would ask for her hand in marriage and that her holding be gifted to me."

At that the king was moved, but not for Lambert. His thoughts went to William, who had taken an impure wife to his marriage bed. William had deserved better for his service. Henry's mind spun to consider other holdings that would suit his man better. It was not that he would give Greneforde to

Lambert, but that he would give William something else. As to Lambert, he would not receive Greneforde as his prize, for he had nothing to bring to the marriage; by law, his portion must be equal, and Henry would not amend the law for one such as Lambert.

"Edgar," Henry said, "I would have William le Brouillard before me when I decide the fate of Greneforde and its lady. Summon him to court."

"Aye, my lord." Edgar bowed before he left to dispatch the messenger.

With Edgar's departure from the room, the subject of Greneforde was closed. The king turned to other matters with other supplicants. Lambert did not miss the significance of the fact that he had not been addressed again. He stood on unstable ground in regard to his claim to Greneforde, even though he had played his game with what pieces were left him, using the swift ruthlessness of one who had nothing to lose.

There was another course of action open to him now, and the king himself had opened it. The ownership of Greneforde would not be decided upon until William reached the king. Apparently another man had a claim to Greneforde. He could intercept this William whom the king had summoned and kill him ere he reached the king. King Henry would perchance be more disposed to gift him with a holding that was free of any other claim. He had little to dissuade him from this course; the king would plainly not give him a holding that he had given to another, but there was a chance that he would not feel so constrained if William were not around to argue the point. It was a chance, his only chance, and he would take it, not bothered by conscience. He had none.

Chapter Fifteen

"Did you not hear something amiss coming from the lord's chamber last night, John?" Marie questioned anxiously.

"Nay," he said, smiling in answer. "I heard nothing that gave me cause to worry."

"Did you not?" She frowned. "I did not think myself dreaming, yet, if you did not—"

"What is it that you believe you heard, Marie? Tell me, and I will seek to comfort you in what way I can."

"'Tis that, as I lay abed with eyes closed, I thought I heard . . . a scream," she finished, wide-eyed.

"Ah," he said with a smile. "You heard a scream and so you worry for our lady."

"But if you did not—"

"But I did, girl. I also heard a scream, and the

sound of it was not unlike Lady Cathryn's voice."

Marie's lovely blue eyes filled with horror as she imagined what it was that Lord William had done to wring such a cry from his wife—she who had not cried out when Lambert beat her and killed her brother.

"Nay," John comforted, "there is no cause for alarm. He did her no injury, and this you will see when she comes down to break her fast."

"But she has not come down," she whispered, "and 'tis past the dawning."

"She will come down," John repeated. "All is well with her." And with William, if he was aright in his thinking as to what had transpired in the lord's bed. "And here is one who looks for you."

Ulrich bounded into the kitchen and stopped abruptly upon seeing Marie. An enchanted light shone from his eyes as he made his way toward her. Marie pushed thoughts of Cathryn to one side and faced him with a shy smile, one she had practiced to perfection in the calm water of her washing bowl.

"And I now have broken my long night's fast, for I can feast again on your beauty, and though I feast daily, I am never full, never sated. I fear 'twill take a thousand lifetimes to drink my fill of you, lovely Marie," Ulrich expounded with drama.

"I fear I am a food that will never build the muscle upon your bone," she coyly answered, giving him the opportunity to deny it.

"Nay, you are wrong," he contradicted gallantly. "You are all the food I need, yet you parcel it out so sparingly that I admit 'tis possible that I could waste away. Yet I do so willingly!" he added when she started to walk away in pretended insult.

"I think you would have food of me that would near destroy me in the giving of it," she said, not allowing him to see her face.

"I would not," Ulrich vowed, "for as you feed me, I would also feed you. 'Twould be a banquet we would share."

"Yet you find it in your heart to complain as to the bounty of the gifts I have already given you."

" 'Tis only that they are the first course, and a man needs heartier food to sustain him, Marie."

"To indulge the way you would like is to indulge in . . . gluttony, and such is a deadly sin," she countered, enjoying their verbal debate and the sensual undertones of it. "Would you have me fat?"

"Marie—" he smiled engagingly—" 'tis hardly possible to grow fat on the banquet of delight I speak of."

"So men say, until the lady of their heart does indeed grow . . . fat."

John watched them as they made for the door, with Ulrich in his constant position of trailing after the coyly enticing Marie. If Marie were not careful, Ulrich might well wring a scream from her.

"And would you say the Lady Cathryn is fat?" Ulrich countered, blocking her progress as she skirted the edge of the enclosure. "She and my lord dine daily at the banquet table of love and yet are not the worse for it."

With the mention of Cathryn, all thoughts of verbal byplay flew from her head and she turned to Ulrich with fear plainly visible in her eyes.

"You make mention of my lady, and I confess to

you that I have a fear for her well-being, Ulrich. Tell me true, has Lord William harmed her?"

Ulrich drew back in surprise and then in indignation; Marie was in grave error to cast a slur upon William, and he was quick to tell her so.

"William le Brouillard is the most chivalric and the most gallant of knights, whether on the continent or this rain-drenched isle! He would never harm any lady, and least of all his wife! He is a true Christian knight, Marie! But whence comes your concern? Do not tell me that you have seen him raise even the smallest finger of his hand to Lady Cathryn, for, as charmed by you as I am and always will be, I will not believe it."

"Nay," she admitted, "I have not seen him be anything but kind to her, yet—" she hesitated before darting into a shadowed corner—"yet I thought I did hear a scream coming from the chamber that they now share. Did you not hear it?"

Ulrich puffed his chest out to its full capacity and wore a smile of male pride as he answered, "Yea, I may have heard something like it."

"And she has not left the chamber though the sun is strong upon the sky. 'Tis unlike my lady," she muttered.

"You worry needlessly, Marie. There is naught amiss."

"So you say, but have you seen her?"

"Nay," he admitted. "Lord William has instructed me soundly that none should breach his door when he and his lady are closeted within."

That information did nothing to calm Marie's fears. They had just increased twofold, for why would a man secure his door when his lady lay within unless he intended to do her harm and wanted none to stay his hand?

"I do not know your lord well, Ulrich, but that does not ease my fears," she said.

Ulrich smiled, understanding her fear yet not able to stop himself from taking advantage of it.

"To ease your fears, I would suggest that we find ourselves a quiet corner where I may comfort you. I promise you that thoughts and worries of Lady Cathryn will fly from your head once you place yourself in my tender care."

On ground again both new and familiar, Marie trilled a laugh and moved off to the sunny center of the yard, enjoying the knowledge that Ulrich followed in her wake as certainly as the moon followed the sun. And so he did, wearing a smile as bright with promise as her own.

Cathryn awoke to the feeling of fingers running through the hair that framed her face. It was not unpleasant as an awakening. There was no confusion as to whose bed she was sharing, or where she was, or what had passed the night before: she remembered all with vivid clarity, though she had not yet opened her eyes to greet the day. And William.

She could scarce believe that any man could call forth such ringing pleasure with his hands; nor could she believe that a woman's body could experience such depth of feeling. She had believed, and had not been discouraged in believing, that the pleasure of sexual union belonged to the man and the pain of childbirth to the woman, as her price for the fall of man in his relationship with God the Father. So wrongly she had believed. So much did she yearn to feel William's hands upon her again, to feel his touch upon her breast and his tongue flicking against . . .

With a slow smile, she stretched her legs fully and her arms above her head, arching her breasts upward. She looked as languorous as a cat, though William would hardly have said so aloud. She looked like a woman well pleased, and he could not help smiling at her.

As he was smiling down on her, his look as washed of arrogance as he could make it, she flipped over and landed upon his stomach, wrapping her arms around his neck.

"You awoke me with your touch, my lord, and so I reply with a kiss, and another, and another. . . ." She giggled, kissing his face, his throat, his chest, and any and all parts of him she could reach with ease.

He was astounded. Cathryn was far now from the lady who surveyed all with an emotionless eye and a cool retort. She had been reborn last night as a woman who exuded a licking heat with her sultry smile and sent sparks of sensuality with every look from her dark and shining eyes. When he had breached her defenses, every last one of her defenses, he had hoped to soften her. He had had no thought as to the warmth and gaiety that lay beneath the ice.

Cathryn had not only been unleashed; she had been uncollared.

"And here is a kiss for bruising your Frankish

pride concerning the wealth of your portion." She kissed his ear, causing him to shiver. "And one for teasing you about your eating habits." She kissed his throat. "And for remarking upon your lack of humility." She kissed his furry chest. "And for being so slow in attending you at your bath. I fear I have much to apologize for in offending your tender, Frankish sensibilities, do I not?" In finale, she kissed her husband quickly on the mouth before moving down to settle comfortably upon his massive chest.

William ran his hands up and down Cathryn's back, enjoying the silken smoothness of her skin beneath his hands. She was transformed, and he was the man responsible for it; he had never been so pleased with both his effort and the result. She was more than he had dared hope for in a wife. He had little thought to find such warmth in the woman who had opened Greneforde's gate to him.

"Strange is the manner in which the English make amends for their misdeeds and thoughtlessly spoken words," he said, his gray eyes sparkling with reflected sunlight from the open wind hole. "In France, we render each apology with solemnity and grace, taking the time needed to truly heal the wound."

Cathryn laughed and rolled away from him to lie upon her own side of the bed. Crossing her arms behind her head, she stared at the ceiling and declared, "Short and sweetly to the point is the only way I know to apologize for deeds," and then added, "once thought to be misdeeds."

William rolled until his weight settled atop her,

his furred chest tickling her nipples to urgent life.

" 'Tis as I thought," he declared into her unrepentant face. "The English are too blunt in their manner, and you, wife, are my latest proof. Your culture is a strange one and in need of shoring up lest you sink back into barbarism. We French have been known to be so eloquent in our dialogue that our listeners are often rendered speechless."

"Perhaps, my lord—" she smiled widely—"they were not speechless, but instead unconscious?"

William braced his weight with bulging arms on either side of Cathryn's shoulders and looked down into her sparkling brown eyes with stern severity.

"And with those blunt and uncourtly words, you owe me another apology, wife, and I will have it in the Frankish fashion. And I do promise you," he said as his mouth descended upon hers, "you will stay awake for the whole of it."

The morn was far gone by the time Cathryn sat upon the stool plaiting her hair, not that she cared overmuch about her tardiness. Her time with William had been too sweetly spent to allow the time lost to curdle the rest of the day. She could live beneath the power and pleasure of his hands for the rest of her days and be glad for the opportunity, but there was no ignoring the duties that called to them both. It was with a light heart that she answered Marie's timid knock and ushered her in.

"Oh, Marie, I am glad that you have come. My hair is one long tangle and I need your gentle help in righting it," Cathryn said, smiling.

"Yea, certainly I will help," Marie answered

slowly, both relieved and confused, happy and surprised, to see Cathryn in such good health and buoyant spirits. It was far from what she had anticipated.

As Marie worked the comb through the tangles that ranged down Cathryn's back, she said, "I am relieved to see you this day. I was anxious when you did not arise with the dawn."

Cathryn smiled and ducked her head. "My sleep was disrupted last night and left me much fatigued. My lord . . . encouraged me to stay abed this morn. I did not think you would worry, but there was no cause."

"Yea, and so John told me when I asked him about it," Marie began, making steady progress with her lady's hair, "but when Ulrich told me that Lord William had forbidden him to enter this chamber when you were here together, I worried all the more, suspecting that he had, that he would . . ." Marie blushed and could not finish.

Cathryn lifted her head and stared wide-eyed into the fire. "What, in specific, gave you cause to worry?" she asked.

"Why, I thought I heard a woman cry out last night and swore the voice was yours, lady," Marie answered. "When I spoke of it to John and Ulrich, they admitted that they had heard such a scream as well, but when I questioned Lan, he said he had heard nothing, and Alys said she thought that she heard a high-pitched wail but would not describe it as a scream. Still," she continued, "I was sore afraid that harm had befallen you, but none who heard the sound would share the fear with me. I am glad that they were in the right and I in the wrong."

Cathryn's mouth hung open. They all had heard her! They had heard her cry out her killing pleasure when William had her spread out beneath his hands and tongue, bucking and writhing like a thing gone wild. . . . They all knew! All except Marie, who in her ignorance and her concern had spread the tale to all, including those who had not heard.

She would never leave this chamber again.

Never.

But that would make it worse, for then the tongues would truly fly concerning her and her scream . . . for it had been a scream, no cry, but a scream in full. She had been cast from a cliff, and a scream was warranted in such a circumstance. It was most reasonable, thinking back upon it, when at the time there had been no reasoning at all.

Marie had finished with her hair and was just tying the ribbons. She must be up and about her day. There was no choice in that. She could not hide for the rest of her days in this cold room, though she did most sincerely wish she could. No, that was a child's escape, and she was no child.

Especially after last night.

Cathryn drew her cloak of composure about her, and it was a cold, cold cloak now. It was most difficult to pull it up and most difficult to keep in place, but she must. She could in no way face them all without it; but it was a misery after the warmth and laughter William had shown her.

She left the chamber and descended the stairs

slowly, not knowing what she would face, expecting the worst—prepared for the worst.

The hall was busy, for it was almost time to sup, so late had she stayed abed. John saw her first and smiled in her direction. He did not come toward her at quickened pace or look at her with stricken eyes. That was good. Cathryn took a deeper breath and smiled in return.

Ulrich bowed toward her in courtly fashion and said, "Good morrow, Lady Cathryn. We dine again on boar, he was so big a beast, but Lan will tell no one in what manner he has been prepared. He is a most proud cook and most secretive of his art."

It was Ulrich at his normal best, in no way unusual. He had eyes for none but Marie, whom he trailed behind. And that was also usual of late.

And she saw Alys and Tybon and Christine and all whom she looked upon every day. All behaved toward her in a manner most right and normal, and she began to loosen the ties of the cloak she wore around her heart.

All was well. They would do naught to shame her. Mayhap they found nothing shameful about it, though when she thought upon that scream, that wail, that wailing and heart-stopping scream . . . well, she simply would not think about it. Cathryn thanked them quietly in her heart, glad they were so thoughtful as to pretend forgetfulness, knowing that they understood her silence for what it was and thanking them the more.

"Lady," John said, touching her elbow with friendly affection, "Lord William bade me tell you that he is meeting with the men of Greneforde in order to devise a plan of attack."

"A plan of attack? With whom? Against whom?" Cathryn asked in alarm. Surely William had knights enough of his own that he did not need to use Greneforde men, who were not trained as warriors.

" 'Tis an attack upon our poverty they speak of, Cathryn, and Lord William is a most aggressive foe. He has asked me to tell you that he will come to you at first opportunity, but that he must needs begin this action now, as the time is already past for the best beginning."

How it caused her heart to fold upon itself to hear that he would come to her and make haste in the doing. He had unleashed a warmth she scarcely could hold within herself without burning.

"Thank you, John." Cathryn smiled. "I shall be in the solar should he seek me. Nay," she amended, changing her mind, "please inform me when Lord William reenters the hall."

Collecting Marie from a very sad-eyed squire, Cathryn hurried to the solar. The acca called to her, and she was eager to see the crimson fabric draped upon her. She was eager to see William's face when he beheld her arrayed in it. She was eager to feel his hands caress her through the flaming cloth and feel his eager fingers plucking at the laces that bound her within it. Yes, she was eager for much.

"Hurry, Marie, for I would wear this before I am too old and fat, before I look like a scuttling beetle skittering across the floor, before I have gray to match my lord's eyes mixed in the yellow of my hair," Cathryn said, half in jest, half in anxiety.

"Before the sun has set," Marie added, understanding her lady's impatience.

"Yea." Cathryn laughed. " 'Tis so, for I am sick unto death of the faded gowns he has . . . that I have been wearing." She did not want to reveal so much to Marie; that she wanted William to look at her and see her at her best. That she wanted to be as beautiful to him as he was to her.

· But Marie knew anyway.

They made good progress, for they were both skilled with the needle. The body of the gown was complete and they were both now working on the sleeves. When the sleeves, good English sleeves, were finished, they would be added to the bodice. If Cathryn had her way, she would wear the scarlet acca on the morrow, but then, if she had had her way, she would have worn it to her wedding. But she had had her way in so little in this life that she was determined to have her way in this; that was why she drove Marie so hard and also drove herself.

She had finished her sleeve and was picking up the bodice when John called from the entrance to the solar, "He comes and he looks for you, lady!"

Cathryn looked up with a start, fought the flush that crept to her cheeks, all but threw the half-finished bliaut into Marie's hands, and rushed out of the solar.

She rushed headlong into William.

The delicious and familiar smell of him assailed her nostrils, and then his arms came around her to steady her. There they stayed and she stayed happily within them.

"My lord, I would have you instruct me," Cathryn

began, leaning back against his arms to look up at him. "Is it the proper fashion in France for a wife to greet her husband by rushing into his out-stretched arms?"

William smiled and bent to kiss the top of her head. "If it is not, it soon will be. You must know that I am a leader of fashion, not a follower."

"That I did already suspect," she answered, "though Ulrich has not been quick to follow your fashion lead in the matter of bathing."

" 'Tis my wife's bathing habits that most concern me."

"Ah—" Cathryn smiled—"that explains much."

"It should," he said, grinning.

"But come," she urged, laughing, eager to draw him away from such close proximity to the solar. She did not want William to know of the scarlet until he saw her in it. "I would hear of your plans for Greneforde and her hungry people."

"Their hunger will not last much longer," William said, allowing her to take his arm and lead him down the stairs to the great hall. "The seeds have been chosen and the planting will begin today, if the weather holds good, for some seeds will endure a late start in the year, even preferring it. That accomplished, we will see to new huts for all outside of Greneforde's wall. 'Twill take most of the winter, but they are eager to begin."

" 'Tis heavy work in cold weather," Cathryn commented.

"Yea, 'tis so, but their bellies will be full. We ride to the hunt daily and will distribute the meat evenly until the crops are in and Greneforde back to its former health."

She looked up at him as he spoke, knowing that he was remembering her words of Greneforde as it had been, knowing that he had heard her that day and was trying to give her back what she had lost. Again.

It was most unusual for the lord to share with all the bounty of the hunt, but she should not be surprised; William le Brouillard was unlike any man she had known. He was a man most generous, most beautiful. She could not take her eyes from him.

"You speak of riding to the hunt," she said as they entered the hall, "but I do not see your favorite companions at the hunt. Where are Rowland and Kendall? Do they dally in the yard?"

"Nay, and they had best not dally on the errand they have undertaken. They go to the king to tell him of our marriage."

"And to tell him the state of Greneforde," she added.

"Yea," William admitted, "I would have King Henry know that Greneforde is firmly in my grasp." And so saying, he wondered if his proud wife would feel rebellion rising within her at hearing him declare that her home was now his.

But Cathryn had never in the past begrudged him Greneforde and she did not now. Especially not now.

"Yea, he should know what you hold." And when William's hand crept down to rub the round contours of her derriere, she laughed. "Mayhap the king does not need to know *all* that you hold."

And, sensitive as they were to the moods of the other, William did not mention Lambert of Brent.

And Cathryn did not ask.

But he was ever in their thoughts.

Cathryn knew Lambert well and knew that he would not leave Greneforde, which he believed already his, without battle, however ruthlessly waged, that was why she had not felt secure even with him gone. That was why she had daily scanned the horizon, searching for the light of his fire and thankful when she had not seen it. But now William was here and lawful lord of Greneforde, and William had stated again and again that he would not relinquish his hold. They were words most comforting. Greneforde needed him, and now so did she.

William, not knowing Lambert but knowing men, understood that Lambert would not give up Greneforde without a fight. And from what he had learned of the man, it would not be a chivalrous fight but a fight of studied savagery. The thought did not cause even the blinking of an eye. William was ready, more than ready, to face the man who had beaten and raped Cathryn.

Yes, he was eager.

297

Chapter Sixteen

Lambert did not have far to travel when he left the
presence of the king to rejoin his companions. They
were waiting for him not far from the Tower of
Montfichet where the rivers Thames and Fleet
joined. They waited without a fire to warm them,
for they would have no unwelcome company join
them in their well-hidden place.

With a movement of underbrush the two rose as
one, hands pulling swords free of restraint. They
relaxed their posture when Lambert's face appeared.

"What says the king?" demanded Guichardet,
known as le Ebon for his long black hair.

"He says nothing of substance," Lambert replied,
removing his mufflers and tying up his horse.

"But you saw him," Guichardet pressed.

"Yea, both saw and spoke, laying my claim to

Greneforde as well as any foundation was ever laid. He will do nothing, decide nothing, until he sees le Brouillard. He gifted Greneforde to him for service well performed in times past. Le Brouillard must find another holding."

"Did you speak of the Cat?" Beuves of Girone asked with a sly smile.

"I did," Lambert answered. "And he did not like what I told him, yet he did not protest or deny the truth of it."

"Then he is certain of nothing," summed up Guichardet.

Lambert nodded, adding, "And he will not be until he speaks direct with le Brouillard."

"Then why allow this meeting to occur?"

"Yea, that is my thought," Lambert said, his blue eyes as cold as a winter sky.

"There are two ways to skin this cat," Beuves said, still smiling. "The king's messenger may meet some calamity and fail to deliver the summons; it has been known to happen, especially when one is traveling swiftly and without the usual caution. Or . . ."

"Or we can wait for le Brouillard to leave his safe enclosure and slice his throat before he reaches Henry," Lambert finished. "For myself, I prefer the latter."

"I have witnessed le Brouillard in battle," Guichardet offered. "He is no soft knight, but battle-hardened. It is not for singing pretty verse at the feet of Henry that he won Greneforde as his own."

"Greneforde is mine!" Lambert spit out. "And all that her walls encompass have I laid claim to."

He spoke of Cat and they all knew it. Beuves

smiled and sat upon a log. "You are eager to fight him."

"I would have Greneforde," Lambert said.

"You did have Greneforde. You left," Guichardet pointed out.

"But there would have been no keeping her without the king's consent," Lambert pointed out. "Henry is no Stephen."

"Nay, he is not, and William is no court dog to run from your stick," Guichardet said again.

"You think I fear to face him in knightly battle?" Lambert said, rising to his feet, his hand going to his sword hilt.

Guichardet said nothing. Lambert had never yet faced a man with sword unsheathed, knowing the result to be death. Lambert had killed, but not that way. Not with knightly honor.

Beuves rose from his perch and stepped to Lambert's side. "Guichardet speaks not of fear but of wisdom. Let us choose the path to Greneforde carefully."

"I have chosen," Lambert said, slowly releasing his sword. "To kill a messenger of the king would cast suspicion upon me. Henry knows I desire Greneforde. He knows I am aware of the messenger."

"And so he would suspect you if his messenger failed to return to court," Guichardet said.

"Aye, but when le Brouillard leaves his nest, he will fly onto my blade. A knight such as he must have many enemies who can be blamed."

" 'Tis easily said," Guichardet said grimly.

"And easily excused," Lambert retorted.

"Some deaths are harder to purchase than others," Guichardet pointed out.

"Yet I can meet its price and gladly. Killing le Brouillard will give me much satisfaction."

Beuves saw the shimmer in Lambert's eyes and knew he thought of the Cat he had trained to accept his hand, and he wondered if Greneforde would call to Lambert so loudly if Cat did not reside there.

"And when he is dead, how will you regain Greneforde?" There was no Philip now to buy them entrance, and most all the rogue knights that had followed Lambert had drifted off. It was as they said: Henry was no Stephen, and England was not such easy conquest as she once had been.

"By the king's command," Lambert declared. "Without le Brouillard to cry his ownership, King Henry will look more favorably upon me, as I already have ties there and a history." Though it would not help his cause if Henry looked too closely into that history. It would be coin well spent to make a second donation to the priest who had once shepherded Greneforde and who had proved so helpful in the past.

"Then we wait and watch," Beuves said, "and when the messenger is both come and gone, we wait with sterner purpose."

"Aye," agreed Lambert, "we wait for le Brouillard."

And when he was dead, Cat would be alone and vulnerable . . . again.

Though Rowland searched most diligently, he did not detect the faintest trace of Lambert between

Greneforde and the king, who, beyond all expectation, still resided in London. Kendall remarked that they were covering four times the ground they needed to find the king, but Rowland would not be moved from his course, nor would he discuss it. Knowing Rowland as he did, Kendall did not take offense at his silence, though he complained loudly that he would have taken his squire if he'd known they planned to tour England.

It was also beyond expectation that they were received into Henry's presence at once upon their arrival. After all, it was no message of great urgency that they carried. Kendall was delighted with the prompt hospitality shown them. Rowland drew down his black brows in foreboding.

The hall was closely packed upon their entering, and the play of light on the bright woolens and silks worn by the court shimmered in the weak winter light. Kendall made good use of the congestion to greet comrades not seen since he had departed for Greneforde with William. He enjoyed the crowds and the intrigue that was never far from a sovereign of such wealth as Henry of Anjou. The vivid coloration of fabric and jewel was a visual treat after the armored knights and ragtag villeins of Greneforde.

Rowland saw the crowded hall with different eyes; the courtiers looked, as they jostled and elbowed for position, like nothing so much as maggots feasting on rotting flesh. He did not waste his energy considering them. Rowland had eyes for none save Henry, but he did wonder why there was so much activity surrounding their arrival.

Edgar of Lisborne, a man of much experience

who had earned Rowland's hard-won trust, caught his eye and communicated with eloquent wordlessness that he should be prepared. Rowland took the warning to heart and approached King Henry cautiously. Not so Kendall.

"You have been expected," King Henry began.

That was so, Rowland reasoned, for the king would know that William would send him word of his taking of Greneforde, yet the hall buzzed with a feverish undertone.

"I do not see William," Henry finished.

"Nay, my lord, for he would not leave Greneforde vulnerable in this time of transition," Rowland said carefully.

"Aye, my lord king," Kendall added with a chuckle, " 'tis no easy matter to part a man and woman newly wedded."

The hall seemed a thing alive with bodies twisting to confer with neighbors and the sound of whispering barely contained. There was something amiss. Edgar's face warned of it even if the very strange behavior of the court had not. Rowland straightened his dark head and put his hand to his sword hilt.

"King Henry," he began, "William le Brouillard has secured Greneforde. The tower is sound and manned with knights loyal to you."

"And he has taken Cathryn of Greneforde to wife?" asked one of the councilors whom Rowland could not name.

Again Edgar's eyes warned him, though it was not necessary. Something was very much amiss here.

The weight with which each word fell upon the air was far too heavy.

"Yea," he said slowly and with great care. "They were married by Father Godfrey the day we did arrive."

"He acted with speed," Henry remarked, his hands folded and supporting his chin.

"My lord," Kendall said with a forced smile, for the crushing atmosphere had finally made an impression on his sturdy spirit, "any man would speedily claim such a beauty as Cathryn of Greneforde."

"As you say," Henry declared, straightening in his massive oaken chair. "Another has laid claim to Greneforde in your absence and has made a strong case for himself."

Rowland stepped nearer the king, ignoring all the flurry of talk and movement that swirled within the confines of the room.

"William is in firm possession of Greneforde, my lord," he announced in a voice unshakable.

"I do not find that difficult to believe," Henry admitted with a slight smile, "yet this other knight spoke quite explicitly of a prior claim."

"His name?" Rowland asked in a firm monotone.

"Lambert of Brent," Edgar supplied with a trace of eagerness. He was glad at heart to be able to supply the name of the man who threatened William's prize with sly manueverings.

Rowland stood unmoving and unshaken by this proclamation. Kendall was at a complete loss, but wise enough to hold his counsel and his tongue.

"Lambert's claim goes deep," the unknown councilor offered, "to the Lady Cathryn herself."

The titter that rose from the corners of the room was all that was needed to cause Kendall to gasp in shock and disbelief. Rowland did not move except to turn and face the councilor with all the blackness of his eyes. The man shrank back behind another and was silenced.

"Would William not prefer another holding?" Henry asked, not unkindly and blessedly to the point.

"Nay," Rowland answered confidently, his voice heard easily by the servants who hovered in the doorways. "William will not abandon Greneforde. He is well pleased with the king's gift."

"The marriage could be annulled. In the light of Lambert's claim . . ." Edgar prompted, giving Rowland another opportunity to stand for William and choke off the raging gossip that had fired the court since Lambert's arrival. Rowland understood the motive behind the question. Lambert had clearly made his claims in public; it would do William no good to have his position announced in private. That would only lead to misinformation and heightened gossip and further intrigue. No, the charge had been public and so would be the denial.

Kendall moved to stand with Rowland, his face uncertain. By God's Holy Word, he had not expected such a tale concerning William's chill wife. Would William not be better off in a new holding, one of thriving vitality, and with a pure wife? William deserved better than what he had been dealt, and it was most kind of the king to try to right the wrong. What was the matter with Rowland that he so doggedly chained William to Cathryn and Greneforde?

"William has developed a bond unbreakable with Greneforde," Rowland stated with elemental force, the power of his statement striking the far-off ceiling of this grand hall. He would not soil Cathryn's name by bandying it about this hall. Let the talk be of Greneforde and of Greneforde only. "William will not give up his claim."

King Henry, far from being displeased, glowed with pleasure at Rowland's response. William was a man, and a man did not hand over what he had fought for and won because the taking proved difficult. Rowland spoke for William, that he knew, that they all knew, but he would see William and hear his own affirmation as well. It would be the best way to silence the speculators and the gossips.

"Nor will he be forced to," Henry said, "but a messenger has been sent to hurry him to court, and I would hear from his own lips that he is well content with Greneforde."

The subject was closed.

Rowland and Kendall, their purpose served, turned and departed the charged atmosphere of the room with a will. Just outside the door, Eustace beckoned. He was a man past middle years with a face lined with the worry that came from frequenting the court. He was a good soul. Rowland knew him but slightly; nevertheless, he followed, with Kendall at his heels. They hardly knew who was friend and who was foe now, so it was best that they stay heel-to-toe until they returned to Greneforde. Greneforde called to them sharply; William had best know what had occurred at court. His rightful ownership of Greneforde was being questioned, and he would not take that threat lightly.

"Rowland, I know you to be hand to heart with William, so I offer you this warning," Eustace said without preamble, his eyes bright with worry. "This Lambert is no man to be trusted. He presented his case to unfriendly ears, and he is clever enough to know it. He also knows of the messenger being sent to Greneforde and that William must needs withdraw from the safety of the enclosure."

"What do you say, sir?" Kendall interjected, his eyes fierce. "Is there a plan to harm William?"

"I know not," Eustace admitted, "yet I know Lambert. William le Brouillard rides toward danger when he leaves Greneforde Tower."

Rowland clasped Eustace on the arm and said, "I thank you for the warning, and we will urge William to caution, but I must tell you"—he smiled in frigid anticipation—"I know William. It is Lambert who should be warned."

Chapter Seventeen

"Marie, slow down! I would wear a gown that falls smoothly without puckering."

"Aye, lady, but did you not just minutes ago urge me to greater speed?"

Cathryn smiled in apology and straightened on her stool to release the tension in her back. It was true. She was impossible in regard to the scarlet acca. It had to be perfect. It had to be finished. William had to find her irresistible in it. Quite a lot to demand of a single bliaut. Marie had convinced her to use the amber sarcenet as a mantle, and from there it was a short step to lining it with ermine. Cathryn was well aware that her fine costume, so close to completion, echoed the colors of her bridal ring. The connection had been intentional. She wanted to glow for William. She wanted him to be consumed with desire. And with love.

The Holding

He was very tender with her, loving and gentle and amusing, but he had told her time after time that he was a man who kept his vows, and he had made a vow to God concerning her. That was a comfort, surely, but ... she was not certain how much of his own heart was given to her.

He was a man who did right, no matter the cost or the reward; that she knew clearly, as did all who knew him long. He had an agreement with Henry that he felt bound to keep concerning Greneforde. He had sworn to love and protect her before God; such a vow was not taken or cast aside lightly. She should be content; nay, she should be well pleased with the man God and king had sent to her, and she was.

She was.

But did he love her of his own will and inclination? If he did not, she would never know it, for he was assiduous in protecting her from hurt, remembered or actual, teasing her until she laughed with giddiness, stroking and caressing her until she shouted out her blood-mad pleasure. He would never tell her if he did not truly love her for herself, because the knowing would rip at her, and he would never do anything to cause her pain. Yet the uncertainty was surely a pain of its own.

So she was set to win him, this husband who showed all signs of being already won. Yet she would be sure.

Marie did not look up from her task; it was entirely possible that Lady Cathryn would politely scold her for dawdling. Cathryn was not as she had been. She was still uncomplaining and brief of

309

speech—that had not changed—but she was more highly charged. Gone was the woman of cool and withdrawn composure. She had been supplanted by a woman of ready fire and a quick grin. And William le Brouillard had been the tinder to ignite her.

Oh, Marie knew well the signs; Cathryn was in love, and with her husband. That was far from a bad thing, yet . . . she lacked the calm center that had so clearly marked her before his coming. Marie had never seen her like this; she was so changed. John remembered well the time before the death and departure of her parents and assured Marie that this new Cathryn was closer to the woman that God had fashioned her to be. Still . . . she did not think her lady happy, truly happy, in her love.

Ah, she was a fool. Did she not know, and from her own experience, both the pleasure and pain of love? Ulrich even now hurried through his tasks to steal time to court her—a light courting to be sure, but a pleasant one for all that. She bent her head closer to her task. If she could just finish this seam, the bliaut would be complete and whole, and Cathryn would rush to her chamber to try it on, and then she could slip down and saunter by Ulrich and then—

"Marie, you look flushed," Cathryn noted with gentle concern.

"Nay, lady," she denied, "but I am finished." Lifting the scarlet from her lap, she displayed it across her arms.

It glowed and sparkled hotly in the warm light of

the solar. Cathryn reached out eager hands to clasp it to her. Such was the effect it had on her; she never could keep her hands away from it. With God's goodwill, it would have the same effect on William while she was sheathed in it.

"Think you I have time to try it before my lord returns from the fields?" Cathryn asked with dark eyes shining.

"Yea, Lady Cathryn," Marie encouraged. "If you hurry."

It was all the prompting that she needed. William had already brought back a doe and four pheasants from his morning's hunt, which Lan had accepted with his usual high humor. William then had joined the men of Greneforde in clearing the distant fields of their wild seedlings. He would be hungry and fatigued at the meal after his full day. He more than deserved a visual treat for all his pains. Her heart hammered at the thought, sending its beat to heat the apex of her thighs. She bolted up from her stool, her newly fashioned finery draped carefully across her arms, and rushed to her chamber.

Marie watched Cathryn leave with blue eyes twinkling, sitting as still and quiet as a hare on her stool until she was alone in the solar. Then she, too, bolted for the door and rushed down the stairs at a pace that would have shamed Ulrich. At this time of day he was usually at the quintain. . . .

Cathryn was ripping at her laces, eyeing the scarlet acca with its amber mantle of sarcenet and ermine draped across the bed, when she stopped. She was a poor wife to see to her own pleasure when she knew that the men, her husband included, were

311

laboring in the frozen earth and would soon come to have their hunger appeased. The acca would wait. The meal would not.

Hurriedly tugging at her laces, quietly mouthing a plague on Marie that she was not near to aid her, Cathryn donned her old mantle of brown wool to cover the white bliaut she wore and rushed down the stairs. In truth, she was becoming as bad as Ulrich about rushing up and down this tower. Where was the stately step that had marked her passage a week ago? Gone, she answered herself with a grin, and William was the thief.

She dashed across the courtyard at a brisk walk and darted inside the kitchen. The warmth and smells of the room were heady after the cold of the open air. All heads turned to her as she entered. Clearly she was unexpected.

"John, did you remember to add honey to—"

"Yea, lady." He smiled, cutting her off. "The honey, the pudding, the pasties, the venison, the hot pepper sauce, the pheasant, the hares that Ulrich snagged this morn—all are near ready and all prepared most deliciously."

At her crestfallen appearance, John added, "We each have our duties, Lady Cathryn, and are well able to perform them. The meal will please you . . . and Lord William," he added with a smile.

"Lady," Lan called as he turned the venison on the spit, "if you seek to occupy your hands, I would give you my place at the fire."

"And what would occupy you then?" Alys asked, stirring the pepper sauce.

"Why, the stool would occupy the bulk of my bottom, or my bottom, the stool. 'Tis no matter; I would be well and happily occupied."

"Aye, I catch your meaning," Alys said seriously, "and would add that my arm tires of stirring and would seek other occupation. That of thwacking a head that has grown too big on a steady diet of meat!"

Christine laughed, as did John and Cathryn, to see Alys walk with heavy and purposeful step toward the fire and Lan, her long spoon held threateningly aloft.

"They need me no longer, John," Cathryn observed quietly.

"Lady," he answered softly, "they need you, but in not so urgent or desperate a manner. If you find yourself at a loss for something to occupy your time until the meal, a bath should be waiting in your chamber for Lord William. If you are quick, you might make use of the water first."

"Thank you, John." Cathryn smiled with tender sincerity and rushed away from them as quickly as she had come.

" 'Tis well you told her of the bath," Christine commented. "She will want to look her best when she first wears the scarlet bliaut that has eaten the hours of her waking these past days."

They all nodded heartily at that. There was none who did not know of Cathryn's fervor over the scarlet and her hurry to fashion for herself a costume worthy of her beauty—none except her husband.

The knights in the yard slowed in their practice to watch Cathryn run with light steps across the dirt. They slowed to watch her whenever she passed. She was a beautiful woman. She was so obviously in love with William. For both reasons, she was a pleasure to see. The word from Ulrich was that she would wear the scarlet today. It was high time. They had waited for nearly a week to see her in it and to see William's reaction to her in it. They anticipated the meal with more than usual eagerness.

Cathryn was across the yard and up the stair tower at such a brisk pace that she would wager Ulrich would be fairly winded to keep up with her. It was a simple matter to remove her bliaut; she had hardly managed to fasten it before, and it slipped easily from her now. The scarlet glimmered on the bed, and she brushed her hand against it just once before hiding it away in her chest and sinking into the water.

It was well that she hid it. No sooner had she soaped herself with the scent that William preferred than he entered the stair tower. He made no noise or shout, but she knew that he was near. She could not explain this sense she had of his nearness; perhaps it had always been so and she had buried it as she had buried so much else within her. Something else she knew: she knew that he sought her. He always sought her out upon returning. He always found her.

The curtain at the door trembled as he entered the chamber they shared. He did not look upset that she had stolen his bath, the bath that awaited him each day before he supped. He did not look angry in the least. William walked across the floor as quietly as he had mounted the stair, stripping the clothes from his body as he came. Cathryn waited, her eyes dark and huge in the smallness of her face.

His mantle was the first to be discarded. William let it fall to the floor—quite unlike him. His hands were dirty, the dark soil of Greneforde sticking to him, as he pulled his tunic up and over his head. For a moment it looked almost like a banner waving in his hand before it, too, fell to the floor.

Cathryn sat straighter in the water, letting her breasts rise above the waterline. The water trickled away from the mounds slowly, almost reluctantly, to lap against her narrow rib cage and form a clear table on which the fruit that was her bosom was displayed for his pleasure.

William, his gray eyes as dark as storm clouds, kicked his boots into a corner of the room and slid down his hose with some difficulty, as the sword of his passion was largely in the way.

He stood over her. She felt quite small against his size. A tremor of passion swept through her at the look in his black-fringed eyes, and she relished every delicate beat of it.

" 'He who finds a wife finds a good thing, and obtains favor from the Lord,' " he murmured huskily.

So he would quote God's word to her? This time she was prepared.

" 'I am my beloved's and his desire is for me,' " Cathryn answered with a sultry smile.

William's surprise was reflected on his face. It was a very sweet moment, and she had Father Godfrey and his patient tutelage to thank for it. If she was going to live with a man who quoted Holy Writ,

315

then she had better prepare herself against the day when he might be tempted to use his knowledge and her lack of it for his own gain. She hardly thought him capable of it, but then, he was a man. And French.

"Father Godfrey?" William asked as he reached for the fruit she so temptingly offered.

"Father Godfrey," she answered, arching toward his hand.

" 'An excellent wife, who can find?' " William challenged, caressing her face with his hand. " 'For her worth is far above jewels. The heart of her husband trusts in her and he will have no lack of gain.' "

He trusted her. Sweet, sweet words from a man so wronged with an impure wife. How much vengeance he had denied himself to so accept her. She would never cease to be grateful for his merciful compassion toward her. She would never cease to want him.

" 'His mouth is full of sweetness. And he is wholly desirable,' " Cathryn quoted, pulling him down to her, kissing his throat and his jaw until she felt a tremor of passion pass through him.

"Cathryn, wait," William said in a throaty whisper. She was undoing him with her words and with her touch.

" 'May he kiss me with the kisses of his mouth!' " she said against the curl of his ear, his black hair brushing against her face. " 'For your love is better than wine.' " Her hand trailed down his torso to the pulsing evidence of his arousal. With gentle fingers, she rubbed the tip, as he rubbed the turgid thrust of her nipple.

With near savage force, he plunged his tongue into her mouth with all the thrusting beat he longed to visit elsewhere on her body. She would not relent in her attack upon his senses; she traced the length of him to cup the sac beneath and then ran both hands down the column of one leg, pulling him down to her with ever-increasing force and urgency.

"Cathryn," he whispered, his eyes alight with a holy fire.

"William," she answered with a smile, her voice seductively low, "I wait for thee."

With a laugh that was more a bark, he answered, "Then wait no longer."

William lifted his wife from her bath. He did not take her to the bed. He sat himself down and sat her atop him, her knees drawn up to his chest, the water sloshing over the sides of the small tub. It was a most odd position. But it worked.

She should have known that William le Brouillard would not relinquish his daily bath.

William loved the scarlet on her. He loved it so much that she had some difficulty keeping it on.

Cathryn could not have been more pleased.

It had taken voices of complaint raised to a near shout from the hall below, voices weakening from lack of food, or so it was claimed, to rouse them from their chamber and propel them below. The men who followed William and the people who served Greneforde stopped all activity to watch them enter. They had waited long to see her in the scarlet acca, and not a man or woman present felt the wait had been in vain.

Cathryn glowed in her scarlet and amber as brightly as a torch that fit one hand only, the hand of the man who held her elbow softly as he led her to the high table. They seemed of a piece, Greneforde's new lord and his lady, as if woven from a single thread, and woe to the man who dared raise a knife to cut them in twain.

William wore his bridal finery of white samite and gray to compliment Cathryn's brilliance, the ruby at his shoulder glowing hotly in the flickering light of the hall. They looked as they should have on the day of their marriage, clothed in richness and suffused with contentment at their state. William presented an image of cool strength to Cathryn's surging warmth as they moved through the hall. In some way common only to the married, they had changed positions.

William would always be courtly in his ways, that would not change, but there was something more guarded in his manner, as if the walls of his personal defenses had been raised to a more forbidding height. His gray eyes were pleasant as he surveyed the hall and his hand light upon Cathryn's arm, but his manner was one of battle readiness and tightly harnessed caution.

Cathryn seemed not aware of any change in her husband, the change in herself so overwhelmed her. Gone was the woman of cool regard and icy stillness. She looked upon the throng awaiting them with a smile teasing the corners of her mouth and her dark eyes shining merrily; she was amused by them and their faces of expectation. She was amused and confident and secure in all things of late. William was warm, very warm, toward her; he more than liked her in the scarlet, and the world was once again the safe place it had been before the death of her mother and the departure of her father. And if anyone heard a cry coming from the lord's chamber in the night, she would not hide her head in shame; rather, she would need to struggle to hide her smile of supreme satisfaction. Yes, William was pleased with her efforts on his behalf; the fact that they had delayed the serving of the meal by an hour was the clearest testimony to how well pleased he was.

It was a happy meal with smiles all around, and made happier still by the return of Rowland and Kendall.

"The sojourners return!" William called in greeting, beckoning them to the table with a wave of his hand. "Sit and eat and relate to me the success of your journey."

Rowland knew well that William spoke only of their reaching Henry; the news, or lack of it, concerning Lambert's whereabouts would wait for a room that housed fewer ears. But there was more to tell concerning William's hold on Greneforde than William knew.

"Our thanks," Rowland said simply.

William waited for Rowland, or Kendall at the very least—for who could muzzle him?—to relate that they had reached the king and told him that Greneforde was safe in his possession. Rowland's black eyes over the rim of his cup told him much.

319

Kendall's silence told him the rest. None but the most disastrous news could subdue Kendall.

William cast his eyes toward Cathryn, knowing that she sensed the disharmony and willing her not to. In vain. She was aware of the changed atmosphere as a bird is aware of a coming storm. Clasping one of the hands that she held so tightly in her lap, William lifted it to the table and caressed it there, in plain sight of all. Whatever would come, they would face together. Never again would he allow her to retreat into the cocoon that had sheathed her for so long, no matter how she longed to fly there. His winning of her warmth had been a battle too long waged to relinquish even one foot of ground, and though he feared the effect Rowland's words would have on her, he would not run from them. Nor would he allow her to run.

"You found Henry?" William asked bluntly, unwilling to delay the inevitable with pointless parrying.

"Aye, William," Rowland answered. "Henry was found."

And Lambert was not, William guessed, stroking with gentle familiarity the softness of Cathryn's hand.

"You were gone long," William commented, reaching for his cup. "Had he traveled far afield from London?"

"Nay, he was in London still, against all expectation, for we covered the leagues between here and there as does the wolf seeking prey, crisscrossing our own tracks," Kendall supplied, annoyance clear in his voice.

Rowland kept his dark eyes firmly on the plate in front of him; there was no need to explain this method of travel to William. His purpose would be well understood. But not what had been found; that William would not understand unless it was spelled out for him, and that Rowland was not willing to do in the presence of William's lady. Not so Kendall.

Kendall had hardly turned his gaze from Cathryn since entering the hall. She was different. He did not know if she was different in fact or only because he saw her with different eyes. Cathryn of Greneforde glowed with suppressed sensuality; her beauty was a beacon fire that was fueled by the lustrous garments that sheathed her. He could well believe, looking at her now, that she had lain with a man not her husband.

She was not fit for William le Brouillard.

"The king ushered us into his chamber as soon as our feet touched the earth," Kendall said.

"You received a warm welcome," William noted.

Kendall smiled coldly. "Nay, not warm, only quick."

Rowland cast a darkly forbidding glance at Kendall and then at William, his eyes beseeching. William returned the look with flinty eyes and raised Cathryn's fingers to his mouth for a chivalrous kiss. She shivered noticeably and reached with her free hand for her wine. William did not stop her.

For all his warmth of expression toward his wife, his manner was as cold as Rowland had ever seen it. William was set for mortal battle, and if Kendall did not watch his tongue, he would feel the force of William's outrage to the full.

Kendall, too immersed in his own outrage, did not note William's.

"Drink, Kendall; your journey has been long," William commanded. "There is time to tell of your audience with King Henry. We are just at the first course."

Kendall obeyed, reluctantly, and while his mouth was thus engaged, Rowland spoke.

"The king was most eager to hear of your possession of Greneforde."

"And most pleased?" William asked with cool detachment.

Kendall plunked his goblet down with force, spilling some of the wine on the cloth. "Nay, for there—"

"Drink, Kendall!" Rowland ordered in a voice quite unlike him.

Startled, Kendall was silenced. But he did not drink.

"You informed Henry that Greneforde is mine?" William asked, his eyes glinting with silver sparks.

"Yea," Rowland answered simply, willing to let William control the conversation. Willing Kendall out of it.

"He knows that Cathryn is mine?"

Cathryn's shivering diminished upon those forcefully spoken words. Could aught harm her if she was so firmly William's? No, for he had delivered her from the black pit of her sin with his tender devotion; none could harm her, and she knew that none could take her from him. Unless it was the king.

"He was told of your marriage," Rowland answered precisely. Too precisely.

"And his reaction to this news that his orders had been carried out to the letter?" William pressed.

"Another has laid claim to Greneforde," Kendall blurted out, his eyes alighting on Cathryn, "and Greneforde's lady."

William kissed Cathryn's hand again with all the tenderness and intimacy of the bedchamber, breathing his warmth into the heart of her hand. He held her eyes with his own as he asked, "Who has dared to claim my lady?"

"Lambert of Brent," Kendall said with some satisfaction, watching Cathryn for her reaction.

He was disappointed, for all he saw was the Cathryn that he had always seen: a cold woman, icy in her manner, distant in her bearing. The doors of her warmth slammed shut with the mention of Lambert. She was no more William's wife; she was Cathryn of Greneforde, and the possession of either was in dispute.

The next course was forgotten in the hall as all eyes watched the play of emotion at the high table. Cathyrn in her icy majesty was well known to them, and they all, Marie included, sorrowed at her return. Rowland, so quiet, looked at William with eyes so large and so black that they seemed unfathomable. And William. They had never seen him so. He was as quiet as the mist. There was no shout from his lips, no cry of denial or rage, no demands or questions. He was as chill as the winter dawn, as still as the frozen lake; he was a warrior. And he was seeking his adversary.

"Greneforde is mine," he stated with whispered force. "Cathryn is mine. There are no other claims."

Kendall, finally, sensed that he had misstepped and was silent.

"The king would hear you say it, though I said the same in your name at court," Rowland said softly. "The king has summoned you."

"Then he shall see me and hear me repeat what has already been declared. I will not relinquish what I hold," William said calmly, squeezing Cathryn's chill hand as he looked out on the faces of the people in the hall. It was a vow, a promise, to them all. He would not leave her or them. He would return when this threat against his possession had been canceled.

"The king waits in London. It would be best to leave quickly," Rowland suggested.

"Yea, I will depart on the morrow. I would have this settled," William agreed.

"Besides myself, who travels with you?" Rowland asked.

William stopped his measured stroking of Cathryn's hand to give Rowland his full attention. He understood the unspoken warning. William needed no escort to the king, unless some treachery was afoot. *Lambert* . . .

The undercurrents at the table swirled around Cathryn until she thought she would choke on her own breath. Ever since Kendall had voiced the name of Lambert, a chill had descended upon the room, seeping into her bones and her heart until she wondered if she would shake in its icy grip forever. *Lambert*. She could feel his hands upon her still, feel his weight pressed upon her, feel the licking unease that writhed through the hall at the mention of his name. He was here again, though William had banished him.

He was here.

Standing abruptly, Cathryn started to move away from the table. She looked down in stunned surprise to see that William's hand still held hers and that she had reached the end of the tether that was his arm.

"I will go and see what has delayed the meal," she informed him calmly. "Continue, my lord."

He released her regretfully, but there was much that Rowland had to tell him, and it was clear that he would not do so with Cathryn present. When she had looked into his eyes, he had not seen her within their velvet depths; he had seen only himself in distorted reflection. Cathryn was closed to him. As closed and chill as she had been upon their first meeting. Lambert was the door that barred her upon herself, away from him.

Lambert had much to answer for.

All eyes watched her as she walked the length of the hall, the shimmering scarlet acca skimming the curves of her body to froth at her feet. All eyes watched her, and she felt marked by the red, marked in a way not pleasing, not flattering. Yes, she was marked. She longed to rip it off.

Father Godfrey would have helped her in her frozen distress; he would have had the words to soften her spirit, but Father Godfrey was gone, gone with two of William's men to search the area for those who did not know of William's coming and who might have need of a priest, for with Greneforde's priest gone these last months it had been a hard time for all. No masses had been read, no confessions heard, and if there had been a death . . . then that man or woman had gone to face Almighty God unconfessed and unshriven. As Philip had gone.

Father Godfrey was gone; there was no use in running to the chapel, for it would be cold and deserted. But Lambert was here and he was everywhere, in every corner, in the stair tower, in the yard as she raced across it to the warmth of the kitchen—a kitchen that would hold no warmth for her because Lambert was here again, and with Lambert, there was no escape.

The men at the high table watched Cathryn leave in utter silence. When she had passed into the stair tower, Kendall spoke, his resolve to save William from his disastrous match renewed.

"Lambert had been at court, William. It was as plain as sun on sea, the nature of his claim on Greneforde."

William looked at Kendall fully for the first time since he had entered the hall, and Kendall sat back sharply at the steely expression in William's silver eyes.

"Are you saying that Lambert spoke of my wife in open court?"

Kendall swallowed heavily; this was not going well. He only wanted William to get what he deserved, and no man deserved a wife soiled at another's hand. It was possible that William did not know what had transpired between Cathryn and

Lambert. Surely if he knew, he would distance himself from her.

"Aye, he was there before us and sang loud and sweet concerning her. His claim is solid. None disputed him," Kendall answered.

"He made for court when he left here, William," Rowland supplied softly, "to lay his claim firmly with the king. It is my guess that he did not know that Greneforde had already been pledged to you."

"But he does now." William smiled slightly in predatory anticipation.

"He does now," Rowland agreed.

"William," Kendall blurted, leaning closer, "an annulment has been suggested . . . the king would not stand against it . . . no one would say a word against you for leaving such a . . . such a"—he clearly had trouble finding a word to express his disgust and finally settled on—"holding."

Rowland, shaking his head ruefully at Kendall's blind insistence on a course that William would sooner die than follow, leaned back, well out of the way.

"An annulment?" William said low, turning again to Kendall.

"Yea," Kendall answered readily, leaning closer still. "Then you would be free to seek a richer holding sporting a cleaner wife. William, the king will give you his finest!"

"His finest," William repeated softly, and then with quiet force, he turned the power of his impaling eyes upon his comrade. Kendall was struck immobile at the raw power he saw there. "King Henry offers me the chance to bleed the blood from my body."

Kendall could only stare uncomprehendingly into William's gray eyes. He had lost the power of speech.

"You do not understand?" William prodded. "Cathryn's blood and mine are commingled until death separates us, and only God shall decide the hour of our parting."

William leaned closer to Kendall in so menacing a way that if Kendall had been able to move, he would have, but William's eyes held him still.

"Our lives are one," he declared, his voice rising. "Our bodies are one. She is the blood running through every part of me, and I pray daily that I am so to her."

Leaning back in his chair, William looked away from Kendall, whereupon Kendall took his first breath in more than a minute. It was a shaky breath, but William had not finished.

"The Germans have a saying," he began almost conversationally, " 'blood is thicker than water.' Lambert was the water." Looking again at Kendall, his eyes as dark as charcoal, he said hoarsely, "I am the blood."

Kendall, stricken, fell to his knees at William's feet. He was truly contrite. He had no knowledge of such depth of devotion as this that William showed to his wayward wife.

"I ask your pardon, Lord William, and will remain on my knees until I receive it."

William, his mind already on other, more urgent matters, tapped him lightly on the shoulder. "Then rise and be pardoned, but talk to me no more of my wife."

"Who travels with you, William?" Rowland asked again.

"Who would obey me if I ordered them to stay?" William rejoined.

"Not I," Rowland quipped.

" 'Tis so, but all others will," William said, "and all others will stay."

"You will not set the hounds upon him?"

"Nay"—William smiled—"I will come upon him quietly. I would have him caught unprepared."

"You would not share him," Rowland observed astutely.

"Nay, I would not," he agreed pleasantly.

"He knows a messenger was sent," Kendall added.

"Sent and not yet come," William observed. "We have the advantage. He does not know that I know."

"So you leave before the messenger. . . ."

"And catch him waiting for me with one eye closed," William finished.

"You think Lambert waits for you to leave Greneforde?" Kendall asked, not keeping pace with this rapid conversation.

"I know he waits," William answered.

"But . . ." Kendall began, his brows furrowed in thought.

"I know he waits, just as I would wait, for a chance at Greneforde again. And now I am off to enjoy my wife's company before I must depart. Rowland, be ready to leave the hour before dawn," was his final instruction before he slipped out of his chair and across the hall, his mantle floating behind as silently as wind-driven fog. Kendall watched him leave with his mouth agape.

"I never suspected that he would want to keep her, knowing what he now knows about her," he murmured half to himself, half to Rowland. "She has been with another."

Rowland leaned forward on his seat and reached for his wine. He took a long, full swallow before turning to glance sidelong at Kendall.

"Yea, she has," he said.

Kendall looked into the face of the older man with something like awe. "William is truly a man of Christ that he can forgive such a betrayal. I have never known a man to forgive so much; 'tis godlike."

Rowland took another long swallow, Kendall's words turning in his mind like twirling knives until he could endure no more. It was time Kendall became more fully a man.

"Cathryn of Greneforde was used by a ruthless man when he illegally occupied her tower," he said with blunt force, ignoring the look of shock that crossed Kendall's features. "During his occupation, she saw her half-grown brother brutally murdered at this man's hand. She submitted herself to him and, in doing so, kept all under her care free from harm." Rowland took another swallow. It went down heavily. "What is more, she gave no thought to the hurt she endured in their stead. She gave of herself with an open hand. Now"—he paused and pinned Kendall with his dark eyes—"should William love her the less for it?"

"Nay," Kendall whispered, the images rolling

through his mind with the force of the surf. "He should love her the more."

Rowland reached over to cuff Kendall with all the gentleness of a mother bear with her cub. "And so he does."

Chapter Eighteen

When William came upon her in the chamber they shared, she was shrugging off the scarlet acca, the amber mantle already buried within her chest. She did not turn to face him as he entered. She did not smile in greeting. Her mood was low. He had known it would be. She had assumed the mien of the woman who had greeted him on that first day with all the slender and cold strength of a sword blade; the Cathryn he had freed from the bondage of abuse and chilling guilt had walked back into her prison at the mere mention of the name of her jailer. Her prison offered one thing that he did not: familiarity. Familiarity could be a warm companion—this he knew firsthand—but he could not allow her to sink back into the icy tomb of total and frigid control, a control that held together the broken shards of her heart. He had sworn to save her, and he must. He must, for he had not saved Margret. He must because he loved Cathryn with a love deeper than the pain of failing Margret in her broken and bleeding innocence. The thought, both new and familiar at once, filtered through his mind. He had sworn to love her from the beginning, and he was a man of his word, but now . . . now he loved her. He did not love her because of his vow. He did not love her because of Greneforde. William did not know how long this had been so; he knew only that his love for her was not new, only the knowledge of it.

William smiled at Cathryn with gentle affection and teased, "You remove the scarlet? I loved you in it."

She had heard him enter. She was becoming accustomed to his near-silent arrivals and departures; and more, she could sense his nearness. But Lambert was nearer. Lambert was in her head and she could not drive him out. Lambert had invaded again, invaded and conquered her innermost thoughts, and though it was not a physical invasion, still it was complete and he was immovable. He had gone to the king to claim Greneforde, claiming her. He would be back. She saw his pale blue eyes so clearly, felt his damp and fleshy hands upon her breasts, heard his voice speaking to her with amused condescension; she heard him call her Cat, and she trembled as if from the cold. But it was not cold. It was Lambert.

Cathryn folded the scarlet, her hands moving swiftly over the rich fabric, and packed it into her chest. It was a cloth too richly colored for her. It was not for her.

"I am more comfortable in my old bliaut," she answered coolly, not adding that she also felt less conspicuous.

The talk of Lambert had shaken her, and with good cause. She was the object in a deadly game and she had no defenses; nay, she had one: William. He would stand for her; he would convince her of it, but it would be done lightheartedly, for Cathryn's spirit could take no more battering this day.

"I love you in the scarlet," he said mildly, moving to kindle the fire in the hearth, "but then I love you better out of it." And he stood abruptly, stalking her with a comical leer. Instinctively she backed away from him, wearing nothing but her shift.

In spite of her heaviness of spirit, he cheered her. Cathryn smiled and answered, "As much as I would love to have you love me better, I draw the line at going about unclothed."

" 'Tis a moot point," he rejoined, catching her and kissing her lightly on the nose. "I do not believe I could love you any better."

The heaviness of her heart at hearing those casually spoken words threatened to crush her. He did not love her. He had never claimed to. He held her as wife and he would not relinquish her, at least not easily, but he did not love her. Oh, he spoke of love in his teasing way, but it was just his way, a word he used lightly. After all, he was French, and they looked at these things with a different eye. She understood. With her emotions suppressed, Cathryn slipped on an old bliaut of bister; what cared she that the color was heavy and dull? It matched her mood. It was a most perfect gown for her.

"I understand," she answered William softly, turning from him to leave the chamber.

"Do you, wife?" he asked, barring her passage. She understood so little. That would change—and now.

"To love you better, I would not slumber so that I could watch you sleep through the night, watch you as you sleep with your hand beneath your cheek and your hair tangled around your throat."

Cathryn started and looked into her husband's eyes. They were the color of wood smoke as it reached for the night sky.

"To love you better," he continued quietly, "I would not travel more than two leagues distant for the ache being away from you brings, though I must find meat to fill your rumbling belly and to fatten your war-starved frame."

Tears filled her eyes and she blinked them away, but it would not work, for they just as quickly filled again, and she saw him through a watery haze.

"To love you better, I would travel to the king with all speed so that I may the sooner tell him that I will not, cannot, be parted from you, my wife, my very life's blood, except by God's own express will."

And now she saw—or thought she saw—William clearly, and the love that poured from him seared her, cauterizing whatever wounds remained. Lambert disappeared in the flame and smoke of William's love as though he had never been. She was clean. William's love had washed her, as he had promised it would.

"I would sooner die than relinquish you, Cathryn," William whispered. "Nay, wife, I cannot love you any better." And brushing back a stray tendril of her golden hair, he added, "But do you ask it, I will try."

She had no words to match his, this man of such eloquence. She had no words that would survive the throbbing passion of her heart and the tears that drowned her cheeks. With a sob, she rushed into his arms, crying out her love, her passion, her gratitude for such a love as his. Crying, crying into the strength of him, her sobs choking her as they ripped up from her soul to beat against his loving strength. William held her hard against him, not permitting even the force of her cries to tear her from his grasp.

Marie, having come to comfort Cathryn over the ordeal at the dinner table, stood listening at the door. She turned away, the tears magnifying the intensity of her blue eyes before coursing down her face.

Chapter Nineteen

At the hour before dawn William and Cathryn walked together into the yard. William wore his mail and gray surcoat; he was a study in gray, almost invisible in the dim and foggy light of the pre-dawn hour. Cathryn, also, was dressed for traveling. She wore a heavy woolen bliaut of burnet, the rich brown as dark as the earth itself, and a mantle of lighter brown. At her waist she wore a jeweled knife, a gift from her husband, and she fingered it lightly as they walked to the horses. Not expecting her, they were one mount short.

Or so they thought.

"You travel with William?" Kendall burst out in surprise at seeing her.

"Yea, she travels with me," William answered for her. "A man so soon wed should not be expected to depart from his bride. Cathryn stays with me," he finished with pleasant firmness.

"The way may not be easy," Rowland murmured seriously, his mind awash with the memory of his Lubias at the sight of Cathryn standing so resolutely by her lord's side.

"No way is easy, comrade," William said gently. "The Lord God has taught me that time and again, but Cathryn has asked to stay with me. I cannot refuse her. In truth, I have little inclination to."

"Lambert waits," Rowland said in a near whisper, turning his face from Cathryn's so that she would not hear him.

"She knows it well, Rowland, mayhap better than we. 'Tis why she is in mortal fear of staying at Greneforde, 'twould be too similar to that other time. I can protect her better than Greneforde's walls; this I know and this she believes. I will not leave her," he finished.

Rowland looked deeply into William's silver eyes; he saw that William would not leave her. As he had not been able to leave Lubias. Even knowing the end, would he have ridden away to leave her in the relative safety of the town? No, he would not, for he could not leave her, such was her love and his weakness.

"Then do not," Rowland said solemnly, "but know that I ride at your back, now as always. She will be well protected." And his dark eyes swore the truth of it.

William clasped the arm of his blood friend in quick embrace and smiled. "Knowing you ride with me made it a simple thing to grant Cathryn's request, but you, Kendall," William continued, his voice rising as he parted from Rowland, "you shall stay at Greneforde and see to her defenses. Your hide will be forfeit if you burn her down in my absence!"

"She shall not burn, William," Kendall answered with his own smile. "But you may return to find the rest of the west field planted, and then I will expect due compensation for dirtying my hands at field labor."

"Nay, Kendall," William contradicted. "Do not leave the enclosure until we return and bring news of our success. Open the tower gate for no man, be he walking or riding, if he is not well known to you. I must know that Greneforde is secure."

"Aye, William," Kendall readily agreed, all the humor wiped clean from his face. William left him in charge of his legacy. He would not fail him. "You shall return to a holding worthy of you."

William smiled and fit his hands into his mufflers. "I would be content to return to the holding gifted me. I am not sure but that I would ride by a holding that was worthy of me, thinking it the bishop's new tower."

And as Kendall and Rowland laughed at William's latest vanity, knowing full well that he sported expressly to lighten the seriousness of his ride to the king, Cathryn spoke in like manner to Marie.

"Nay, it has been decided," she said again and for the final time. "I ride with my lord and you remain within Greneforde's walls."

"But lady, there is danger without. I would be with you," Marie pleaded.

"Marie, I will be safe with him," Cathryn said with all the confidence of a woman in love, "but would not ask too much of him. What man, no matter his merit, can handle two women?" Smiling at her joke, cajoling Marie into smiling with her, Cathryn said more seriously, "I would know you are safe, and it will be easier for me if I have only myself to worry over. Do you comprehend?"

And in a flash of understanding, she did. Lady Cathryn had endured much, sacrificed much, to protect her. An image of being hustled into an open chest before Lambert came bursting through the door rushed upon her, causing her to live that day again. How much easier would it have been for Cathryn if she had not been compelled by her own nature to act in defense of Philip, of Marie, of John, of them all?

"Yea, Lady Cathryn, I comprehend," Marie said humbly in her new understanding. "God go with you and keep you from harm," she whispered, and quickly kissed Cathryn's hand in effusive affection and gratitude.

Cathryn returned the affection of Marie's kiss with a quick embrace and whispered in her ear, "I pray that God will also keep you from harm." And when Marie pulled back to gaze questioningly into her face, she added, "I thought to keep you safe within Greneforde's walls, but now I wonder if a greater danger does not dwell under my own roof." And with her eyes, she directed Marie's gaze to Ulrich, engaged now in whining conversation with William over his being left behind.

Marie, with a swift change of mood, giggled lightly. Mayhap staying behind would not be so onerous.

Their good-byes said, they were mounted and gone before first light, though their departure had been delayed. William rode in front, leading Cathryn's mount, as it had been many years since she had ridden and she was unsure of herself, and Rowland followed close behind. For all that she knew Lambert lurked somewhere in England and that he still desired Greneforde for his own, Cathryn could not subdue the heady joy that rippled through her. She was exploring the land outside of Greneforde's walls; truly, she felt freer than she had since her childhood. The open land of England was not as safe as it had been in the days of her father—this she sensed though it had not been explained to her—yet she could not fear. Did not William ride before her? And did he not love her? She smiled fully, hugging the knowledge to herself, afraid the pounding joy within would topple her from her horse.

The day was clear but cold, the rising sun striking the frozen earth with weak force, warming it not at all. But it was clear and sunny, the rain absent as it had not been for many weeks. She could not help but be joyous on such a day. And why try?

The barren trees were a gray tangle against the brightening blue of the sky, no breath of wind stirring against their nakedness. The ground was frozen and firm and brown beneath the hooves of the horses they rode, the constant rain having washed away the snow long ago. The air smelled clean to her; it had no aftertaste of wood smoke or soap or manure, as did the air of Greneforde. It was a clean day, as cleanly clear of blemish as she. What a glorious day!

The day passed quietly for them, she enjoying her freedom, Rowland and William alert to danger so that she should remain so. It was coming on to dusk when she must have made some noise of pleasure, for William turned to smile at her; or mayhap she had made no noise and he just looked for the sheer joy of looking.

"You are bright today, lady, brighter than the struggling sun." He grinned, slowing until her mount had come abreast of his.

" 'Tis a bright day and I am the brighter for it," she answered cheerily, holding her face to the sun.

"I am much afeared that I have a traveling woman on my hands, one not content to remain at home, but ever about and restless to be off. Pray, deny it, wife, that I may sleep at night in my own bed."

Casting him a coquettish look, one she had borrowed from Marie, Cathryn smiled. "And why, pray, would you want to sleep at night when there are so many other diversions that await you in your bed?"

Rowland, smiling softly, let his horse trail farther behind, giving them privacy.

William raised his brows in mock astonishment and answered, shaking his head with pretended woe, "Oh, I have unleashed far more than a traveler. You, lady, are insatiable; you are fortunate in having me for a husband, for I have the cure for what is your malady."

" 'Tis no malady." She laughed.

"Mayhap not for you, but for your aging and weary husband?"

"Is my husband truly so weary?"

William's gray eyes twinkled with all the shine of polished steel. "Nay, not so weary as all that, but you have not heard the cure."

"I have not been convinced that there is a malady."

"You may be convinced of the malady when the cure becomes known to you," he responded, pulling her closer to his side.

"Is this a French malady?" Cathryn asked suspiciously.

William shrugged arrogantly. "I make no claim that we French have exclusive rights to the malady, but we most assuredly have the market on the cure. Would you hear of it?"

"Mayhap I had better, before you puff with Frankish pride upon this additional feat of your people; verily, the list of your . . ."

"Superiority?" he supplied helpfully.

"Arrogance," she answered, "grows longer by the hour. You had best tell me, though I have near forgotten what you intended to say."

"Then allow me to remind you," he said softly. "You, dear wife, have a malady, and its name is hunger, insatiable hunger."

"I am not hungry."

"But you are. I can hear your body's call."

"My body makes no sound," she denied, afraid

that her stomach rumbled and that he could hear.

"Nay, there is no sound, but still I hear it call. You are hungry for me, Cathyrn." His fingers brushed the rim of her delicate jaw, and his mouth hovered close above hers. "Is that not so?"

"Is this the malady?" she hedged.

"Do you hunger for me, wife?" he demanded gently.

"And what is the cure?" she countered.

"Do you want me, Cathryn?" he demanded again, with greater force.

His face was so close, and it was a closeness she yearned for with greater intensity with each hour she spent with him. The sun gleamed with blue light on his black curls; his eyes were as darkly gray as thunderclouds, his skin as fine as silk. Yes, she wanted him.

"I want you," she said in a whisper.

William smiled in satisfaction. Strangely, she was not the least offended by it.

"Then here is the cure: the best and most proven method for curing insatiability of any sort is over-indulgence." Cathryn's eyes widened as she leaned into his caressing hand upon her face. "Aye, wife," William said into her dawning comprehension, "you will be given a steady and abundant diet of me. I will fill you to completion and you *will* be satisfied."

"This cure will not work," she said with a smile.

"Because it is Frankish?" William asked with a slight frown.

"Nay, William," she said softly, "because I will not be cured of you."

Her dark eyes glowed her love and passion for him, yet he was ever conscious of Rowland. Leaning down to her, William kissed her softly and sensually on the lips for a brief moment and then let her mount fall behind. It was folly to have baited her that way; if he'd let his body have its way, they would have tumbled from their horses and rolled upon the path like two animals. If Cathryn kept looking at him the way she was now and saying such provocative things, he just might tumble her anyway.

"I suspect you say such because it is a French cure," he teased when she was well away from his hand.

"I say such because I have a French husband," she answered very quietly, looking at his back.

He heard her. He made no reply, but he had heard. And he smiled in full satisfaction.

"We must make camp," Rowland called. "There are no houses near or monasteries where we might be welcomed for the night. I am sorry, Lady Cathryn, that you must sleep upon the ground."

Thinking of her conversation with William, she had little expectation of sleeping on the ground, but she said nothing to Rowland.

"Nay, be not sorry. It is high adventure for me," she called back happily.

Rowland, knowing what he did of her, should not have been surprised by her answer, yet he was. She was a woman of remarkable character and resiliency of spirit. William had been given a gift most fine when he received Greneforde and its lady.

Yet there was danger. Lambert lurked and could

not stay his hand much longer. Tomorrow, late, they would reach the king. If an attack was made, it would be better neither too close to Greneforde nor too close to court.

Rowland watched as William pulled off the small cart path they followed. There was an abandoned and derelict remnant of a shepherd's hut just visible in the waning light. The wind had kicked up with the passage of the sun across the sky and the weather was brisk. Cathryn needed shelter in which to rest, even such shelter as this.

William looked back, and Rowland nodded his approval. Rowland watched as William's eyes lingered on his wife. He was decided with that look. Once settled and fed, he would circle the area for signs of recent human passage and he would sleep, however lightly, in full view of the night sky. Let William and Cathryn have their privacy.

The meal was cold—venison, bread, wine—but it was rich fare on such a cold night, and the company was sweet. William would allow no fire, but the night sky was clear and bright with stars. Even in the gloom of the hut, through the open wind holes and the large hole in the roof, Cathryn could see the silvery gleam of his eyes.

She knew that she would taste of "the cure" tonight.

Rowland wiped his fingers on a scrap of cloth that had been a part of their bundle and rose quietly. William watched him expectantly.

"I will go now," Rowland declared, "but I will be near."

William and Cathryn watched him go with inhospitable eagerness, with no words offered to delay his leaving. Rowland took no offense; in fact, he smiled. Those newly married were not known for their manners.

A gust of wind heralded his passage into the darkness of the doorless doorway, and then he was gone. Cathryn looked at William, a smile of anticipation lighting her features.

"How do you fare, wife?" he asked, keeping his distance from her. "Did the venison suit your tastes?"

"Yea, 'twas most succulent," she answered demurely.

"And the wine? I note you did not consume your usual portion, but a bare two cups," he prodded. "You are not ill?"

Never again would she need wine to bolster her courage to face the rigors of the bedchamber, and well he knew it, but she would play this game with him and not be found the loser.

"Nay, I feel quite well," Cathryn answered easily.

"No malady afflicts you?" he asked just as easily.

" 'Tis strange the meaning you French twist onto a word," she said to the air, "but, nay, I lay claim to no malady."

"With no malady, there need be no cure," he said in a low voice.

"Again the twist, but I say again that I cannot be cured. What say you, husband—will you attempt the impossible?" Cathryn challenged.

"Yea," William answered, rising to his feet, "I attempt any and all."

Cathryn rose with him, ready to accept his embrace, gleeful that she had not risen to William's bait but had instead taunted him into rising to hers. Her back was to the doorway as she stood, and William had taken only one step when she felt a blade pressed against the line of her jaw. William stopped and drew his sword free in one motion, yet he did not proceed beyond that. The blade was sharp that pricked Cathryn's flesh.

Cathryn felt the knife shift against her throat, and the man holding her from behind came into view.

The night was black, but the stars were bright in that cloudless sky. She saw him clearly.

"Nay!" she whispered, the blood chilling within her at the sight.

"Yea, Cat, I have not forgotten you, as you can see. Would I be vain if I assumed that you have not forgotten me?"

It was Lambert, his massive ring gleaming in the cold light of the night. His ring caught her attention as the knife could not. She had so many memories of the hand that bore that ring. It was that hand, that ring, that had scarred her brow and that marked her still. Cathryn reached up a tentative hand to feel the ridge of the scar. Yes, it was there still. He had marked her.

Nothing had changed.

Lambert was here, touching her. His hand was heavy, so unlike William's. He stared at her, his eyes so pale a blue as to be almost white, paler than a winter sky, so different from William's stormy gray. Lambert. He was back. He was touching her. He had her.

And there was room in her mind for none other,

not even for herself. There was no thought of the jeweled knife that was within easy reach of her hand. She had no defense and would offer none.

The cold descended not from without, but from within, as if the eternal and irreversible coldness of all the dead that had ever died rose from within some secret part of her to welcome her to their number.

She embraced the cold willingly.

She went with them eagerly, for who could harm the dead?

And William saw her swift and icy retreat into herself and feared for her. This danger was greater than the knife at her throat; this was the death of her spirit.

"Still the quiet cat, but that is one of your virtues, Cat," Lambert said with silken insincerity. " 'Tis well you still have it. You have so little virtue left."

The sound of malignant snickering pricked something within her, and she turned to the sound. As if through a long tunnel, she saw that William was being held by two of Lambert's men. Two swords were pressed against him, each against his torso. He was unarmed. William made no move, no sound, but his eyes never left her face. She scarcely noticed. But some small voice inside of her remarked upon the fact that those two knights were dirty. Very dirty.

A shiver of laughter shook her. She was mad to notice such a thing, for it did not matter. Could anyone be as dirty as she?

"You still tremble for me, Cat." Lambert grinned. "You have not forgotten."

No, she had not forgotten, though she had thought so for a small span of hours, but that had been a dream and this was waking. William was the dream, and she looked at him with eyes of glassy stillness, eyes empty of thought and of emotion, and then she looked away as she felt Lambert's hand trace with heavy precision the curve from breast to hip. She knew what was to come and she could not bear for William to witness it. In looking away, she closed the door on William and locked it.

Lambert would have her; she could only pray that he would take her where William could not see her degradation. Somehow that mattered more than anything. She could almost accept his invasion of her body, almost. . . .

She did not understand that her cold submission was evidence of the dying of her spirit. But William understood.

He had never seen her so cold, so detached from her surroundings; she was becoming detached from herself. She was distancing herself from him with every breath she took, shunting him to one side along with all the newly found warmth that he had kindled within her. This withdrawal was blindingly swift and mortally deep. She would not survive this.

William, silent in battle, never voicing a cry, watched the woman who shared his soul being pushed to the hard-packed dirt of the hut.

"Cathryn!" he said hoarsely, pressing against the points of the blades, unaware that they pierced him, unaware that his blood stained his tunic before running in a fragile stream to the floor.

Guichardet and Beuves dared press him no further. Lambert had claimed the right to kill le Brouillard, as he had claimed the right to his wife, yet they knew no other way to keep him immobilized.

"Cathryn," William repeated, "he has no claim on you!"

The swords pierced deeper into the muscle that banded his ribs, unnoticed. Guichardet and Beuves looked at each other in growing discomfort. How to stop a man who did not heed a sword in his side? Guichardet enjoyed a moment of rueful self-congratulation; had he not said again and again that le Brouillard was a knight to reckon with?

"You have been given to me by God and by king and I will not relinquish you, wife!" William shouted, demanding that she hear his words and know their truth.

Beuves and Guichardet threw down their useless swords in tandem and grabbed William's arms to keep him back from his wife. And then William knew that they would not kill him, at least not yet, and that gave him the advantage, for he had no compunction about killing them at any time.

"Fight for yourself as I fight for you!" he commanded her. "Wife!"

And, as if through a deadening fog, she heard him.

She was William's wife. She belonged to him. She did not belong to Lambert.

Lambert's meaty hand was upon her skirts, pulling them up, the air chill on her skin. With her hand, she grabbed his wrist to stop him.

Nothing that she could have said or done would have shocked him more.

Cat did not resist, not after that first time when he had cuffed her and sent her brother to his grave. He had cured her of fighting him.

And when Lambert did nothing to her in his shock, Cathryn gained courage. She pushed against his bulk with her arms and kicked at the hand that was held motionless against her leg. Lambert came out of his shock. What had worked once would work again. Mayhap Cat had forgotten a few things. He would remind her.

With brutal force, Lambert lashed her face with the broad back of his hand.

Her head rang with dizzying pain for many seconds, and she stopped her resistance. Lambert chuckled his satisfaction and drew her skirts up to her hips. The rush of air on the juncture of her legs cleared her head quickly enough and she lunged, trying to throw him off.

She had not seen the blow coming, though she had expected it. With the strike, knowledge burst upon her with such blinding clarity that it rivaled the force of the blow: Lambert could not kill her. To kill her would be to lose all chance at Greneforde. If he would not kill her, then she had nothing more to fear from him; he had already done his worst. Again and again she had endured his worst. She would not endure it even once more.

William was only steps from Cathryn, yet they seemed leagues apart, and the battle that Lambert had initiated with his entry into the hut had lasted no more than two dozen heartbeats. It seemed to William that they were caught on the threshold of eternity. Lambert had swung back his ringed hand

and cuffed Cathryn as casually as a man would cuff a begging dog. The sight of her dazed expression burned into his mind. He would not forget. Lambert would not live long enough to remember.

William drew free the knife that hung from his belt with swift and deadly silence. He turned and jabbed downward toward the open and vulnerable point where mail did not quite cover throat.

Guichardet fell dead, his windpipe severed.

Beuves backed up a step, releasing his hold on William. This man was more than he had planned for. Guichardet was dead. To be dead was not what they had discussed when planning to retake Greneforde.

The look in le Brouillard's eyes when he turned from Guichardet, the blood a vivid red line on his blade, caused a mortal heaviness within Beuves. This man would kill him. There was no fury, no rage, no blood lust in those gray eyes. There was just cold death. His death.

Beuves turned to run, running not from the act of dying—all men must face that, and there was no escape—but from death personified in that cool and solemn face before him. Only the dark and fathomless eyes showed any sign of life: the tormented life of the damned. Le Brouillard's face was enough to drive him into insanity.

Before even one frenzied step was completed, Beuves fell dead, the shaft of an arrow protruding from his neck. Rowland appeared behind William through the open wind hole, the bow in his hands.

"Your pardon, William. I strayed too far afield."

He did not say more—indeed, he had said that

much on the run—and William did not bother to answer. They both raced to where Cathryn lay near the portal of the hut, Lambert straddled over her, her skirts akimbo. He had struck her once, the side of her face already showing a swelling darkness, but it was Lambert who was howling in pain. Cathryn, certain only that he would not kill her, was taking her revenge.

Her thumbs were pressed against his eyes and she applied pressure relentlessly. Lambert had thought to pry her off. He could not. He had thought to beat her off. She was not to be dissuaded for so paltry a price.

It was William who ended their battle. With killing ferocity, he kicked Lambert off of his wife, robbing him of breath in the doing. Following, holding his sword ready, William waited until Lambert lay still and dazed. When Lambert could see and understand his death in William's face, William did what no knight did to another: he gave Lambert no chance at gallant battle. William slashed downward with his sword, beheading Lambert where he lay.

Rowland stood to block Cathryn's view of what was happening. It was well he did.

With cold disdain, William kicked Lambert's lifeless head into a far-off corner, and then, the gleam of that brutal ring catching his eyes, he hacked off Lambert's hand and kicked that into the same corner to keep morbid company with its head.

Lambert was dead.

That was the last thought William would ever give to Lambert for the rest of his days.

Rowland, knowing William well, knew that Lambert would no more occupy William's thoughts than a dead mayfly. Cathryn and her welfare would consume him, and so it should be. Rowland lifted what remained of Lambert of Brent and tossed the body out of the wind hole. With calm detachment, he located the hand and head and got rid of them in the same manner. Once outside, he would gather the parts and bury the man who had reached once too often for Greneforde. The other two nameless knights would be buried with him, unshriven and unconfessed. They would be joined together throughout eternity, whether they wished to be or no.

William was only dimly aware of Rowland's movements in the hut. His entire attention was focused on Cathryn. She had gone far inside herself to cope with this latest abasement. He was greatly afeared that he had lost her forever. She lay now as one in a heavy swoon. She had not stirred when he had kicked Lambert from her. If she had noted his death, she made no sign. Blood ran in a slow line from her mouth, and she made no move to wipe it.

He was completely unaware that he bled from two small wounds to his rib cage. His thoughts were all for her.

She was gone from him; he could see it. There was no recognition in her dark and lovely eyes. There was scarcely any sign that she lived, except for the heavy rise and fall of her chest. She had battled, this wife of his, battled her greatest and most feared foe. She had done well. She had heard him in her fear, for it was when he had commanded her to fight that she had fought.

She had heard him.

William felt the beginning of hope flower in his mind. If she had heeded him before, she would heed him again. It would be so.

But how to reach her?

Lightly, he almost thought he heard the God of all whisper softly. Yes, he must not smother her with care or she would die with the weight of it. There was one way in which to reach Cathryn, one way that had proven itself time and again.

"Up, wife!" he commanded in gentle reproof, "you must learn not to roll in the dirt the day before you meet England's new king."

Cathryn sat up before the words had completely left William's mouth, and then their meaning registered in her mind. Up, she must get up. William had said so. And why? Because Lambert was dead.

Lambert was dead. She had fought him. William had killed him. William le Brouillard had not relinquished her, as he had promised her countless times that he would not.

She believed him; after all, he was a man who had no history of losing.

Slowly a smile wrinkled her eyes and turned up her mouth. She wiped the blood with the hem of her bliaut and touched with tender fingers the swelling near her eye. She was covered in dirt and bruises and dried blood, but she was looking at him with all the richness of her character shining out of her dark eyes. She had never looked more beautiful to him.

His Cathryn was back from that dark place inside

herself where she hid when threatened. She had gone far, but she was back.

"I will vow," Cathryn said, raising herself to her feet by slow degrees, "that the king did not know how fastidious you are when he sent you to me." She stood straight and pressed her hands to the small of her back, sighing heavily before pinning William with her gaze. "I say this with all affection—your love of water is become a burden to me."

William raised his black brows in scandalous shock, loving her bedraggled looks, her sweetly barbed speech. Loving her.

"I? A burden to you?"

"But"—Cathryn smiled up at him—"your love of me is no burden at all."

William crossed his arms over his chest in a pique of royal proportions.

"You deliver a kiss with the blow," he said. "Still, 'tis a blow."

"Which warrants an apology?" Cathryn grinned.

William raised one raven eyebrow at that.

"Frankish or English?" he questioned.

" 'Tis yours to choose." She shrugged.

William glanced around the hut. All signs of battle and death had been removed. The place was much as it had been when they first alit here; mayhap it would be a healing balm to her to join their bodies now.

"I would choose a blending of the two," he said seductively and very diplomatically, "to combine the best of both."

Cathryn reached behind her, thrusting her breasts out invitingly, to untie her laces. The bliaut gaped and fell down around her shoulders, her skin warm and golden even in the blue of night.

"Quick or slow, William?"

There would be no compromise.

As she shifted her shoulders, the bliaut fell to her feet to rest on the dirt floor. Her shift quickly followed. Like a gay flirt, she kicked them away from her to land at William's feet and toyed with the shining length of her hair, cloaking herself against the night air with it, caressing herself with it. She knew she would not feel the chill of winter for long.

William had only one answer to give, and he said it heavily.

"Quick."

Cathryn smiled and sauntered toward her husband, confident and at ease in her nudity and in herself. She lifted her arms and wrapped herself around him.

"You will be an Englishman yet, le Brouillard."

They are pirates—lawless, merciless, hungry. Only one way offers hope of escaping death, and worse, at their hands. Their captain must claim her for his own, risk his command, his ship, his very life, to take her. And so she puts her soul into a seduction like no other—a virgin, playing the whore in a desperate bid for survival. As the blazing sun descends into the wide blue sea, she is alone, gazing into the eyes of the man who must lay his heart at her feet. . . .

Lair of the Wolf

Also includes the fourth installment of *Lair of the Wolf*, a serialized romance set in medieval Wales. Be sure to look for future chapters of this exciting story featured in Leisure books and written by the industry's top authors.

___4692-X $5.50 US/$6.50 CAN

Viking!

CONNIE MASON

The first time he sees her she is clad in nothing but moonlight and mist, and from that moment, Thorne the Relentless knows he is bewitched by the maiden bathing in the forest pool. How else to explain the torrid dreams, the fierce longing that keeps his warrior's body in a constant state of arousal? Perhaps Fiona is speaking the truth when she claims it is not sorcery that binds him to her, but the powerful yearning of his viking heart.

___4402-1 $5.99 US/$6.99 CAN

the Black Knight

Connie Mason

He rides into Chirk Castle on his pure black destrier. Clad in black from his gleaming helm to the tips of his toes, he is all battle-honed muscle and rippling tendons. In his stark black armor he looks lethal and sinister, every bit as dangerous as his name implies. He is a man renowned for his courage and strength, for his prowess with women, for his ruthless skill in combat. But when he sees Raven of Chirk, with her long, chestnut tresses and womanly curves, he can barely contain his embroiled emotions. For it was her betrayal twelve years before that turned him from chivalrous youth to hardened knight. It is she who has made him vow to trust no woman—to take women only for his pleasure. But only she can unleash the passion in his body, the goodness in his soul, and the love in his heart.

___4622-9 $5.99 US/$6.99 CAN

IONA

MELANIE JACKSON

Isolated by the icy storms of the North Atlantic, the isle of Iona is only a temporary haven for its mistress. Lona MacLean, daughter of a rebel and traitor to the crown, knows that it is only a matter of time before the bloody Sasannachs come for her. But she has a stout Scottish heart, and the fiery beauty gave up dreams of happiness years before. One task remains—to protect her people. But the man who lands upon Iona's rain-swept shores is not an Englishman. The handsome intruder is a Scot, and a crafty one at that. His clever words leave her tossing and turning in her bed long into the night. His kiss promises an end to the ghosts that plague both her people and her heart. And in his powerful embrace, Lona finds an ecstasy she'd long ago forsworn.

____4614-8 $4.99 US/$5.99 CAN

MANON
MELANIE JACKSON

Alone and barely ahead of the storm, Manon flees Scotland; the insurrection has failed and Bonnie Prince Charlie's rebellion has been thrown down. Innocent of treason, yet sought by agents of the English king, the Scots beauty dons the guise of a man and rides to London—and into the hands of the sexiest Sassanach she's ever seen. But she has no time to dally, especially not with an English baronet. Nor can she indulge fantasies of his strong male arms about her or his heated lips pressed against her own. She fears that despite her precautions, this rake may uncover her as no man but *Manon*, and she may learn of something more dangerous than an Englishman's sword—his heart.

Lair of the Wolf

Also includes the eighth installment of *Lair of the Wolf*, a serialized romance set in medieval Wales. Be sure to look for future chapters of this exciting story featured in Leisure books and written by the industry's top authors.

___4737-3 $4.99 US/$5.99 CAN

The CHANGELING BRIDE

LISA CACH

In order to procure the cash necessary to rebuild his estate, the Earl of Allsbrook decides to barter his title and his future: He will marry the willful daughter of a wealthy merchant. True, she is pleasing in form and face, and she has an eye for fashion. Still, deep in his heart, Henry wishes for a happy marriage. Wilhelmina March is leery of the importance her brother puts upon marriage, and she certainly never dreams of being wed to an earl in Georgian England—or of the fairy debt that gives her just such an opportunity. But suddenly, with one sweet kiss in a long-ago time and a faraway place, Elle wonders if the much ado is about something after all.

___52342-6 $4.99 US/$5.99 CAN

Bewitching The Baron

Lisa Cach

Valerian has always known before that she will never marry. While the townsfolk of her Yorkshire village are grateful for her abilities, the price of her gift is solitude. But it never bothered her until now. Nathaniel Warrington is the new baron of Ravenall, and he has never wanted anything the way he desires his people's enigmatic healer. Her exotic beauty fans flames in him that feel unnaturally fierce. Their first kiss flares hotter still. Opposed by those who seek to destroy her, compelled by a love that will never die, Nathaniel fights to earn the lone beauty's trust. And Valerian will learn the only thing more dangerous—or heavenly—than bewitching a baron, is being bewitched by one.

___52368-X $5.50 US/$6.50 CAN

Dorchester Publishing Co., Inc.
P.O. Box 6640
Wayne, PA 19087-8640

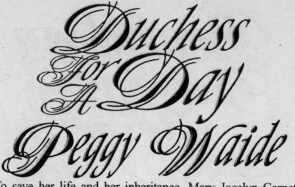

Duchess For A Day

Peggy Waide

To save her life and her inheritance, Mary Jocelyn Garnett does what she must. She marries Reynolds Blackburn—without his knowledge. And all goes well, until the Duke of Wilcott returns to find he is no longer the king of bachelors. As long as the marriage is never consummated, Jocelyn knows, it can be annulled—just as soon as she has avenged her family and reacquired her birthright. Unfortunately, her blasted husband appears to be attracted to her! Worse, Reyn is handsome and clever, and she fears her husband might assume that she is one of many women who are simply after his title. After one breathless kiss, however, Jocelyn swears that she will not be duchess for a day, but Reyn's for a lifetime.

___4554-0 $4.99 US/$5.99 CAN

Dorchester Publishing Co., Inc.
P.O. Box 6640
Wayne, PA 19087-8640

Please add $1.75 for shipping and handling for the first book and $.50 for each book thereafter. NY, NYC, and PA residents, please add appropriate sales tax. No cash, stamps, or C.O.D.s. All orders shipped within 6 weeks via postal service book rate. Canadian orders require $2.00 extra postage and must be paid in U.S. dollars through a U.S. banking facility.

Name_____
Address_____
City_____State_____Zip_____
I have enclosed $_____ in payment for the checked book(s).
Payment <u>must</u> accompany all orders. ☐ Please send a free catalog.
CHECK OUT OUR WEBSITE! www.dorchesterpub.com

PEGGY WAIDE
POTENT CHARMS

She is the most frustrating woman Stephen Lambert has ever met—and the most beguiling. But a Gypsy curse has doomed the esteemed duke of Badrick to a life without a happy marriage, and not even a strong-willed colonial heiress with a tendency to find trouble can change that. Stephen decides that since he cannot have her for a wife, he will convince her to be the next best thing: his mistress. But Phoebe Rafferty needs a husband, and fast. She has four weeks to get married and claim her inheritance. Phoebe only has eyes for the most wildly attractive and equally aggravating duke. But he refuses to marry her, mumbling nonsense about a curse. With time running out, Phoebe vows to persuade the stubborn aristocrat that curses are poppycock and the only spell he has fallen under is love.

___4694-6 $4.99 US/$5.99 CAN